HALF
LIFE

ALSO BY LILLIAN CLARK

Immoral Code

HALF
LIFE

LILLIAN CLARK

Alfred A. Knopf   New York

THIS IS A BORZOI BOOK PUBLISHED BY ALFRED A. KNOPF

Visit us on the Web! GetUnderlined.com

Educators and librarians, for a variety of teaching tools, visit us at RHTeachersLibrarians.com

Library of Congress Cataloging-in-Publication Data
Names: Clark, Lillian, author.
Title: Half life / Lillian Clark.
Description: First edition. | New York: Alfred A. Knopf, [2020] |
Summary: Sixteen-year-old overachiever Lucille Harper agrees to be a beta tester for a secretive human cloning program, hoping her clone will meet her academic and family responsibilities and leave her free to figure out who she really is.
Identifiers: LCCN 2019022643 (print) | LCCN 2019022644 (ebook) |
ISBN 978-0-525-58050-8 (hardcover) | ISBN 978-0-525-58051-5 (library binding) |
ISBN 978-0-525-58052-2 (ebook)
Subjects: CYAC: Cloning—Fiction. | Identity—Fiction. | Individuality—Fiction. | Science fiction.
Classification: LCC PZ7.1.C59413 Hal 2020 (print) | LCC PZ7.1.C59413 (ebook) |
DDC [Fic]—dc23

The text of this book is set in 11.5-point Whitman Roman LF.
Interior design by Stephanie Moss

Printed in the United States of America
June 2020
10 9 8 7 6 5 4 3 2 1

First Edition

To everyone who's ever needed to hear that you're already worth it. You're already enough.

CHAPTER ONE

Truth is a funny thing.

It's fluid, relative. A self-fulfilling prophecy. What you want, what you need, what you believe, what people believed before you: welcome to your truths.

Truths like, say, the sky is blue. Easy, right? The sky is blue.

Except, it isn't. The sky *appears* blue because of the way specifically coded cells in our eyes collect data that is then interpreted by the specifically coded cells in our brains which are programmed from birth to "know" that when we're speaking English, that specific hue of scattered light is "blue."

Outside of your brain, the sky isn't blue. The sky is a mess of molecules and light waves that are only "blue" when seen by a creature with the correct ocular structure and conscious context needed to *interpret* the sky as "blue." *So what the hell color is the sky, anyway?*

Think about it. "Truth" is subjective. It's perception. *Repetition.*

Tell yourself a lie enough times and *poof!* it becomes your truth.

Like me. My brand. Who I Am™. Case in point:

"Lucille Harper, always the overachiever," my social studies teacher says, dropping my graded final paper facedown on my desk, grin tinged with resentment. Well, maybe it's resentment. Maybe it's end-of-the-school-year ennui. Or heartburn.

I flip my paper over—knot in my chest going tight—read the "95" he's written atop it in his trademark green pen, and flip it back like I don't care. Except, I do. Care. About this specific paper? No, though the grade makes my knot loosen. About jumping through this hoop, the couple thousand that came before it, and however many will come next? Yes. Hoops, hurdles, a yawning expanse of boxes to tick. I care about them all because they're what sits between me and my goals, me and college, me and proof that all of this "overachieving" is worth it.

Take my classmates. Really, conduct a poll:

What do you think of Lucille Harper? Is she:
(A) Super awesome. Everyone loves her, wants to date her or be her or somehow both.
(B) An uptight, overachieving kiss-ass.
(C) Who?

My bet would be on a sixty-forty split between B and C.

To them, to *everyone*, I'm either No One or who Mr. Fitch says I am: Lucille Harper, Overachiever.

And I own it, even if I hate that term. *Overachiever*. How *exactly* does one "over" achieve? Is there some line I'm not supposed to cross? Like, whoa, hold on there, little lady, you're awfully close to appearing *ambitious*. You're one quick skip shy of *trying too hard*. And we all know what a horror show *trying hard* is, right?

"Lucille," they say, "stop trying so fucking hard."

I open my messenger bag, pull out my binder, and tuck my paper neatly into the front pocket. Why? I don't know. Class is over, the *year's* over. It's literally Friday of the second-to-last week, with only one useless week left to waste time, turn in final assignments and books, and clean out lockers that are already clean since no one uses them anyway. There is a zero percent chance I'll need this thing again. But I slide it in there anyway—all neat and crisp—then put my binder back in my bag and turn to talk to Cass.

She's twisted around in her seat talking to Aran. Because of course she is. How do I keep forgetting he's in this class? Legit all semester. I'd say it's because he never talks and does little more than slouch back in whichever of his revolving skate-brand hoodies he's wearing that day, but really it's willful ignorance. I choose to forget he's in this class like how I choose to forget he's Cass's boyfriend.

They look through his paper together, probably because he's worried about his grade. Cass's sits on her desk, a "94" written in the top left-hand corner. How Mr. Fitch decides percentages on analytical research papers is beyond me. I get one tiny extra point, yet my paper's twice as long.

Cass doesn't look like she's turning back around anytime soon, so I pull out my phone to wait out the last five minutes like the rest of the class. I tap in my passcode, and feel the knot cinch tight.

There's a text from Dad saying he's already waiting out front and four new emails: one from some company called Life^2 that keeps dodging my spam filters, an updated syllabus and e-classroom group assignments for my summer college business course, a "hello" from my SAT prep tutor, and an update from Reach the Sky, the day camp for low-income and at-risk kids where I'm volunteering later this summer.

I trash the first, move the next two to their folders to deal with later, then open the one from Reach the Sky. Is this masochism? Knowing it'll hurt me but doing it anyway because I kind of want the hurt. Or, I don't want it. I *earned* it. Because of course the message is for the first-session interns. Which is really all of the interns except for me. I only got selected for the second session. Off the wait list.

The message is bland—prep suggestions and reminders about meeting times and final requests for paperwork—but it feels like a hand reaching out to tug at the tangled mess in my chest. I flip over to my Instagram app and pull up Bode's page.

Call me pathetic, because obviously there're no new posts since I last checked at lunch, but I don't care. *I do care. Like, really. Please don't call me pathetic.* I browse his website next, scrolling through his store of hand-screen-printed products, knowing I'll never buy any because he'd see it was me from the order form and who cares that half the school wears his stuff, I know he'd read my name and sense my near-debilitating crush through the screen and wouldn't that just be the worst?

I mean, it's one thing to pine in private. Private means he only says no inside my head. Private means the unflappable Lucille Harper brand remains unflapped.

Still, I see the warning "only three left in stock" under my favorite one—a purple ombré octopus printed on a white V-neck tee—and hesitate, my finger above the buy button.

The bell rings. I close the page and sling my bag's strap over my shoulder as my classmates shift and stand around me. Mr. Fitch raises a hand in farewell as we file out. "Have a good weekend," he calls over the din of footsteps and chatter. "Make good choices!"

In the hall, Cass catches up with me and loops her arm through mine. "So, how'd you do? No, wait. Let me guess." She pretends to consider. I grin and think, *Is this condescending? Am I this predictable?* "Ninety-seven."

"Close. Ninety-five."

"Kick-ass." She holds up her free hand for a high five. I oblige.

"You?" I ask, though I already know.

"Ninety-four."

"Nice."

She skips a step, not like missing one but bouncing, and nudges me with her shoulder. "Want to know what Aran got?"

No. "Sure." It's awful, and I'd never tell her this, but sometimes Cass exhausts me. I love her. Like a sister. LYLAS: Love Ya Like a Sister. That's how we used to sign all our notes/texts/ et cetera. It's the best-friends-before-birth thing, thanks to our platonic-soul-mates-since-college moms. In a lot of ways, it's awesome. In others—like the she's-prettier/funnier/more confident/ popular/wanted-than-me way—it's not.

Cass looks back at Aran, who's currently walking a pace behind us in some asymmetrical third-wheel configuration, and beams. "Ninety-eight," she says, and turns back to me. "Ninety-freaking-eight! He did his whole paper in verse."

I try to stop it. Like holding in a sneeze. But my brow rises and eyes widen and my traitor open-book face gives me away.

"Wow, Luce," Cass says, "someone crop-dusting ahead of us or are you really that petty?"

"Sorry. I just—" *A ninety-eight! God, I— And what was with Cass guessing I got a ninety-seven?* "I just worked really hard."

She stops, making me stop with her by yanking our linked arms. "And Aran didn't?"

"That's not what I said."

"Yeah? Tell that to your face."

"Sorry for my face, then."

She rolls her eyes and starts again toward the west lobby, where the sophomores congregate. Aran follows, the same pace behind. I'd guess he looks uncomfortable, but I don't check. Cass unloops our arms and falls back a step to walk the rest of the way beside him.

Sometimes I'm pretty sure she hates me. The other side of the LYLAS thing. Like how sometimes you act the worst to the people who are closest to you. You know it's awful, but you do it anyway. Maybe because you trust them to keep loving you. At least, that's what I tell myself. Because the other answer is that when you're not actually sisters, LYLAS is little more than silly shorthand for a feeling you're doomed to outgrow.

Or it's Aran. Texting Cass while we're hanging out. Laughing with her and their theater friends about jokes I haven't been in on since September. Getting a better grade than me on a paper I spent two weeks writing for a class I don't even like.

I round the corner into the sophomore lobby and hesitate, stopping so quick the kid behind me rams into my back. Because three people wait for Cass and Aran at their usual bench. Louise and Finn, two of Cass's theater friends, and Bode.

Bode's not a theater friend, more theater-friend-adjacent. Or, rather, everyone-adjacent. Because Bode, with his achingly cool screen-printing designs and generally palatable self, is universally adored among the sophomores and beyond. A universality that includes yours truly, as I've had an unrequited crush on him since the seventh grade.

If I'd managed to slow down in the hall, let Cass and Aran pass me, it'd have been easy. I'd have followed them over, like, *hi, yes, look at me coming over because I Belong.* Because we are all Friends here.

Instead, there's the aforementioned freeze. Total deer-in-the-headlights. Which is pathetic. I know this. Even more pathetic? Rather than resuming my progress after being rammed into, I look at my phone—though I have exactly nothing new to look at—until I see Cass and Aran walk over to the bench out of the corner of my eye.

They join the group and ease into the conversation like water mixing with, well, water. Seamless. While I wander over and stick to the outskirts. The five of them all laugh about something, then Cass turns to me. "Your dad still picking you up?"

"Yeah, he's already outside. You're not coming?"

"Nah." She nods back at Aran and the other three. "We're going to find something to do."

"Okay."

"Do you want—"

"Can't." I swallow. Why is my mouth so bitter? Oh, right, because "bitter" is the taste of pity-invites. "My parents have some sort of announcement, remember?"

"Oh, yeah." And I can tell she's relieved. She didn't want me to say yes. Since her new—if an entire school year still qualifies as "new"—friends don't like me. "Talk later?" she asks.

I nod. She nods. There are smiles and waves. And the five of them head out the doors while I stand there. I need to go that way too, but I'd rather fake that I forgot something for a minute than trot awkwardly along in their wake.

The weight of my bag tugs at the fabric on my shoulder. I resituate the strap, fix my Peter Pan collar and the lay of my dress, then start toward the door. I hope Bode liked it. My dress. Black with short sleeves and a shadowy geometric print. I try to remember if his eyes lingered. If he'd looked at me at all. He had, hadn't he?

I like to think our styles are complementary. Him with his thick-rimmed glasses of various colors and assortment of artistic tees. I'm not artistic, but I am composed, so Bode and I make aesthetic sense. Like mixing patterns you think would clash but enhance each other instead. Pinstripe and paisley. Micro polka dots and toile. Chevron and filigree.

My dad's parked in the pull-through, against the rules, with the engine off and the radio on. When I climb in, he pushes the ignition button and turns down NPR. "Greetings, Kid," he says.

"Salutations, Parent."

"No Cass?"

I shake my head and wait for him to do his thing: tipped head, pointed gaze, awaiting elaboration. But he doesn't, only shifts into gear, checks his blind spot, and pulls away from the curb.

We're silent through the lurching stop-go procession of cars leaving the lot. I reach over and turn the radio back up. A woman reads an update about the latest political indictment, and Dad uses the steering-wheel buttons to switch the station from NPR to classic rock. I try doing the tilted-head-staring thing to him, but he doesn't notice. He's too busy looking like he's sleepwalking. The car ahead of us at the stop sign turns onto the street and he doesn't even pull up.

"Dad."

"What? Oh. Right," he says, then rolls forward and flips on the turn signal, waits for a break in traffic, and accelerates out onto the road.

I spot them halfway down the block. Cass is on Aran's skateboard, arms out, balancing as he pushes her down the sidewalk with a hand on the small of her back. Louise and Finn follow behind, huddled together, watching something on one of their phones, each with an earbud in one ear, oblivious.

Bode's up ahead on his own board. Cruising lazily toward the corner and currently red light. We pull up even with him as he stops and toes the back of his board to pop the front up into his hand. My insides clench. *Turn green, turn green, turn green.*

I slouch down.

Hold my breath.

Open my bag on my lap and pretend to search through it.

Glance at the side mirror though all I can see is my own filtered reflection.

Wait for a knuckle to tap the glass.

The light turns, and we roll forward. I exhale, looking back as we accelerate through the intersection to see the five of them bunched up on the corner, unaware that the light's even changed. With no clue that I'd been there at all.

I drop my bag onto the floor and stare out the window. An ad for American Furniture Warehouse plays on the radio. Then one for Elitch's. Then my mom calls, my dad's phone ringing through the car's Bluetooth, interrupting the first few bars of a Pearl Jam song.

I tap the answer button on the touch screen. "Hi, Mom."

"Hey, Luce." Her voice is weird. Not just car-speaker weird, but taut. And I think, *Maybe it's in the water.* A parasite. Alien microbes using my parents as hosts. "You almost home?"

I glance at Dad, and he looks the same as before. Like, should I slap him? Not hard. Just a snap-out-of-it tap. "Yeah," I say, "almost there."

"Great," she says, and hangs up.

We ease to a stop at the last light before home, and I ask, "Did someone die?"

Nothing. Like he's not even in the car with me. I'd been joking—*halfway*—but now my stomach shrinks and my pulse rises. *"Dad."*

He gives his head a slight shake. "What?"

"Mom. You. This conference in the middle of the afternoon on a workday. *Did someone die?*"

He shakes his head again. "No."

We turn onto our block and pass a series of densely landscaped, oversized houses. The Gilberts' Maltipoo sprints across their front yard to bark at our car through their wrought iron fence, a frenzied sentient cotton ball. "Then, *what?*"

"Your mom and I will tell you inside."

"Awesome. Not at all ominous."

He doesn't say anything. Not as we pull into the garage stall next to my mom's car—leaving the door open, I note—or as he climbs out, forgetting his work bag in the backseat. Nothing as I follow him into the house. Nothing as Boris, our five-year-old Great Pyrenees does his groaning delighted dance in the kitchen, shoving his massive body first against Dad's legs, then mine. Nothing as Mom comes into the kitchen, as they pass each other without a glance.

No, worse than "without a glance." They pass each other like two negatively charged magnets, with a repulsed barrier between.

"Hey, Lucy Moosie," she says, leaning over Boris to give me a hug.

"Mom. Please."

"Right." She straightens and picks dog hair off her navy skirt. "Sorry. *Lucille.*"

Navy skirt and crisp-not-crumpled blouse means she probably wasn't on call, but I ask, "Usher forth any new life today?"

"Not today." She crosses the kitchen in her nylons, taking a mug from one cabinet and our basket of assorted teas from another. She sets those on the island and grabs the kettle off the stove. "Ava offered to take most of my patient load today so I could make it home in time."

Does that mean Ava, Cass's mom, knows what this is about? Does *Cass?* I watch my mom fill the kettle in the sink, set it on a burner, turn said burner on, then shake her head and turn it off again.

But, not death. So, are we moving? Is Mom pregnant with some midlife-crisis baby? Is someone sick? *Does one of them have cancer?*

"Come on," she says, walking toward the living room. "Your dad and I need to talk to you about something."

The knot in my chest is pulled so taut, it's vibrating.

Dad's in one of the accent chairs arranged to face the couch, elbows propped on his knees, tie dangling in the space between. Mom moves to sit in the second accent chair beside him. They wait. I stand behind the couch, arms crossed, holding myself together. Boris plods into the room and lies on the rug with a full-chested sigh. *Likewise, Bubbo. Likewise.*

"Luce," Dad says, not looking at me. "Please."

I sit.

"So," Mom starts, then swallows whatever she planned to say next. Her eyes are wet.

She and Dad share a look, and he says, "We've decided—"

"Together."

"Right. We've decided, together, that it'd be best for us to separate."

I blink. "What?"

"Well, not best," says Mom. "That's not—"

"Okay. Poor word choice, but—"

"Wait. Separate or divorce?" I ask.

"Divorce," they say at the same time.

Dad shakes his head.

Mom rolls her eyes.

And I feel the bottom of my world fall out.

"Lucy." My mom's watching me. "Say something? Please?"

"I—" They were perfect. College sweethearts, married after graduation, each other's cheering squads through MBAs and MDs and working at the same hospital, perfect. Jobs, house, kid, *perfect.* "I thought you were happy."

Mom flashes a look at Dad, but he's staring at his hands, linked in his lap. "We were. For a long time. Then it . . . faded. Until we were just going through the motions. And once you realize you've been pretending at something like that, like happiness, well. It's pretty impossible to go back."

For the last year or so, since I got my learner's permit, I've been having this recurring stress dream. I'm driving my mom's SUV, with her in the passenger seat, and the brakes give out. It's not dramatic. Or even exciting. Instead, it's so basic it's almost boring. I'll be preparing to turn or slow down on a hill, press the brake pedal, and . . . nothing. I can feel the weight of the vehicle around me, impossibly heavy, pushed forward by its momentum. And I have to stop it with the sheer force of my will.

I slam my foot down on the useless brake and *urge* the SUV to stop. All two and a half tons of it.

Sometimes I manage to make it slow.

Most of the time, I don't.

This is like that. If I try hard enough—*stop trying so fucking hard, Lucille*—it'll stop.

"Is someone moving?" I ask. "You? Dad? All of us?"

Dad blinks some focus back into his eyes and clears his throat. "I am. I—" His voice breaks. He coughs, falsely, to cover it and pats his chest with an open palm. "I took a job over in Aurora."

"We thought it'd be . . . easier," Mom says.

Easier?

Dad rubs his eyes. "I signed the lease on an apartment yesterday."

I try to take a deep breath. *Try, try, try.* But the knot's so tight, the room's gone airless. Standing, I say, "I have stuff to do," and walk away.

Behind me, Mom calls, "Luce," while Dad says, "Let her go."

I cross the entryway and climb the stairs to my bedroom. Close my door, squeeze my eyes shut, ball my hands up so tight it hurts. And silent scream.

But it does nothing. When I open my eyes, the knot's still cinched tight, and my room's a brittle void, a vacuum tailored to me alone.

CHAPTER TWO

A favorite mug. A set of end tables. A vase. A smattering of picture frames from the walls and shelves. Then the bedroom set from the guest room, the entire contents of Dad's home office. Gone. In his car and a U-Haul towed by Mom's SUV, leaving our house three-quarters full.

It feels fake. I mean, I've been over this—what's real, anyway? What's true?—but this is the ground tilting. Or finding out the ground has always been tilted and all the while you've been happily, obliviously walking up the incline. Then *poof!*, awareness. And now you're struggling. Legs aching and unsteady on your feet. While you ask yourself, *Has it always been this hard?*

But of course it hasn't. Because maybe the foundation of your life shifted, but it did so gradually. *Quietly.* Behind closed doors and when you weren't home. Sunday, eavesdropping from the top of the stairs, I wonder, *Would screaming have helped?* A few blowouts, accusations and vitriol, muffled by my bedroom walls while I did my homework. Brittle silences and sidelong glares at dinner. Would that have made this . . . better?

"What about this magnet, Ryan?" my mom asks, painfully polite. Like, yes, this is torture, but make sure it's *nice*. "The one from the Grand Canyon."

"Sure, I'll take that one," he answers, followed by the sound of said magnet being tossed in a box.

Or, later, my dad: "What should we do with the wedding china?"

"Save it for Lucille?"

A pause. "You think she'll want it?"

Nope.

"Leave it," my mom says. "I'll ask her later." Then I hear her sigh. There's the sound of a dish being set on the counter. Soft footsteps. Dad murmuring. It's gentle. Sweet.

This can't be real. Divorce is for hatred and infidelity and not being able to stand sharing the other person's air. Not this amicable shredding. This painstaking courtesy. Like my seemingly happily married parents are playacting at divorce.

Then, more footsteps. Closer, crossing the dining room toward the stairs, so I sneak back to my room thinking, *Lucille Harper, Overachiever; Nancy and Ryan Harper, Perfect Couple; Nancy and Ryan Harper, Bitter Farce.*

If perfect's not perfect, then . . . what's the point?

●

Friday again, the last day of the school year, and Cass claps her hands in front of my face. "Earth to Lucille," she singsongs.

"Sorry."

"What planet were you on?"

Planet My Dad Spent the Last Five Nights in His New Apartment. Which I'd tell her except I'm honestly not sure how. At some point in the last nine months, I stopped knowing how to talk to

Cass. And every time I picked up my phone to call her last weekend, every time I thought to bring it up this week, I'd hesitate, imagining opening my mouth only to have nothing come out. Knowing that if—*when*—I managed to tell her, it'd go from "real" to *real*. Official.

"Preoccupied," I say.

"Obviously." She half smiles. Half-indulgent, half-annoyed. "But with what? School's over." Sitting hip to hip on the bench, she nudges me, teasing. "Nothing left to be uptight about for three whole months."

"Funny," I tease back. At least, I hope it sounds like teasing because it feels like bullshit.

"Come on," she says. "I'm trying here. Are you okay?"

She got her hair done last weekend. Fresh cornrows on the sides with strands of purple woven in and her natural hair styled in a Mohawk up the middle. It looks incredible. Which I told her, of course, Monday when I saw her in English. But now I wonder if, while I went through SAT vocab lists and listened to my parents haul boxes outside, Aran went with her. Or even Louise or Finn. And I feel jealousy slurp the marrow from my bones, then fill the hollow left behind.

"I'm fine," I say, and force a smile. She smiles back, lips stained a bright purple that looks amazing against her brown skin. I can't wear colors like that. I'm too—*self-conscious*—pale. Purple lipstick would turn me corpselike. But maybe that's what I need. Purple lips, neon hair. A new look, a new everything.

Aran and Bode stroll up, and Cass stands to wrap her arms around Aran's neck, kissing him in a grand display of school's-over-can't-get-in-trouble PDA. I lean back against the wall. Bode catches my eye, nods toward the pair, and rolls his eyes extravagantly.

He sits next to me, and I stare at his red Vans, matched to his red-framed glasses and the blood dripping from the horn of the unicorn on his T-shirt. It's rearing, preparing to stomp a half-mashed Starbucks logo beneath its hooves. A Bode original.

Don't blush, don't blush, don't blush. "Subtle," I say.

He glances at Aran and Cass. "'Subtle' is not the word I'd use for that."

"I meant your shirt."

"Oh." He looks down at it. "Yeah. And a little passé."

I breathe a laugh.

"Seriously," he says. "I made this screen in eighth grade."

"Really?"

"Sure."

I smile. "It's really good!" *Gross, Lucille, no.* Way too enthusiastic.

His brow creases as he grins. A closed-mouth grin, the paradoxical kind where the corners turn down like he's not sure if what I said was a compliment or an insult. "Thanks."

My cheeks heat. I consider becoming incorporeal and sinking back through the wall.

"You coming tonight?" he asks.

"Where?"

"Lava!" Aran cheers.

Cass unhooks her arms from around his neck. "A bunch of us are going to play it in the park. You should come."

My knee-jerk is to say no. Because when she says a bunch of

us, she means her theater friends. Such as Louise, who isn't my biggest fan. Like, rolls her eyes at half the things I say, and I don't talk much around her. But even with everything—I'm caught up with prep and nothing starts till the week after next—I have none of my typical excuses. And my house feels like living inside that ache in your throat when you refuse to cry. So I say, "Okay."

I walk home. My mom's still at work. I let Boris out, empty my messenger bag, unload the dishwasher, vacuum Boris's daily layer of shed fur, then sit in front of my laptop in my room. I reply to my SAT tutor, update my calendar with the new info from my Intro to Business syllabus, send a "hello" message to my group through the classroom portal, and try not to panic as the knot creaks with tension in my chest. Writing it all out helps. Four hours of class each day, chapters to read, weekly assignments, quizzes, tests, the course-long group project.

Dad was supposed to take me. Drop me off, pick me up. But now he's in Aurora. I pick up my phone to call him, make a new plan.

There's a thin layer of dust on the moose figurines arranged along the back of my desk. I watch a single mote—rainbow, flickering in the late-afternoon sunlight spilling through my window—float down and settle atop the one from my sixth birthday, a bobblehead with the moose sitting like a person on a rock and holding a banner that reads COLORADO. There are seventeen total. One for each birthday, including the day I was born.

"Lucy Moosie." What a ridiculous nickname. Who wants to be called a moose? But, for some reason, from that first one—bought by my dad in the hospital gift shop—it stuck. It was that or geese, I guess.

I set my phone down and pick up the moose from the year I turned twelve. It's the most fragile. Glass. With brittle antlers and spindly legs. I weigh it on my palm, consider throwing it at my wall. Then put it back and schedule in enough time each day on my calendar to take the bus.

The Reach the Sky email from Friday is still in my inbox. I should've moved it, trashed it. Instead I scan it one more time, like picking a scab. Like I might read between the lines why— with a perfect GPA and a list of accolades and extracurriculars as long as my arm—I'm only an alternate.

Not like I didn't already ask. I did. And the answer I got back read like a form rejection from a college: "With limited positions and a record-sized applicant pool, we were forced to be exceedingly selective" and "we invite you to reapply next year" and "should a position open up, we'll be in touch." Thankfully, someone has a scheduling conflict in the second session, so yeah. I'm happy. And I was able to swap an evening class for the daytime one with more credits. But it won't fix the pockmark on my applications made by missing the first session. It doesn't explain what about me doesn't hold up. A privileged, straight white girl with a four-point-oh from a Mountain State? Boring. One in a hundred. Less. I need perfection. And then some.

My phone and computer ding with a message from Cass: *Pick you up at 8!* I make myself wait a full five-count before answering that that sounds great—*behold how calm and collected and not frantically convincing myself not to bail I am*—then close my phone in a desk drawer to focus on the practice SAT test my tutor sent over to assess my existing skills.

I'm only six questions in when my computer dings with a new email. From Life². Again.

I hover my cursor over the notification, ready to click delete for the tenth time in as many days. Instead, I open it.

The message is topped by a banner ad. Silver, sleek, enigmatic, and animated so that when I move my cursor over it, the Life² logo switches to a slogan—*Do more. Be more.*—with a flash of light like a lens flare. The body of the message is congenial. And less generic than I expected. "Dear Lucille," it reads, "I realize this is unconventional. And I hope you'll forgive my persistence despite your lack of response. Thanks to your history of dedication to excellence, we at Life² are eager to extend to you this opportunity of a lifetime and . . ." blah blah blah *delete*.

An "opportunity of a lifetime" to hand over my Social Security number and end up with a few dozen credit cards opened in my name. But I stare at it in my trash folder thinking, *Only an alternate, exceedingly selective, dedication to excellence* while the knot in my chest goes *creak, creak, creak.*

I hear the door to the garage open and close downstairs. My mom calls, "Luce?" and I head down.

"Hey," she says, dropping a bag of fast food on the counter. Her hair's falling out of its messy bun and her eye makeup's smeared, like she's been crying.

"Hey," I echo. I don't know what else to say to her. The divorce, her sadness, it all makes me feel so unprepared and insufficient.

She dumps her work bag on the floor, letting it fall off her shoulder, not even trying to catch it, then unpacks the food, pulling out two cartons of French fries, then a burger and a salad. She pushes both toward me. "Your choice, Lucy."

I must make a face, because she wilts. Sitting on a barstool, she drops her head into her hands. "Sorry, *Lucille.* Sorry, shitty dinner. Sorry, sorry, sorry." She laughs. "I am so fucking tired of saying sorry." She turns her head, still propped on her hands, and smiles at me. The world's saddest, smallest smile. "It's been the week from hell. And today was the sixth circle, at least. Maybe seventh."

"Harpies and blood rivers?"

She stuffs a couple of fries in her mouth and, chewing, answers, "Less Dante, more calling customer service and getting an endless series of robo-menu prompts where you're screaming *Talk to a person!* over and over while the lady's perky recording-voice intentionally misunderstands you every single time."

"Brutal."

She nods, focus drifting to the burger. "You have plans tonight?"

It's a funny—as in sad—question because I basically never have plans anymore. I wonder if I should stay home. Offer to watch a movie with her. Eat ice cream. Help populate the TV room downstairs with its walls left barren after my dad took all of his framed concert photos. But then I think about canceling on Cass and how that feels barren too. "I'm going out with Cass and some of her friends in a bit."

"That's great! I'm glad you two are spending some time together. I know things have been . . ." She shrugs a shoulder.

"Yeah." I sit next to her and open the salad. "Hopefully, it'll be fun."

There's a *thud* on the roof of my hiding spot. I slap a hand over my mouth, swallowing a squeal.

Play Lava, they said. *What, the game where you can't touch the floor? The favorite of rowdy four-year-olds? Sure! Why not?*

This is not that game.

Take the horror-movie scene I'm in right now. The squeak of shoe soles on the hollow plastic roof of my tiny turreted room. The clatter of swing chains. Muffled laughs drifting through the dark like fog. The echoing "hoot, hoot" of Aran taunting Bode—said roof dweller and current "It"—from across the playground.

And me.

Breathing shallowly, silently, through my nose with my mouth clamped shut lest Bode hear me, tag me out first, and make me the next "It." I will do literally anything not to be "It."

The playground's a maze. One of those wood-and-plastic-composite monstrosities; part cabin/part castle, with half a dozen slides, swings, a climbing wall, monkey bars, bridges, and a labyrinth of raised walkways and elevated rooms like the one I'm in. Floodlights cast erratic patterns of dark and light. A shadow moves across a walkway to my left. Bode shifts on the roof, his weight denting the plastic with a baritone *thunk*.

He jumps.

Off the roof, onto the platform outside my room, sprinting across a wobbly bridge in the direction of the shadow—Finn's boyfriend, Matt, I think—who flees up a narrow staircase to a tall slide. I scoot across my little space to peer over the half wall in time to see Bode charge up the stairs after him while Matt runs down the slide, then leaps off the end toward a set of swings.

He makes it. Grabbing the swing's chains with outstretched hands, foot finding the swing's seat. A few people cheer. And he keeps moving, from one swing to the next, aiming for the four-person teeter-totter at the end. Bode pauses atop the slide, ready to follow, when Aran starts hooting again.

"You know I'm the best 'It'!" he yells. I look out and see him, perched atop a crow's nest and silhouetted by the white glow of the floodlight at his back.

Bode climbs up onto the hard plastic awning above the slide, and hollers back, "Is that a challenge?"

I don't care that all of this is ridiculous; watching him, I feel my crush bloom in my gut like a flower. *Oh my god I just referred to a portion of my anatomy as a flower.* It's the way he stands. Back straight—sue me, I like good posture—and hands in his pockets, the picture of nonchalance despite balancing on a bubble of plastic a solid fifteen feet off the ground. I mean, it's not a skill, is it? Standing? Or, like, *extreme* standing. But, still, it's sexy.

Aran shouts back, "Of-fucking-course!"

Bode laughs. "Fine!" He jumps off the slide's awning and sprints back the way he came. As in, straight toward me.

I panic.

I will not, *cannot*, get tagged out first. I'll cry. Seriously. Hot, pathetic stress tears. No wonder Cass never invited me before. I can't handle it. Everyone depending on me, uptight, hyper-responsible, nonathletic *me*, for the fun part? Absolutely not.

I look for an out, but he's already coming. Charging across one walkway, then the next. And I go for the roof. He did it, right?

I crouch on the half wall, gripping the underside of the pyramid-shaped plastic roof, then stand, warily. Even as Bode sprints toward the bridge.

Now what? The roof's slick plastic! And I'm just standing here. Waiting. In full freaking view while—

Bode runs past.

He clatters across the planks of the bridge and continues through the little room, straight past my legs, without missing a beat, traversing a sideways rope-ladder-thing between my room and the next walkway, where he pauses, looks back at me.

And *winks*.

I hide for the rest of the game. At least until after Bode chases Aran down, tagging him out first, Cass second, then, while chasing Finn, pauses in my tiny room to tag me out, too. This time without a glance.

Which, as I wander over to the sidelines to watch the last of the game play out, makes me rethink the reality of a wink that might've just been an exaggerated blink. Which makes me second-guess my gut reaction that he'd not-tagged me out of kindness and instead skipped me out of a desire to pick a competent "It" and continue having actual fun.

Welcome to my head.

I feel like I'm in one of those scenes in a movie where the main character stands still while everything else moves around them. A blur of happy activity around that one, stagnant soul. Through each of the next few rounds, while the others maintain that one-step-shy-of-breaking-their-necks bar, I remain low-hanging fruit. Shitty at hiding. Easy to catch.

Yet, I go out third or fourth every single time.

Which I take as confirmation that Bode's skipping me wasn't kindness, but a tactic. A fact that settles in my gut. By the time we—they—finish the last round and congregate in a loose circle in the grass, it feels like a sour weight, pulling me down.

"A-plus session, team," Aran says, lying on his back next to Cass.

I sit cross-legged beside her with Bode to my left and Finn, Matt, and Louise across from us. "Definitely," Bode says. "Matt's slide evasion was *epic*."

"Hey," Cass says, "don't forget how Lou hid *inside* the rock wall. Like a freaking spider."

Louise grins. "And how Luce just hid."

Matt boos quietly.

"Yeah," Bode says. "Boo, Lou."

Cass changes the subject. "Okay, but is anyone even going to mention my monkey-bar-balancing skills?"

It's September all over again. Me, feeling like Cass and I are still a package deal. Louise, taking jabs: *Oh my god, she laughs! . . . Who knew you were capable, Luce? . . . Careful, Luce, or your face will freeze like that. . . . Who asks for homework the first day? Any ideas, Luce?* Cass, picking no one and thereby picking everyone but me. Me, adding an independent study and eating lunch in the library for the rest of the year.

They move on, keep talking, but I stew in the awkward—Lucille Harper, Feels Like Her Skin Doesn't Fit—until Bode and

Aran get up to do skate tricks in the parking lot and Matt and Finn wander away. After a too-long beat of silence, Cass asks, "Why didn't you tell me?"

I look up from the plucked-grass pile I've been making on my legs. "Me?"

She chews the end of one of her sweatshirt's drawstrings. "Yeah, you."

"About what?"

"You're kidding, right?"

I shake my head.

She lets the string drop from her mouth. "Your parents, Luce. Why wouldn't you tell me something like that?"

I don't know why I say it. Maybe because she didn't back me up in front of Louise. Maybe because this whole night has felt like an exercise in proving I don't belong here, and it's left me feeling hurt and mean. Maybe the "why" doesn't matter. "We don't tell each other plenty of things."

"That's not fair."

"Fair or not, it's true."

"This isn't like not waiting to watch the next episode of our favorite show together. It's your parents' divorce." She shakes her head, huffing a breath out her nose. "My mom assumed you'd told me. Because why wouldn't you? Except, you didn't. So this afternoon, when I told her you were coming with us tonight, she goes, 'That's really good, Cassandra. I bet she needs it.' And I was, like, 'Needs what?' And she said, 'You. And to have some fun.' And I had to ask my *mom* why my *best friend* needs me. It was . . ."

"It was what?"

"Embarrassing."

"Embarrassing?"

She shrugs and I fill my lungs with a slow breath. "So why didn't you just tell her?"

"Tell her what?"

"That we aren't . . ." I purse my lips, deflate.

Between us, Louise is too still. Cass shifts up onto her knees, facing me, and says, "And whose fault is that? That we 'aren't'? My mom says your dad *moved*. And you didn't tell me!"

The knot's so tight my chest burns. I want to tell her about it. The heat. The pressure. How perfect's not really perfect, how all of my truths suddenly feel like lies, how every step she takes away from me leaves me even farther behind. And how ridiculous that makes me feel. To have what I have and still feel like I'll never be enough.

But even as I think them, the words go acrid and thin. Because while I know I should be thinking about *My Little Pony* birthday parties and sleepovers and bike rides and days at Elitch's and Water World, thinking about all the good stuff that makes us *us*, all the stuff that should've made her the first person I told, all the stuff that should've made me feel guilty that she wasn't, instead I think of Louise. Louise, who's hated me from day zero. Who's sitting *right there*. Listening. Like she's part of this? Like there's *nothing* that's just Cass's and mine anymore? Even our *drama*?

Then, to the backing track of his and Bode's laughs and clattering skateboards, I think about Aran.

No, I'm riding the bus with Aran.

Not tonight, Luce, Aran's coming to dinner and it's going to be weird enough.

Sorry, that was a text from Aran, can I call you back later?

Aran, Aran, Aran. Tugging my best friend away from me in stretches, one arm length, inside joke, coy smile, and shared secret at a time.

So I don't say anything, I just shrug.

Cass's jaw drops. "Really?"

"What?"

"What do you mean, 'what'? Are you *trying* to hurt me?"

"Hurt *you*? They're *my* parents. It's *my* life."

"Your parents, sure, *Lucy*." She does it on purpose. "But I'm your best friend! And your mom and dad—" Her voice cracks and I look to find her crying. "They're not just your mom and dad. They're Nancy and Ryan. The people who've picked me up from school a thousand times, who took me to the hospital when Micah was born. They're my family too!"

I scoff. "Are they? You haven't been to my house in months, *Cassandra. Months.* Since early March, to be exact."

"*To be exact,*" she mocks. "Of course you'd freaking know. I bet you know the date. I bet you know the *hour*. Do you make friendship study guides, too? 'Cause it's not like there'll be a fucking test."

Louise snorts.

"Good," I say. "Great. Make fun of the fact that I study. At least I give enough of a shit to keep track."

"I'm sorry, are you saying I don't give a shit about you?"

Dimly, I note that the sound of skateboards on the pavement has stopped. "You, my best friend of sixteen years."

"Stop calling me that," I snap. "Your best friend. How can you still call yourself my best friend? Sure, I didn't tell you. But it's not like you tell me shit either. You've spent the last nine months—"

"Of course!" Cass throws her hands up. "Bring up me and Aran." She stands. "I'm guessing you know the date for that one too, right? Made a note in your calendar." She mimics typing something into a phone. "Cass gets boyfriend and stops giving me her undivided attention."

"Right, ha ha. Look at Lucille, so ridiculous and uptight. Isn't that hilarious."

"It's not funny." She wipes the tears from her cheeks. "It's fucking sad."

I don't know why she's crying and I'm not. I guess I should be, but I don't feel like crying. I feel like burning something down. "Yeah, it'll be super sad when all my ridiculous uptightness gets me into Harvard. But, hey, you and Aran enjoy DU."

"God, Lucy!" she shouts. "No one cares that you want to go to Harvard or Yale or where-the-hell-ever! And *what* is wrong with D—" She shakes her head and holds her hands up. "You know what? Not worth it. It's *not worth it*."

She walks away.

Louise follows a pace behind.

And I stare at the ground, letting my vision blur.

I add some more grass to my pile. The sound of Bode's and Aran's skateboards—oh my god, they heard all of that—starts up again. I roll a wad of grass between my palms until it turns into a pulpy mess, then stand and wander into the playground.

To find her? To apologize?

I don't know.

I kick at the wood chips as I go, thinking, *I don't know, I don't know, I don't know.*

"Screw her," Louise says, loud enough that I know she doesn't care who hears her. "She's pathetic. And just jealous because she can't get a boyfriend."

I stop.

They're around a corner of the castle/log-house structure from me. Through the gaps, I see them sitting on the edge of a short platform.

"I mean," Louise continues, "she's had a crush on Bode forever, right? And he doesn't give a single fuck about her."

My breath stalls.

I spin on my heel and head for the parking lot to grab my phone off the backseat of Aran's mom's minivan. He and Bode are still doing skate tricks in the parking lot. Neither looks up. Mom answers on the first ring. "Luce?"

"Can you come get me?"

She doesn't ask why, just where, then says she's on her way.

I walk down the street away from the park, stop two intersections down, send my mom a pin, and type out a text to Cass, thumb hovering over the send button.

There's a picture of us in the upstairs hallway, on the wall across from my room. We're six, cheek to cheek, smiling with teeth stained purple from the overdyed icing on my *My Little Pony* birthday cake.

I remember so much of that day. The table of presents. The plastic *My Little Pony* gift bags. Mixing bites of chocolate cake with strawberry ice cream, and how that purple icing—overly sweet and somehow greasy—felt in my mouth.

Then, a few months ago, I dropped that memory into a conversation with my mom, like, "Hey, remember that *My Little Pony* birthday party I had?" And she crimped her brow and asked, "What?"

Because it wasn't my party.

It was Cass's.

Tell yourself a lie enough times and it becomes your truth.

I hit send and wait, forgiving her for the first five minutes, ten, fifteen even, because her phone's probably in Aran's mom's car like mine was. But then my mom's here. Then I'm home.

The first thing I do is open my laptop, my email, then the trash folder. There are three of them in a row. Ten total, starting a week and a half ago. The newest is the only one I've opened, so I go back and start from the beginning.

"Dear Lucille," I read, brow tightening with every subsequent line. There are the buzz phrases, that "opportunity of a lifetime" plus "ideal candidate" and "free trial." All signs pointing to click-the-link-get-a-healthy-dose-of-malware. Except, the more I read, the more real they sound.

Conversational, direct, informed, signed by a "Dr. Thompson" who says they found me "through a targeted search for the most ambitious young people with the most promising prospects in the area," based on my participation in a list of groups and programs included in the second email. All of which sounds

ridiculous but apparently makes me a "highly desirable candidate" for some program that they swear—again and again—will
be the "advent of a new human era thanks to unprecedented scientific breakthroughs."

I know what I should do. I know how I *should* feel. I should
delete the whole lot of them, feel creeped out that they admit
to snagging my email off the—likely not publicly accessible—
business-class roster, block the address, empty the digital bin. I
should laugh, close my laptop, and go to bed.

But I don't want to. Because it feels *real*. Like they want *me*.
Like they know *me*. Like they *need* me. And maybe that's a symptom. The fallout of my shitty night and feeling like everything's
falling apart. But I keep reading, and when my computer dings
with a new message from Life^2 right as I'm finishing the last one,
it doesn't feel like a warning, it feels like a sign.

"Lucille," it reads.

This will be my last effort. While I'm confident that you
are the perfect fit for this opportunity, time constraints
and your silence have forced me to reach out to alternate
candidates. I understand that within the context of our
modern world, my approach may seem unbelievable or
disconcerting, but as this is my only known contact for
you, I've been forced to make do.

Life^2 sits at the precipice of the greatest advancement for humanity in modern history, and I would hate
for you to lose out on an opportunity to be an integral
part of that thanks to confusion about our intentions or

misguided doubts about the company and our program. If anything I've said now or in previous messages piques your interest, do not hesitate to call, day or night. The position is yours until it's claimed by another.

I reread the message until I can recite it from memory, then stare at the banner logo, moving my cursor onto it and off again to watch the animation work, keeping the arrow equidistant between *Do more* and *Be more*, knowing that if I click through it'll be like taking a running swan dive into the rabbit hole.

Acres of red flags and a thousand questions . . . yet.

Do more. Be more.

Exactly what I want, what I need, served up on a shining, enigmatic platter.

Lucille Harper, Overachiever. Lucille Harper, Pretending at Perfect. Lucille Harper, Insufficient Daughter. Lucille Harper, Left Behind. Lucille Harper, Pining Over a Guy Who *Doesn't Give a Single Fuck About Her.* Lucille Harper, Checks Her Phone at 12:32 a.m. and There's Still No Text from Cass Because She's Not Even Missed.

Lucille Harper, Says *Fuck It* and Clicks the Damn Link.

CHAPTER THREE

The building is nondescript. Think a giant gray Lego plunked down in the middle of nowhere northeast of Denver, designed to make you forget what you're seeing even while you're looking straight at it.

I cross my arms tighter around my chest, blow out a breath while I watch my Lyft car do a rolling stop at the end of the access road, turn west, and drive away, then check my phone: 9:55 a.m. Five minutes until my appointment.

Plenty of time to turn back.

But—even staring at the fifteen-foot chain-link fence topped in coils of razor wire, the mechanized gate, surveillance cameras, and accompanying video-com screen—I don't want to.

Clicking that link was like solving one mystery only to find another, then another and another. The site was sleek, minimalist like the email banner, with nothing but a portal to a contact page through the Life² logo. So, I went to Google.

And found rumors. Conspiracy sites. Reddit threads. A Wikipedia page prefaced by the "needs citations" warning. All signs pointed to a hoax. A fantastically effortful phishing scheme. Or, darker, a trap. Except every single lead shared the same uniting thread: Life² is a multibillion-dollar company leading the charge on biological advancement. Those "breakthroughs" Dr. Thompson kept mentioning. But in what? Pharmaceuticals? No. Biomechanics? Not exactly. Human-animal hybrids à la *The Island of Doctor Moreau*? One guy was convinced.

Evolution, biosynthesis, singularity. Cryogenics, immortality, regeneration, gene editing.

Do more. Be more.

Each answer led to five more questions. It was like trying to piece together what something is, based on what it isn't. Like looking for a picture in an image's negative space. But instead of feeling bored or warned, I felt *invigorated*.

The deeper I went, the more ridiculous the conjectures— aliens, supersoldiers, clones—the more I needed to know.

So I called. And even at two in the morning, someone answered.

Three minutes until my appointment, and I take a deep breath and step up to the screen.

It flicks on. *"Hello, Miss Harper."*

I recognize the voice. Isobel, no last name. The same one who answered my call last night. I clear my throat. "Hi."

The woman—brown-skinned with a perfect face, like facetuned perfect—smiles. *"We're delighted you came."*

"Uh, yep. Here I am."

"Please," she says, and the gate buzzes, clinks, swings open. *"Come in."*

One gate, two doors, and I step into a room with that blinding white aesthetic Apple always has. Sleek. Monochromatic. Seamless.

The second door closes, and it's what I imagine having an air-lock seal behind you feels like. My ears even pop. It's too still. Too silent. I can hear Isobel breathing, the sound of her mouth when she smiles, the *shush* of her sleeve brushing her side as she gestures to a stark white couch. "Please," she says. "Sit."

I sit.

"Would you like a refreshment?"

"No thank you," I say, though my tongue's so dry it sticks to the roof of my mouth. Ingesting something here feels final. Eating the "Eat Me" cake. Sipping faerie wine, then falling under some enchantment and dancing till my feet bleed.

Still smiling, she dips her head once, then hesitates. Like she's unsure what to do next. Like the only answer she's prepared to accept is yes. And sure enough, she turns, crosses the slick white floor to a white sideboard against the white wall, and fills a single slim glass with water from a matching pitcher.

Her footsteps echo faintly as she returns. She sets the glass on the coffee table—also glass—in front of me. Then stands, waiting. I look between her and the glass. "Thanks?"

She offers another dip of her perfect head, then clasps her hands behind her back. "Dr. Thompson should be here shortly."

I eye the glass of water on the table. Stare at it. Because I can feel Isobel staring at me.

I lick my lips, try to swallow, but my spit's gone tacky. My palms are slick, and the knot in my chest is yanked so taut it rings. I think, *What am I doing here, what am I doing here, what am I doing here,* on a loop.

But I already know the answer.

I'm here because I need to know what "here" is. I'm here because even *thinking* about more, being more, makes the knot calm.

I'm here because *they* need *me*.

It's what Dr. Thompson said when we spoke on the phone after Isobel—chipper and bright—asked me to hold and the line went quiet for less than a minute. "We need you." She said a load of other stuff too, but that's the line that echoed in my head. Intoxicating—*don't call me pathetic*—validating. They need *me*. They want *me*. I am their first pick.

And I know, I *know*, how that sounds. I hear it even clearer sitting on this rigid white couch under the gaze of a woman standing so stiffly, I swear her joints creak. I sound deluded. Delusional. Ridiculous and reckless and like I might as well lie down on the floor, dig into my own gut, and hand them my organs to sell on the black market myself. I mean, if my being here—secret building, secret company, secret plans, I probably should've left my mom a note—says anything, it's that self-preservation isn't my strong suit.

But.

I lean forward, grab the glass of water off the table, and take a long drink.

A door opens—I'll use "door" in the technical sense because, legit, a section of the wall *shinks* open, the sound like a sword being pulled from its scabbard—and a white woman, exquisitely dressed in a slate-gray wrap dress under a white doctor's coat, enters the room followed by a man in a white coat, crisp slacks, and a tie, with an oversized tablet in his hands.

"Lucille, welcome," the woman says, extending her hand. I stand to shake it. "I'm Dr. Thompson, and this is Dr. Kim. We apologize for the wait."

I take my hand from her and fight an urge to hug my arms around my chest. "At least the accommodations are cozy."

"Would you believe me," Dr. Kim says, his voice deep and loose with the slightest Southern drawl, "if I said we're still decorating?"

"I'd believe you if you said that door leads to an alternate dimension."

He breathes a laugh. Dr. Thompson smiles superficially and says, "Thank you for taking the leap of faith to join us today. I'm sure you have a lot of questions."

Understatement. "Yeah, I—"

"First"—she waves Dr. Kim forward—"the formalities I mentioned last night." He offers the tablet to me, a nondisclosure agreement already open on the screen.

There's an awkward moment where I pause, unsure. I prepared for this. She told me, asked me specifically, to bring an ID verifying that I'm over eighteen so I can legally sign the "necessary paperwork." And when I tried to tell her I can't, I'm not, she interrupted, saying, "Bring what you can, and I'll make it work." So I thought of the fake ID hidden in a box in my closet, procured last summer for a concert at an eighteen-and-up venue that Cass just *had* to go to, a card that was flimsy then and will no doubt be worse now, under this bright, unforgiving light. But, Thompson knows. She has to. *She* found *me.* And if she doesn't care that I'm only sixteen, should I?

I meet her eye and she dips her head, slightly, conspiratori-
ally, and says, "You can give Dr. Kim your ID after you sign."

"Right." I stand there and read the NDA.

The print's small. The prose convoluted. And their attention
makes my hands shake. I scan it—catching phrases like "all information, written or otherwise conveyed, owned by or pertaining to
Life^2, its assets or investors, whether having existed, is now existing, or will ever exist, whether tangible or intangible" and so on
for another two thousand words—then sign with my finger and
pull out my wallet and fake ID.

Holding my breath, I hand it to Dr. Kim. He takes a photo of
the ID with the tablet, then hands it back.

"Fabulous," Thompson says. "Shall we?"

I take a moment, tucking the ID back into my wallet and my
wallet into my purse. If I follow them through that creepy sci-fi
door, there's no going back.

I think of my dream. The SUV. It's always so heavy. On my
shoulders, against my back. In my stomach. Fighting against me
as I press my foot to the brake. And the thing I never do, the thing
I always wonder: *What if, instead, I push the gas?*

I follow Drs. Thompson and Kim through the portal and down
a hall. The walls emanate the same bright glow as the lobby. It's
giving me vertigo. And I think, *Ninety percent chance I never see
the sun again.* Then Dr. Thompson turns a corner into a bright,
sunlit room.

I stop in the doorway and exhale. Long and slow.

A wall of windows looks out onto a courtyard, maybe half an acre square and empty except for a single pathway running through plush summer grass. A conference table—white, of course—dominates the center of the room. A video screen is built into the wall at my left.

Dr. Thompson chooses the first chair on the window side of the table and gestures for me to take the seat across from her as Dr. Kim sits at her left. I pull the chair out and sit, purse still over my shoulder and phone in my hand. I wore one of my nicest semicasual outfits this morning—skinny black dress pants with a flowy blouse—with my hair curled and makeup done, but every sterile surface in this place makes me feel like a stain.

I press the home button on my phone. For comfort? Force of habit? And see the tiny "no service" notice up in the corner.

A matchstick of panic lights between my shoulder blades, flaring up my neck and across my scalp. I raise my eyes to them again and find them watching. Expectant.

It's not funny. It's fucking sad.

I take a deep breath, set my phone facedown on the table, loop the strap of my purse over the back of the chair, and square my shoulders, hands linked atop the glossy white table. "You called me the ideal candidate."

Dr. Thompson nods. She mimics my posture. Or maybe I'm unconsciously mimicking hers. "You are."

"For what?"

"Welcome to Life Squared," says the man in the video. White, with salt-and-pepper hair and wearing an expensive-looking dark-gray suit, he stands on a path winding through a park. Sunlight falls on the vividly green grass around him, shimmers on the blue surface of the lake at his right. The foliage—scattered bushes and trees lining the path—glows in autumn hues. "Do more," he says. "Be more. You know our slogan." There's a gentle backing track, ignorable instrumental music alongside the quiet *shush* of the lake and occasional trill of a bird. It's soothing. Hypnotic. "And I'm sure you know what those words mean to you as they echo, right now, in your mind. Maybe what you need more of is energy. Space, time. Freedom."

Hands in his pockets, the man starts walking. The camera follows. "Maybe, with your responsibilities, the weight of your life's expectations, what you really need . . ." He pauses, staring into the lens, and takes a wide step to the side, revealing . . .

A second him.

Together, they finish, ". . . is to be in two places at the same time."

I glance at Drs. Thompson and Kim across the table. Both watch the screen. The corner of Dr. Thompson's mouth curves up.

"With RapidReplicate," the first man continues, "the product of Life Squared's countless revolutionary scientific and technological advancements, you can do that—"

"And more," the second man finishes.

The setting changes, leaving the park for a stark white lab filled with technicians in biohazard suits working at long tables populated by an array of intricate equipment. Alone now, the man tours the space in his fine suit, weaving casually between the scientists. An ignored observer. The room's only color. Narrating as he goes: "Using groundbreaking methods, Life Squared can duplicate you. In entirety. In adult form."

He pauses beside a seemingly unaware scientist bent over a microscope, and the camera switches perspectives, following the scientist's line of sight down the microscope to the magnified contents of its slide.

"Your DNA, collected in a procedure that's as painless and minimally invasive as possible, will be inserted into new cells"— the tip of a needle appears among the cells on the screen, piercing the wall of one—"then, through a process of directed growth and formation, your Facsimile, your second self, will be . . ."

The scene changes again, this time to a lab populated only by the man and a person-sized capsule. Hands still in his pockets, the picture of nonchalance, he saunters over to it, and frees a hand to press a button on its side.

The lid lifts. The camera angle shifts, hovering above a second man—utterly identical to the first—lying prone and seemingly unconscious in the capsule. The background music intensifies. Crescendos. Then, at its fullest moment, goes silent.

The second man opens his eyes, and says, "Brought to life."

The screen goes black.

I blink.

Across the table, Drs. Thompson and Kim watch me. Waiting.

Clones.

A hysterical laugh bubbles in my chest, but I swallow it.

Do more. Be more. With a literal second self. It's . . . "Not possible."

Thompson tips her head. "It is."

"No. Some cartilage. An ear. Part of a clavicle. Sure. But a heart? A whole body? A *brain*? Not possible." I'm shaking my head. Shaking, shaking. "No way that guy's real."

"You're right," she says. "He's an actor. Which is why we need you."

I purse my lips, take two slow breaths in and out my nose, then say, "Tell me more."

Enucleated oocytes. Somatic-cell nuclear transfers. Induced pluripotent stem cells. Dedifferentiation and reprogramming. 3-D bioprinting. Vascularized cellular constructs. Cell-laden hydrogels. Biodegradable polymers. "But while they pioneered the use of microchannels to deliver nutrients to the tissue," Dr. Kim continues, referring to the group of scientists he's been telling me about as we walk—a group that, a few years ago, managed to fabricate human parts using an integrated tissue-organ printer, or ITOP, "their processes limited the size and stability of their fabrications. Think about the complexity of the human cardiovascular system. Or the nervous system! Forty-six miles of nerves in the human body. *Miles.* And approximately one hundred billion neurons in the brain. Think about replicating not only your adult skeletal structure but also your marrow, each of your blood vessels, your skin." He pauses before a massive observation window built into the hallway's wall.

I stand between him and Dr. Thompson and watch as the technicians within—dressed as they had been in the video—go about their business.

Business like growing a human arm.

An *arm*. Complete from just above the bicep to the hand.

I step closer, my nose a half inch from the glass, and watch a scientist reach into a tub of translucent blue goop and carefully, oh so carefully, detach a set of tubes connecting the arm to a machine, then pull it out and set it on an exam table. I expect it to be wet with the goop, like Jell-O, but from the window, it looks dry. The scientist peels a semi-opaque covering, like plastic wrap, from the raw section above the arm's bicep where it would meet a shoulder. They touch the area with a small tool.

And the arm's fingers flinch.

Its fingers flinch.

"Dr. Adebayo is testing the appendage's nerve functions," Dr. Thompson says.

My stomach rolls. "What *is* it?"

"The final stages of testing for complete appendage transplant. Science has made impressive leaps in transplantation: female reproductive organs, hands, faces, male genitals. But the difference here, of course, is that Life Squared's appendages will be true replacements, not donations. Here, we can grow you a new, genetically identical arm."

"No risk of rejection," adds Dr. Kim.

"And a complete return of all motor functions." Dr. Thompson starts down the hallway again. Dr. Kim and I follow. "Nerve damage, hearing and sight loss, compromised internal organs from injury or disease. Not merely repairable, but *replaceable*. All of which brings us to . . ." She gestures to the observation window of the next laboratory.

I step up to the glass and peer inside. It looks like the lab from the last scene in the video. With one major addition. "What am I looking at?"

Dr. Thompson grins. Proud. "That," she says, pointing past the capsule at a massive machine with more than a dozen articulating arms, "is the full-sized ITOP."

She shifts her finger down, pointing at the capsule from the video. A high-tech glass coffin. Or, the exact opposite. "And that, is the incubator."

"One of them," Kim says.

"Why do you need more than one?"

Dr. Thompson crosses her arms. "We have yet to master the contiguous fabrication of a Facsimile."

"What does that mean?"

"The Facsimile's organs require individuated replication. With bodily integration after the fact."

"That sounds like a fancy way of saying cloning, but with some assembly required."

Kim smirks. "It is."

Dr. Thompson tips her head. "For now."

I think about my heart, my lungs. My brain. "So you . . . grow me. Print me. Then what? She's an . . . *infant*? A neurological blank slate?"

Dr. Thompson turns her attention from the room beyond the window to me, looking almost amused. "Our tour isn't over, Lucille. There's still more to see."

They lead me back to the conference room, where Dr. Kim uses the tablet to pull up a digital image of a brain on the wall's screen.

"We call it MimeoMem," Thompson says. "The process we use to digitize your connectome, the sum of everything that makes you *you*, and upload it to the Life Squared supercomputer, ready to be downloaded, or more accurately, *incorporated* into your Facsimile's wetware."

"Brain," Dr. Kim clarifies.

I nod, touching the white tabletop, matching my fingertips to their reflections, one at a time, again and again. "That much computing power," I say. "They . . ." *They*. A ridiculous concept now that I'm sharing a room with an iteration of "them," that catch-all moniker for those nameless, faceless people out there, somewhere, making discoveries. Advancing the narrative of humankind. The things you glimpse in headlines. Take bites of by watching TED talks or reading your mom's copies of *Scientific American*. "I read that scientists have only begun to digitize the connectome of a mouse. That there isn't enough computer memory in the whole *world* to do what you say you're doing."

Dr. Kim smiles. "The world doesn't know about us."

"Why not? If you can do all of this, why keep it secret?"

"The subject is . . . contentious," Thompson says. "And Life Squared believes that we can do the most good off the public stage. You've had the barest glimpse of our capabilities. We wouldn't want prolonged international furor over issues the average person is incapable of comprehending to curtail that progress."

I tap my fingers to their reflections in order, pinky to index, again and again. "Say I agree. What does that look like? Rapid-Replicate. MimeoMem. All of it."

"It is a ten-week process, counting from the date of your

stem-cell retrieval. Eight for RapidReplicate, which includes a series of procedures to procure the necessary genetic material for duplication and to facilitate the Facsimile's growth, such as body scans, the Mimeo, and memory tests for future verification. You'll need to make yourself available for these, but otherwise the time requirement is modest. Following consciousness, there is a two-week adjustment period during which we'll assess the Facsimile's structural and mental integrity in preparation for integration.

"Upon completion, this trial requires that you and your Facsimile embark on a four-week field test, during which time it will live with you and perform duties as would be desirable to our future clients. Spend time with your friends and family, fulfill your obligations. Be you without detection."

"You mean don't get caught."

"Yes. It's imperative, not only for the success of the trial but for our general purposes, that all of your dealings with us remain confidential. Hence the NDA." Thompson smiles at me, close-lipped and blandly congenial. "Your Facsimile's trial will be our final test before taking RapidReplicate to market. With your help, we'll cross the line from experimentation to implementation. And a vital aspect of that is secrecy.

"Our clients don't want a twin, they want an expanded self, the capacity to exceed lofty expectations without sacrificing anything. They want to be attentive spouses, parents, friends, while simultaneously running companies and leading nations. They want to explore their truly limitless potential. And they want the credit for it, as a *single* individual. Detection, even among those closest to them, would defeat that purpose."

"And if she is? Detected?"

"The trial terminates."

Kim adds, "And we do damage control."

"If it's successful, then what happens when it ends?"

"The asset returns to us," Thompson says, "to be decommissioned or repurposed as we see fit, and you continue on with your life knowing you were an essential aspect of the greatest achievement in history."

I can't name the feeling in my gut when she says that. Excitement? Apprehension? It's a chimera. Motley and surreal. If I weren't sitting here, touching this table, breathing this air, I wouldn't believe this place exists. Even with all of that, it's part figment. Reality, but one with a purple-tinged sky.

"I still don't understand. Why me?"

Dr. Thompson's brow creases as she tips her head. "Lucille," she says, holding my eye, "surely you know that you are an exceptional young woman. And we are in the business of exceptionality.

"You will be our capstone. Your Facsimile, the first fully functional, adult human duplicate, a scientific marvel that will change the world. Would you give that position to anyone but the best?"

The best. I want to believe it. I want to believe it so bad.

I drop my focus to the tabletop, so perfect and smooth and reflecting the doctors' images keenly enough that I can see their features, their expressions as they watch me, and the moment they share a brief, expectant look.

All the shoulds. Should've deleted that last email, but I didn't. Shouldn't have clicked, researched, called, but I did. Should feel skeptical, nervous. Afraid. But I don't.

For as long as I can remember, I've felt this tug. Pressure, the knot in my chest, whatever. Pulling at me, whispering, *Keep up, keep up, keep up.* A current of expectations I've kept my head above, but only just. Only barely. Or, maybe, not at all. Because every time I excel at one thing, I fail at another.

But this. A second me. Four hands instead of two. Two minds instead of one. Forty-eight hours in a day. I could do anything. I could do *everything.*

Four whole weeks to be me, but better.

To be me, but *more.*

CHAPTER FOUR

Before and after.

That's how I think of it. It's that revolutionary.

Before, I thought about this summer and felt . . . dread. A whole summer of me? Solitary, daughter-of-divorcés, left-behind me? Yep, crushing, weight-of-an-SUV-bearing-down-on-me dread.

But that was before.

And this is after.

After I signed a contract with a multibillion-dollar science and technology company on the brink of altering the course of human life as we know it. Well, for a minuscule subset of "human life," to be known about by almost no one. Because Life²'s advancements are "proprietary," Thompson told me. "We have to protect our financiers' investments. And ensure that our technology doesn't end up in the wrong hands."

"Not to mention," Dr. Kim added, focusing on drawing what would be the first of many samples of my blood, "that global shit-storm we mentioned going public would cause."

I'd watched the vial fill with deep black-red liquid, and made a mental note to google cloning laws when I got home.

Because that's another part of after. Watching old interviews and reading articles about Dolly, the first animal successfully cloned using adult cells, and newer ones about Zhong Zhong and Hua Hua, the macaque monkeys cloned in China a few years ago. Learning that in 2005, the United Nations called for a nonbinding ban on human cloning, that seventy countries forbid it, but that no law prohibits it in Colorado. And that there's an ever-present moral, ethical, secular, and religious debate about it, including concepts like "human dignity" and, as the Vatican itself put it, a person's "right to be born in a human way."

But what about a clone that isn't born but made? *Assembled?*

Before, I thought about assignments, grades, college application hooks, SAT prep, and whether or not Cass would invite me to whatever her friends planned next.

After, I think about assignments, grades, hooks, prep, whether or not I'll ever actually talk to Cass again, and the semantics of "reproduction" in the context of zygotes and fertilization versus literal duplication, like printing two copies of the same page. Personhood, individuality, and if it'll work to keep her in the mother-in-law suite above the garage for a month.

So, okay. A revolution, but one that's still in progress.

It's all progress. Swimming with that current of expectations but feeling like someday soon, I'll finally be able to touch the bottom, and maybe even stand.

I focus on that as I settle into my seat for my first Intro to Business class. My stomach's tight. I'm the first one here, twenty minutes early, and I check the schedule three times to make sure this is the right room. A medium-sized lecture hall with tiered seating and tables instead of desks—I picked the one that's front and center. Beside my laptop, I open my textbook to the first chapter, and wait. Wondering who will sit in the three other seats at this table. Hoping the professor's nice. Soaking it in because this is where I've worked so hard to be.

Not this class, specifically. But college, the future, this feeling. A place that's big and limitless. Where I'm not an overachiever or Cass's plus-one or a daughter too oblivious to realize her parents' perfection is a lie, I'm just me. Whoever I am.

I stretch my arm out on the table and stare at the tiny scab in the crook of my elbow from the latest blood draw. Glucose, cholesterol, LDL, HDL, triglycerides, STI screening, and a pregnancy test, though I told them that was pointless. Saturday's the stem-cell retrieval, then they'll start.

I wonder if she'll remember this. The cool surface of the table growing warm beneath my arm. The bite of the needle drawing my—*our*—blood. The nervous flop of my stomach as the door opens behind me and a group of students starts down the stairs, talking while they pick their seats without a glance at me or my empty table. I wonder if any of them are in my group. No one responded to my message, though it shows that three of the four have seen it. More people file in now, and I turn forward, opening a new doc on my computer to take notes.

Ten weeks from Saturday, and she'll be here.

Ten weeks, and I'll be more, enough, no longer alone.

I don't get used to it. The white. The general starchiness. Like the designer said, "I want the place to look like the feel of squeaking your finger across a clean plate." Each time I walk through the doors feels like the first time, like I'm tripping through a crack into a skewed universe. One where I'm Lucille Harper, eighteen-year-old freshman at DU and subject LH2010, an identifier given to "maintain your anonymity," Thompson said, "for when I present our progress to the Board."

The lying turns out to be surprisingly easy. At home, because my parents are so busy being mid-divorce and I'm so good at being self-governed that apart from being driven around, I'm basically a nonentity already and my extra absences go utterly unnoticed. And at Life^2, because I don't think they give a single shit. Not about what I'm studying or how my life looks, only that I'm here.

And when I'm here, I'm meat.

Today, I'm *tenderized* meat.

They throw around words like "extraction" and "multipotency" with accompanying needles. It helps "streamline" the process, Dr. Thompson tells me as I lie on an exam table, wearing a Life^2-specific set of white scrubs, with a numb scalp and aching hip. "The somatic cells found in your blood may be multipotent, meaning they have the capacity to develop into any of several cell types, but their primary purpose is to regenerate damaged tissue or replace dead cells."

I swallow. My throat's dry, and my jaw's sore from clenching my teeth. "Not to grow a second brain."

"No." She smiles thinly. It curves her lips, lifts her cheeks, but that's all. Mechanical. Intention and physical response, not the consequence of an actual feeling. "Which is why we retrieve samples from as many locations as possible. To speed up the process and better ensure success."

I lift a hand to touch a fresh bandage stuck to my hair, holding a cotton ball over the hole Dr. Adebayo, the resident neurosurgeon, cut in my head. "Constructive criticism to benefit paying clients?"

"Yes?"

"Contrary to what the video suggested, that was neither painless nor minimally invasive."

She arches an eyebrow.

"Knock people out. Or at least give them the option."

She stands. "Noted." And leaves, the door sliding shut behind her.

For a while I stare at the ceiling. Thinking about needles and samples and vials and ten short weeks, then slowly I sit up. The door opens again, revealing Isobel this time, holding a bin filled with my neatly folded clothes.

I move, shifting my legs off the table and pursing my lips at the pain in my hip where they took hematopoietic stem cells from my marrow. "Administrative assistant *and* nurse?"

"I called you a car."

Hands gripping the edge of the table, half-numb head hanging, I say, "Thanks."

"I remember—" She cuts herself off, and I look up. The moment my attention brushes her face, her expression flips from frustrated to beatific. She takes two efficient strides across the room, sets the bin on the table beside me, and says, "I hope you aren't too uncomfortable," then goes.

I run down the hall, but the door's already closed, and I can hear Professor Mathieson lecturing inside.

Hand on the door, I pause to catch my breath, then squeeze the handle oh so slowly, like that'll make me invisible or rewind time twenty minutes or, hell, an hour, so instead of waiting for my dad—"I promise I'll be on time, Luce. Promise!"—I could've taken the bus like I usually do, anything but this: opening the door into a dim lecture hall, flooding the space with light, drawing every eye including Mathieson's, who turns from his video presentation to raise a significant brow at me.

I ease the door closed behind me and hurry down to my table—where I still sit alone—and pull out my stuff. As I open my laptop to take notes, Mathieson, still lecturing, grabs a paper from his desk, steps down from the raised teaching platform, and drops it on my table.

My mock business proposal.

With a C on it.

The knot in my chest goes so tight I can't breathe. My right hip still aches, and I lean into it. Feeling the pain like an anchor, a promise. Just last night, I stood in the mother-in-law suite above the garage, a full studio complete with a love seat, bathroom, and kitchenette, and thought, *It's perfect.* Now I'm looking down at my first C.

When class ends, I pack my things and stand by the platform, waiting to catch Professor Mathieson's attention.

"Yes, Miss Harper?" he says.

I hold out my paper. "Can I talk to you about this?"

"Of course."

"Okay. Well. What did I do wrong? I followed the example perfectly?"

"You did." He crosses his arms and leans back against my table. "But that's *all* you did."

"Isn't that what you wanted?"

He takes a slow breath. "Miss Harper, do you want to study business?"

"I—"

"You're young. High school, right?"

"Yes. A junior next year."

His brow rises. "Wow, okay," he says. "Why'd you pick this class? Be honest."

I purse my lips.

"For your applications?" he guesses. "Taking a summer college course ticks a box, right?"

I nod.

He uncrosses his arms and presses the palms of his hands together. "Listen. That's admirable. You're ambitious and following through. But there's nothing innovative in that." He waves at the paper in my hand. "Nothing original or interesting or, well, *outside* of the box. It reads like you're checking items off a list, because that's what you're doing. You took the example and filled in the blanks with new answers. That's it. And that can get you by in a lot of life. But if adding a gold star to your college applications is the only reason you're here, maybe this class isn't for you."

"It's only one assignment."

"It is. And it isn't. It's an outlook. Your *approach*. Filling in the blanks is the bare minimum. If you're not willing to push yourself to come up with something new, then you're doing little more than warming a seat." He holds his hands up, palms out. "Tough love, I know. But we both know the paper's not your only issue here. A couple of members of your group say you keep missing meetings."

I huff a breath. "That's because two of them are roommates, and they're always getting together at, like, midnight or meeting downtown with no notice, and I live in Lakewood and don't have a car."

He shrugs, like *not my problem*, and says, "I think you just need to ask yourself why you're really here. Is it to learn something you're actually interested in? Or to earn that gold star? It doesn't make any difference to me. But I'm willing to bet that figuring that out will make a big difference to you."

Sitting on a bench out front, I flip through my proposal, reading comments like "uninspired" and "unoriginal" and "needs fleshing out" before folding it up and shoving it into the bottom of my bag.

I have twenty minutes until the next bus, and I should be going through the math problems my SAT tutor sent over last night or brainstorming extra credit to make up for my C—*my god, a C*—but I open my phone and Instagram instead, pulling up Cass's page to sink the knife a few serrations deeper.

We haven't talked since that night three and a half weeks ago. The longest we've ever gone. Based on a series of sunlit photos, they went to the lake last weekend. Looking at them, I swear I can smell summer. Sunscreen and campfire smoke, and I think, *Sure, that's cool, but I'll raise you a living, disembodied arm.*

The joke echoes once, then fades out in the solitude of my head.

There's a vase of flowers on the sideboard today. Orange vase, orange dahlias. I touch a petal. They're real.

"You like them? They were her—"

I flinch. Turn. Isobel.

She blinks once, slowly. "They're my favorite, too."

"They're beautiful," I say, and her smile widens a fraction, losing a bit of its falseness. She's wearing dangling earrings the same color as the flowers. I've never seen her wear jewelry before, never seen her deviate from her professional, grayscale uniform.

The door opens, and Dr. Kim waves me forward without pre-amble.

I follow him down the hall. "No Thompson today?"

He doesn't look up from his tablet. "No. She's presenting a progress report to the investors."

"On me?"

He nods.

"And?"

He turns into a room dominated by a single enormous piece of equipment. "All good," he says. "We haven't hit the hard part yet."

I snort. "Sure. Brain tissue samples are the easy part."

He breathes a laugh out his nose. "When you're building a human from scratch, they are."

"True." I wave a hand at the thing in the room. "What's this?"

"Full-body scanner."

"Like a CT?"

"Yes. Like one. But . . ." He taps around on his tablet before turning the screen toward me. On it is an image of someone's body, a 3-D digital rendering of their entire physiology from the inside out. "See?" he says, shifting around to stand beside me, moving his fingers on the touch screen, tapping sections of the image to highlight, enlarge, isolate, and rotate them. "Organs, skeletal structure, nervous system." He pulls forward the image of the body's large intestine, then uses his thumb and index finger to pull the coiled mass apart, stretching the intestine out straight. Next, he double-taps on it, and a section enlarges. He taps again, once, and an array of data shows up on the screen, numbers correlating with things like width and density, measuring the thickness of the intestinal wall, the variations in texture and contours.

"So, this thing will make you a 3-D Paint-by-Number 'Lucille.'"

"Cool, huh?"

"Incredible."

"It's one of a kind."

My brow rises, though I don't know why I'm surprised. This place is inside a schism in reality, after all. "And you'll use that to make molds of my kidneys and liver and such?"

"Pretty much."

"After which bio-goop imbued with my specific and specially

extracted 'Lucille' goop will be extruded by the ITOP into said molds, so it can start growing into extra kidneys and livers and such."

"Basically." He closes out of the scanner image on his tablet and opens a different one, this one a photo of what looks like a kidney. But, a kidney *in progress*. Nestled in the blue, not-quite-Jell-O like the arm, it's pale, bloodless, and . . . partial. The shape of a kidney, even with the shadow of where the renal artery should be, but it's semi-translucent. And textured like a grid. "The ITOP uses your 'Lucille bio-goop'"—he grins—"to build the structure of your kidney. A detailed blueprint. Then we encourage the cell growth that fills it out."

"Wow."

He tucks the tablet under his arm. "Ready?"

Back in my white scrubs, lying on the scanner's platform with my head, shoulders, hips, and ankles strapped down, I listen to the machine's percussive whir, loud even through the headphones Kim gave me.

I think about kidneys.

Printing kidneys. Cells growing over the printed blueprint for kidneys like mold on bread. Or do the scientists layer them on like strips of papier-mâché? A kidney. A heart. Vertebrae, ribs, lungs, trachea, skull, nose, ears.

Ears. Orange earrings, flowers on the sideboard, and a non-plastic smile. *I remember,* Isobel said Saturday. But, she remembers *what?*

If I run after the car, right now, I could catch him. Tell him I'm going to be sick, that I can't do this. I look from the Reach the Sky building to the road and see Dad's car already halfway down the block. I can't remember anymore why I even signed up for this. Well, no, that's a lie. It's because this is *the* most competitive volunteer opportunity for high schoolers in the area, because recommendation letters from its director are basically golden tickets. But what good is that when you're the alternate? Like, cool, I'm in, I'm here, but only barely. Only because the one they really want can't be.

Which, super fun, also makes me the only one who won't already know everyone else. The only one with something extra to prove.

I close my eyes and think, *Ideal candidate, the business of exceptionality, the best.* I wonder if this is what Bruce Wayne feels like. The whole double-life, alter-ego, secret-lair thing. Does he ever doubt himself while he's Bruce and think, *Wait, I'm Batman?* Like how while I stand here debating my merit, thirty-odd miles from here a supersecret mega company is literally growing me a second self.

So what if I'm starting this session as the odd one out. So what if Cass hosted a Fourth of July party at her house on Saturday and didn't invite me. So what if my business-class group practiced our final presentation without me and I had to do my part separately like some sad—albeit obsessively prepared—dingleberry. So what if my "this class isn't for you" ass then went on to get a C overall, basically making the whole thing pointless, since who the hell brags about getting a C in their first college class on their applications?

So. What.

That supersecret mega company, a few short weeks out from changing my life and altering the course of human history, picked *me*. Not me, Lucille Harper, Barely Keeping Herself Afloat, but me, Lucille Harper, Worthy of Being Duplicated.

It's early enough that the halls are still quiet. I wander until I find the director's office and introduce myself. Adaline's welcome is warm but brief, since her phone starts ringing midsentence. She tells me where to find the break room where the interns meet and not-so-subtly ushers me out of the office.

The break room is home to a coffee station, fridge with magnetic poetry already arranged into a mess of jokes, and a single table in the center of the space surrounded by a dozen chairs. I hesitate, worrying I'll pick someone's favorite seat, then opt for one in the back corner.

The others start showing up around ten till eight, walking in in pairs or groups like they carpooled or met up beforehand. A few carry coffee cups and snacks. And everyone's talking, catching up on what they all did over the weekend like it's just another Monday because for them it is. Some wave at me, others nod, but no one goes out of their way to talk to me. Their chatter drowns out the twang of the knot yanking tighter in my chest.

Usually, in a situation like this, I'd be sizing up my competition, wondering about their hooks, what they have that I don't to float them to the top of their Ivy League application baskets. Sports stars, maybe. Tragic pasts. Maybe the one with the reporter-style notebook is a politician's kid, state representative or something. A legacy. Maybe the girl with perfect hair runs track. Maybe the guy with dark, messy curls, leaning back in his chair with his eyes closed, seemingly asleep, is . . . Okay, that one's got me stumped.

Then there's me. *To whom it may concern, please enjoy this essay on how I cope with my life's greatest tragedy: my inability to tan. Sincerely, Mayonnaise Incarnate.*

Though, of course, I'm the new blood now, and I swear I can feel *them* wondering about *me.* If only I could wear my currently-being-cloned status around like a hat. A flashy one, with glitter and blinking lights.

At five till, Adaline comes in with a clipboard, gives a quick welcome back, then says, "Everyone say hi to Rachelle's replacement, since she's abandoned us in favor of an exchange in Italy, poor girl." There are mock groans, and glances at me. "Lucille, you'll be with Marco since everyone's already paired up." She waves a hand at the dark-haired guy—who's now awake and mashing the heels of his hands into his eyes—then at a bulletin board on the wall by the door. "The new schedule's up on the board. I switched your class orders to make sure everyone works every session and with each teacher, so make sure you check where you're supposed to be. There's also a list of a few new campers up beside it; check their names against your class rosters and help them find their way around and fit in with the others.

"Otherwise . . ." She scans her clipboard. "Oh! Two peanut allergies this session, noted on class rosters, so beware. And that's it!" She looks up, smiling. "As always, do your best, be your best, and . . ."

"The best will follow," the interns finish. All of them but me.

Then they move, checking the new schedule and filing out in pairs.

I get up and go stand next to the dark-haired guy's chair. "Hi."

He drops his hands, blinks—long, dark, ridiculous lashes—melodramatically, and looks up. Gorgeous dark lashes, gorgeous dark eyes. Curly dark hair that's a little too long. And *tousled*. Really. Like, run your hands through it and oh my freaking god what if I just crawl under the table and die. "Hey, Lucy," he says.

I purse my lips, look at my feet, and think, *Screw you, Lucille Harper, Overachiever, you knot of insecurity, you champion of self-consciousness. So, he's hot. So what? You're Batman! This guy doesn't know* you. *You can be whoever you want to be!*

So I sit on the table next to him and stick out my hand. "Actually, it's Lucille."

He grins one of those awful—*awesome*—cute-boy grins where only half of his mouth curves up. "Okay, Lucille," he says, and shakes my hand.

"Your eyelashes are ridiculous."

He blushes. "Thanks?"

I blush too. "Statement of fact."

"Should we be done shaking hands now? Or go for a record?"

"Well"—I pull out my phone with my free hand—"let's see."

Still shaking—subtly now, so it's more like we're just holding outstretched hands—I google it. "Fifteen hours, thirty minutes, and forty-five seconds."

"*That's* the record? Sounds fake. Fifteen, thirty, forty-five."

I set my phone down on the table. "Right? Like they planned it."

"Probably did," he says.

"I would."

"My arm's getting tired."

"Yeah." My hand's getting sweaty, which is sort of mortifying? But I'm deciding, right now, that Lucille Harper, Flirts with Reckless Abandon, is *done* being mortified. "And my hand's getting sweaty."

He's grinning again. "Maybe we should stop."

"Probably should."

"On three?"

I nod. We count to three. Together. And drop hands. It's the corniest—*cutest*—thing I've ever done. *God, my bar is low.*

Smiling, he shakes his head, then pulls his phone out of his pocket—older model, cracked screen—and reaches for mine. I unlock it, hand it to him, and he programs his number into my contacts, then hands it back. "Now text me, so I have yours."

I read the new contact name and cough a laugh. "Marco—Gorgeous Lashes?"

"Hey, you said it."

I text him: *Ridiculous. I said ridiculous lashes.*

His phone dings. He opens the message and types an answer back.

My phone buzzes: *semantics*

I laugh. "Fine. Marco dash Gorgeous Lashes it is. But, then, who am I?"

Sirens in my head scream, *Wah! Wah! Wah! What are you doing? Who the hell do you think you are? Fraud, fake, sham, shame. Flirting with a stranger, and one who looks like—*

My phone buzzes again. I open the message. It's a screenshot of his contact entry for me: Lucille—Beautiful Smile. And he says, "Statement of fact."

It's good. Too good.

Him. The day. It's easy, fun. He leads me from session to session, introducing me to the teachers and students—all of whom seem to adore him—catching me up on what and how and when to do what we need to, all without seeming bored or inconvenienced or condescending. We spend the morning making papier-mâché, setting up badminton nets, acting as team leads for an ongoing math tournament. And I keep waiting for the punch line. Waiting to say something awkward. Waiting for him to say he's not single or straight or allo. Waiting for some sign that I can't have this if only because I never have this.

Gorgeous boys do not flirt with me. I do not make gorgeous boys laugh by telling jokes about stuff like how the advertising for Teddy Grahams is weirdly cannibalistic. But that's what happens. Jokes and sitting with him at lunch, where we chaperone our group of campers, opening yogurts and bags of chips, mitigating mini arguments, and he asks me what I did the first half of the summer. I tell him about tutoring and the business class and he whistles, impressed.

"Save it. I barely passed. And the professor pretty much told me I didn't belong there."

"No shit?"

I shrug. "Maybe he was right."

"Why'd you take it?"

I surprise myself by being honest and saying, "I don't know."

He breathes a laugh. "Like you forgot? Signed up in your sleep?"

"Yes," I say. "Sleep college. Sleep registered? Whatever, yes. That's what happened."

"Like those people who take Ambien and order shit online."

"Or drive."

"Or murder."

"Damn, Marco, take it there."

He laughs, and I'm grateful when his next question is "What else?" and not some follow-up about the class.

Because, truth is, I'm not proud of my other answers. Why do you try so hard, Lucille? So I can get into a great college and finally make some sense to myself. How do you feel about your first college experience being a truly epic letdown? Well, awesome. If "awesome" means that every assumption in my life from my happily married parents to my best friend since birth to my very hopes and dreams is turning out to be a lie.

But it's not like my answer to this one's easier. Can't casually drop "stem-cell retrieval and full-body scans to facilitate the 3-D bioprinting of my fully functional duplicate" into the convo. So I say, "Very little. You?"

He tells me about watching his little brother and sister—nine-year-old twins, Ariana and Sam, who attend the program and are half the reason he works here—and his job at a coffee shop, his mom, his friends, then we help clean up lunch and herd our group on to the next class. We spend the afternoon assisting with science experiments, supervising a scavenger-hunt-cum-history-lesson, and continuing work on set pieces for the end-of-session play, then it's five, and I'm a balloon. Floating, lighter than air, and fragile.

It's too much. Too good.

Out front, waiting for the twins, we watch my dad pull up. "Farewell, Marco dash Gorgeous Lashes," I say. "See you tomorrow."

He smiles. "Until then, Lucille dash Beautiful Smile." Then he puts a hand on his chest and bows.

I hurry to my dad's car, anticipating a sharp stick or dropped string.

Thursday after Reach the Sky, and the gate and doors of Life² open for me—*I'm Batman*—the moment I approach, clanking and swinging wide in time with my footsteps so I don't even have to slow. It's awesome, like a slo-mo moment in a movie, complete with a breeze in my hair. It's also weird. Because it's not automatic, or specially Lucille-keyed, it's Isobel.

"Good afternoon, Lucille," she says—always chipper, always crisp and neat—and leads me across the glowing white lobby like she always does.

"Hi."

She pauses by the wall, hand hovering over the door's incorporated touch pad. "Making the full-body mold today?"

"Yeah." My eyes flick to the orange vase on the sideboard, drawn to the room's only color. It's filled with tiger lilies today, the same mix of hues as the scarf tied like a cravat around Isobel's neck.

"Slow breaths," Isobel says. "In through your nose and out your mouth. It helps with the panic."

"Wait. What? Have you—"

"Lucille," Dr. Thompson calls from down the hall.

I look to her, then back at Isobel, and find her watching me, face a perfect void. The door slides closed between us.

Dr. Thompson doesn't say anything when I join her at the end of the hall, just starts walking, expecting me to follow. Which, of course, I do.

"So, Isobel," I say over the knock of Thompson's heels. "She's . . ."

"Yes?"

"She's done this before. What I'm doing."

We pass the first labs, heading toward the one with the full-sized ITOP and incubation pod. Through the observation window, I see Drs. Kim, Adebayo, and Karlsson, the kinesiologist, waiting inside. Thompson presses her hand to the touch pad. "Not exactly."

The door opens. All attention turns to us.

"Not exactly," I repeat. I feel it in my chest. Like a skipped heartbeat. "You mean she's not an Original. She's a clone."

"Facsimile. Yes." She motions to Karlsson, who steps forward with a plastic-wrapped bundle in her hands.

"Then . . ."

What happened with her that makes them need me?

But Thompson doesn't give me time to ask. She takes the bundle from Karlsson and holds it out to me. "Change into this," she says, pointing me toward a privacy screen in the back corner.

I take the bundle, plastic crinkling in my hands. No one says anything. No one acknowledges what I just learned. Only Adebayo bothers to meet my eye.

I change behind the screen, setting my purse and clothes on the floor, listening to the scientists' quiet discussion out in the room. They talk about growth rates and CRISPR. Thompson's voice goes tense when Kim mentions something about Shanghai. "No setbacks," she says. "We have to be first."

I rip open the plastic and pull out what looks like a wet suit, only the material's thinner and slick. It feels like trying to yank on a second skin, covering everything but my hands and feet, complete with a hood that pulls up over my hair and fits tight from above my brow to just below my chin, leaving nothing but the circle of my face bare.

When I step out, they barely pause their conversation, Thompson drilling Kim about Shanghai's dates for their subject's Mimeo and him responding that they're only rumors.

Dr. Adebayo skirts them, smiling as he walks toward me, while behind him, Karlsson opens the cover on the incubation pod. It's already half-full of translucent blue goo. Standing beside it, Adebayo fits one breathing apparatus into my nose and another in my mouth. "Practice," he says in his thick Yoruban accent. "In through your nose. Out your mouth. Calmly."

I do it, in and out, five times.

"Good," he says. "It will be cold at first, but the hydrogel will adjust quickly to your body temperature." He holds my eye, intent. "You cannot move. Keep your eyes closed. And remember to breathe slowly. The sensors in your suit will track your heart rate and alert us if you begin to panic."

"Don't panic," Karlsson adds, her accent Scandinavian. "If you do, you ruin the mold and we have to start over."

Mouth and nose full, breathing in and out, I nod.

Finally, Adebayo shows me a wireless earbud, lifts the edge of my hood, and tucks it gently into my right ear. Then, with Karlsson standing on a stool on the pod's opposite side, he helps me up the steps and they both help me climb into the pod.

The hydrogel is thick, cool. Viscous. My feet sink into it, but slowly. Karlsson and Adebayo help me sit and then lie down, physically shifting my limbs, arms set six inches from my sides, fingers splayed, and feet shoulder-width apart, body buoyed a few inches above the bottom of the pod by the goop.

I swallow, fail to suppress a shiver. But the gel compensates, slowing my vibrations before they cause a ripple. It's already beginning to warm, from cool and damp to a thick nothing, the same temperature as my skin.

Adebayo attaches tubes to my nose and mouth apparatuses, then leans back. "Ready?" he asks. "Blink twice."

I do.

And they close the lid, the clear, rounded length of it descending slowly from its anchor down past my feet. It settles and suctions closed.

"Slow breaths," he reminds me in my ear. "We'll fill the pod now."

The gel rises around me. Blue goop encasing me, inch by fraction of an inch. Over my fingers. Up my ankles. Seeping in over my collarbone and around my neck.

I close my eyes.

Recite SAT vocabulary from last night's tutoring session.

Aberration: not normal, deviation

It reaches my hips.

Derivative: not original

My stomach.

Inscrutable: mysterious

Touches my cheeks.

"Slow. Breaths," Adebayo's voice says, deep and calming. "Count with me. In, one, two, three. Out, one, two, three."

Over my lips, around my nose, pooling into my eye sockets.

In, one, two, three.

Teeming: abundant

Out, one, two, three.

Covers my forehead, coating me completely.

"Twenty minutes for the gel to set."

Predecessor: someone who came before

Isobel did this.

No, Isobel *remembers* doing this. Remembers doing something she's never actually done. Like mine will.

It's hot, ninety-something at least. From my spot on the side of the field supervising a flag football game, I can see heat waves rising off the Reach the Sky parking lot. I lift my sunglasses to wipe the sweat from the bridge of my nose for the eighth time in the last five minutes.

"Hey," Marco says, joining me. He has a bag of orange slices in each hand and a Gatorade under each arm.

"Hey." I grab the bags and together we head over to one of the nearby picnic tables to finish setting up the snacks, dumping the orange slices into a giant plastic bowl and making sure the water cooler's full.

"Sorry, armpit Gatorade," he says when we're done, and holds out the bottles, one red, one blue.

I laugh and pick the red one, twisting open the cap to take a long drink. "Thanks."

We turn back to the field. "Letting Ariana play flag football is a terrible idea," he says. On the field, her long hair pulled back in a tangled ponytail, blue jersey hanging longer than her shorts and cinched tight at the waist by her flag belt, Ariana sprints straight at the kid—opposite team, yellow jersey, eyes going wide with terror—holding the ball. He hesitates as she nears. Eyes searching, knowing he should throw it, then when she's a pace or two off, panicking and chucking it up in the air. Ari stops, catches the ball, then runs back to score a touchdown.

The blue team cheers. Marco and I cheer, too. A teacher blows a whistle.

"*Damn*, Ari!"

Marco laughs. "You're telling me. Do not get on that girl's bad side." He takes a drink of blue Gatorade, then sets the bottle in the grass at his feet and crosses his arms, standing close enough to me that his elbow brushes my arm.

He asks, "Do you ever think about how many people have walked or sat or slept or peed or even died, right here, where we're standing? Like, in history?"

I breathe a laugh. "I am *now*."

He grins. "You're thinking about pee, aren't you?"

"And dead people."

"In which case it'd be both, thanks to the evacuation-of-your-bowels thing."

"Delightful. The one thing this moment was missing was a graphic mental image of a corpse that's soiled itself."

"Who am I to deny you graphic mental images of historical deaths and subsequent shatting?"

"Don't try to pretty it up with your fancy poop words, Marco. The damage has been done."

He laughs and uncrosses his arms. Ridiculous arms. Not "ridiculous" like, *Damn, look at that guy's ridiculous arms. They're the size of my leg!* Marco's arms are just . . . Whatever, I like his arms.

He clears his throat. "Plans this weekend?"

A spark rolls up my spine to settle in my cheeks. Is he going to ask me out? Is that ridiculous? Conceited? Why am I assuming he likes me? We flirt, sure, but people flirt. For fun, when they're bored. And boys do not ask me out. Like, ever.

"Just staying at my dad's." *Oh, and getting my consciousness digitized. No big.*

"Ah, Camp Divorcé."

"Yes. Where there are, like, five pieces of furniture, and three framed pictures sitting on the floor waiting to be hung."

"And one lonely houseplant, still in its store-bought plastic pot in the corner?"

"More like *no* plants because my dad has decided he's done trying to keep things alive."

"*Now* who's being morbid?"

A kid from the blue team scores a touchdown, and Marco and I cheer again.

"That's less morbid and more bleak reality." It's weird, but I can't remember when I told Marco about my parents. It's like that with us. Spending so much time together this week, of course we talk. Anyone would. But this feels different. That, or I'm delusional, and I want this to be different, special, so badly that I've skewed it in my head. Like Bode's wink that night in the park. Tell yourself a lie until it becomes your truth, right? Marco's stuck with me either way. Maybe he's just being nice.

"Well," he says, "you've got to earn those two Christmases somehow. Or in my case, one Christmas and one Hanukkah. I mean, come on. It can't all be guilt kittens and pity rainbows."

"What on earth is a pity rainbow?"

"Fine. Pity . . . I don't know. Whatever love-me-more-than-my-ex bribe you want. The sky is the freaking limit."

"Reach for the rainbow?"

"No, that's not a thing. You're thinking Skittles. *Taste* the rainbow."

We watch the teachers set the kids up for a final play, and I take another drink of Gatorade. I'd feel bad complaining about it, since at least my dad still lives here, while Marco, Ari, and Sam's is all the way in Seattle, but the first time I tried to apologize, he brushed it off.

"It's weird only seeing him once a week," I say. "Though it's not like I see much of my mom either. With her work and this and everything else. My family's a Venn diagram, but the circles no longer overlap."

"Damn."

I shrug.

"I mean it," he says. "That's tragic. I'm picturing it now: three bubbles floating in the same void, together but totally alone. That's like Bing Bong-dying-in-the-Memory Dump sad."

"It so is not."

"Who's your friend who likes . . ." He waves his hand, beckoning me to finish the lyric.

"No."

"Sing it with me, Lucille. Honor his sacrifice."

"Stop it."

"Here." He reaches for my Gatorade, uncaps it, and pours a sip onto the ground. "For Bing Bong. 'Cause it's basically sugar water, which he'd like."

"Glorious," I say. "I'm sure Bing Bong appreciates it."

"He better. Cotton-candy punk."

I laugh. The teacher blows the whistle again, calling the end of the game—no official winner since they don't keep score, but Ari's smug expression suggests she knows who won, anyway—then announces that it's time for snack. The kids shed their gear and sprint for the table, followed by two teachers who'll help fill up water cups and pass out the granola bars we hid in the shade. Marco and I hang back to clean up the flag belts and jerseys left all over the field.

"So, that it?" he asks. "Sitting around your dad's sad apartment staring at unhung pictures?"

"Yep. In the dark, probably."

"Obviously. Since I'm sure he keeps forgetting to buy lightbulbs."

"And eating bologna sandwiches on stale bread because he

never remembers to grocery shop." I try to take the Gatorade back from him, but he takes a long drink first.

"Hey," he says, offering me the Gatorade, cap still off. I take it and drink, overly aware that his lips just touched where my lips are touching, because apparently I'm in the fifth grade and sharing spit means something. "Bologna is delicious."

I grab the bin for the jerseys and head out onto the field. "It's slices of giant, cold hot dog."

"Exactly," he says, following with the one for the flag belts. "Delicious."

"You're a horror show."

He smiles, overly wide, showing too many teeth.

"Not helping," I say.

Will my Facsimile get this? This perfect image? This sun-soaked moment? I don't know how I feel about that. I've never had anything like this. Something separate and special. Something I, delusion or not, want to keep all my own.

Except, she'll be me. Does that mean she'll feel about Marco the way I feel? Will feelings transfer the same way memories will? Or will she get the image, but not the emotional context? Will she hear all this internal rambling and *feel* it? Or will it be like remembering facts from a textbook?

As Marco and I fill our bins, I realize I don't want her to feel this. What I feel for him. But I certainly wouldn't mind having someone who understands the rest of it, even if only for a month.

"Everything," I say, repeating Dr. Kim. "She'll know everything I know."

Dr. Kim nods while Dr. Thompson says, "The Mimeo gives us a complete digitized copy of your brain, every wrinkle and synapse. The purpose is to create an exact replica of your connectome as it is at the time of the scan, for use in building and operating your Facsimile's wetware."

Hardware, software, wetware.

"The 'me' part of—" I wave my hand, gesturing to my head, my body, *me*. I know this. I've known this. But with the actual procedure happening in two days, I crave clarity. We're in the conference room. Outside, the courtyard is shadowed. I check the time on my serviceless phone. Dad thinks I'm getting coffee with some Reach the Sky friends before I grab my stuff from Mom's and head to his place for the night, and if it gets too late, he'll worry and try to call.

"Yes," Thompson says.

"Your specific physiology," Kim says, "plus your memory. It's chicken-and-egg, since brain configuration and function are two parts of the same whole. But, yeah. Memories, experiences, genes, all of it bundled together into your nervous system. *That's* your connectome."

Dr. Thompson smiles. "MimeoMem *is* Life Squared's crowning achievement. Of all our discoveries and advancements, it is our most monumental."

"And it works," I say.

They pause.

It's the final major procedure. Arguably the most invasive.

The most important. *And they freaking pause.* I think of Isobel and those huge, unanswered questions: If they have her, what happened that they still need me? Isn't *she* the "first fully functional, adult human duplicate"? Their "capstone"? But I don't ask. Partly because I don't want them to doubt me, my commitment, my "ideal fit," and partly because I'm not sure I want to know.

"Of course," Thompson says. "Brain science is delicate. But we have refined the process to within a few percentage points of perfection."

"What?"

They share a glance, and Kim says, "We have a ninety-eight percent success rate."

"Like, it works ninety-eight percent of the time? Or the Mimeo will copy ninety-eight percent of me?"

"With anything at this level of complexity, there is room for error," Dr. Thompson says. "But as with RapidReplicate and SemblanceSync, we at Life Squared have made it our mission to flout impossibility, to perfect the unperfectable."

She sounds like a freaking infomercial. Or a politician.

I look at my reflection on the glossy table, and everything's there on my face: my doubt, my worry. Then I relax my brow. I want this, and they want me. That's answer enough, right?

"How does the scan work?"

Kim and Thompson share a second look before he asks, "Want to see?"

I nod, and they stand. "It started with serial block-face scanning electron microscopy," Kim says as I walk between them through Life²'s pearlescent halls. "But that wasn't an option for us."

"Why not?"

"Because you'd have to be dead."

"SBFSEMs use small samples of brain tissue," Thompson explains, "sliced by the ultramicrotome to a thickness of less than fifty nanometers, that are then scanned by focused beams of electrons to create an image. Images that are stacked together to create a 3-D digital portrait of the sample."

"The trick to the Mimeo," Kim says, "is doing all of that. For your whole brain. While you're alive. It's the kind of discovery that will—"

"Alter the course of humanity?"

"Exactly."

We turn down the hall of laboratories, and Kim pauses before the first observation window. "Pit stop?" he asks me.

I step up to the window beside him. Thompson joins me, crossing her arms. Inside, the team works—Adebayo, Karlsson, and the others I've yet to meet—spread throughout the lab, monitoring a handful of ITOPs and incubation pods, smaller versions of the ones next door.

"Patel's our cardiologist. See what he's working on?" Kim asks. He nods to one of the sterile-suited scientists that I don't recognize standing over an incubation pod roughly the size of a beach ball. The pod's full of the same bluish hydrogel I lounged—suffocated—in to make my Facsimile's full-body mold. And suspended in the middle?

A heart.

My heart.

I try to take a slow breath in through my nose, try to pull the air deep into my stomach—*in, one, two, three*—try to exhale slowly out my mouth. Then I lean over and vomit all over the pretty white floor.

We cut the tour short. Thompson told Isobel to call a car, then left me to wait for it, saying only, "Be here by seven a.m. on Sunday. Prepare to stay all day."

Now, an hour and a half later, Mom squeezes me tight over the center console of her SUV. "Love you," she says into my hair. "Have a good weekend."

My intestines.

I pull back and grab my bag from between my feet. "You too."

My rib cage.

When I get to the lobby door, she leans down and waves at me through the passenger window.

My kidneys.

I wave back, go inside, and watch her drive away through the glass door.

My ovaries and uterus.

A couple crosses the lobby, holding hands. Both men nod to me as I shift out of the way of the door.

My eyes.

"Eleven," I say to the woman who asks for my floor when I join her in the elevator.

My spine.

It wasn't that I hadn't thought about it. I had. But in a cartoon way. In a *plastic* way. Like the anatomical horse my parents gave me for my birthday one year. Its exterior horse shape was clear, with a skeleton and an assortment of organs that I was supposed to paint and assemble for the inside. That's how I'd pictured it. Clean and neat with parts that clicked together and lungs you could paint blue.

I hadn't thought about muscles. Tendons, ligaments, cartilage. Marrow and blood. A tank of it. Waiting to fill her up.

The woman gets off the elevator on the tenth floor. Two breaths later, I get off on the eleventh, then walk down the hall toward my dad's apartment, digging through my purse for the key he gave me.

At the door, I close my eyes and take a slow, deep breath. No more organs. No more Batman. Back to regular life.

●

I wake up the next morning to the smell of pancakes. Dad's specialty, he makes them any day there's something to celebrate or apologize for. Someone's birthday? Pancakes. Missed my History Day presentation? Pancakes. It's his go-to, yet I can't remember the last time he made them.

I throw off the comforter—too stiff, too new—and join him in the kitchen. When I sit at the counter, he smiles, expression like Christmas morning. Not that oozing sentimental feeling people sum up as "Christmas morning," but like how he literally looked every Christmas morning when he woke me up—yes, *he* woke *me* up—to bring me downstairs.

"What?" I ask.

He grins. "Hungry?"

I nod, and we eat. I'm never sure how to act here. It still feels like staying at a stranger's house, some distant relative's or the friend of a friend's. Like I should tiptoe and be careful not to touch anything. It smells different, and even the fork feels odd in my hand, flatter or heavier or something-er than the silverware at home.

But maybe the weirdest part is knowing it's all stuff he picked out on his own. Like the leather recliner couch and navy-blue dinner plates, the fluffy white area rug and the wood-and-steel coffee table. He's hung his concert photos and there's an aloe plant—in a real pot—on a little table by the TV. I think about texting Marco a picture, but I'm not sure we're there yet.

It's not that I don't like any of it. Or that I actually expected him not to try. It's that it's him. *Only* him. Not Dad's taste filtered through Mom's, or *their* taste, a separate thing altogether, but all his own. And it makes me wonder, how well do I even know him? Or Mom?

Seeing how I totally bought into the "happily married" façade, I'm guessing the answer's "not well." Which makes me wonder how well they know me. How well they *think* they know me. Eating dinner last night after seeing my disassembled, duplicated self, Dad asked how hanging out after Reach the Sky was. I answered with some bland lie I can't even remember now. And he believed me. That simple.

Which is maybe a trust thing. Or maybe it's a subjective-truth thing. Happy parents, thriving daughter. We see what we want to see. It makes me wonder if anyone really knows anyone. Do I even know myself?

I breathe a laugh. Guess I'll find out soon.

"What's funny?"

I shake my head and stand to clear our plates. "Nothing."

His glowy face is back. "I have something for you. Well, it's from Mom, too. Put some shoes on. We're going outside."

Standing on the sidewalk around the side of the building by an older Honda Civic, arms outstretched and grinning, Dad says, "Well? What do you think?"

"The car?"

He nods.

I smile, wide and bright. "Really?"

"Yes, really! Your mom and I know how—"

"Tired you are of driving my ass all over the city?"

"Funny. No." He bows—super regal in basketball shorts and flip-flops—and says, "I'd happily play your chauffeur forever."

"But."

"But, yeah, this'll save time."

I laugh.

He holds out the keys. I hug him. Thank him. And we climb in—me in the driver's seat—to go for a drive. *Guilt kittens and pity rainbows.* But even thinking that makes me feel like an asshole, so I say another few thank-yous and enjoy the drive.

"Do you have plans today?" he asks when we get back.

"Just a couple practice SAT tests."

"Not hanging out with Cass or anything?"

I shake my head. There's so much he doesn't know. "No. But we're going to the lake for the day tomorrow. If that's okay."

"Of course. You can take your hot new ride."

"My hot ride?"

"No air-conditioning. *Hot* ride. Get it?"

"Oh my god."

He laughs. "Ah, I crack myself up."

We climb out and head toward the lobby. "We could see what's playing at the IMAX? Drive up to Fort Collins or something?"

"Actually, some of my new coworkers invited me to play on the company baseball team." He makes a fake scared face. "And we have a game this afternoon. You can come if you want. Some of the other families will probably be there."

I quicken my pace a step to hide my face. Why does this hurt so bad? He said I can come. But it feels like Cass. Like, *hi, wanna tag along while I enjoy my new, Lucille-less life?*

"That's okay," I say, forcing a smile as we get in the elevator. "I have plenty of stuff to do."

The apartment's too quiet without him. Too empty without Boris. I realize I've never been here alone before. I play one of Dad's grunge records. Can't focus. Turn it off.

It's nervous energy. Like the day before I got my tonsils out in sixth grade. Knowing something's coming but having no real clue how it's going to go. Sure, Thompson explained it. Scary machine, special scrubs, general anesthesia, tube down my throat, body restrained, skull held steady by screws and a halo brace. I mean, who *wouldn't* feel at ease, right? Ready, set, focus on this set of data-analysis problems for your practice SAT, Lucille!

Instead, I spend an hour in an obnoxiously counterproductive loop: Pick up pen. Read math problem. Put pen down. Open phone. Stare at Marco's contact. Talk self out of texting. Stare at Cass's contact. Feel stab of loneliness in chest. Remember guts in incubation pods. Isobel's plastic smile. *Helps with the panic. Ninety-eight percent success rate.* Laugh maniacally. Pick up pen. Read math problem.

Until I can't stand it anymore.

Out on the street, new keys in hand, I still don't know what to do with myself. Every thought I think feels like ringing a bell. *Ding.* Will she remember this? *Ding.* What about this? *Ding, ding, ding.*

I eye the car, but I can't think of anywhere to go, so I just start walking. I don't know Aurora yet. I wander toward the main road, then head left for exactly zero reasons. It's hot. Traffic's constant. After a couple of miles, I'm sweating and my feet hurt, but my mind slows.

The road complicates, the traffic thickens. I cross a major intersection, pass a KFC, then see signs for a Target and make that my plan. Buy a drink, take a break, then walk back and get to work.

The stretch of car-packed blacktop bakes under the July sun, its heat wafting up my legs. By the time I reach the doors, I can feel sweat in my hair. Inside, I pause, drying out in the artificial cool.

"Lucille?"

Oh my god.

I blink.

Turn.

"Bode?"

He walks over from the row of cash registers, tan and dressed in cut-off jorts. With a T-shirt—a Bode original, of course—that has the sleeves ripped off, an American flag bandanna worn like a headband, and face paint.

"Wow," I say. "Nice outfit."

"Thanks." He smiles and my stomach does its flopping thing. Of course it still does. Marco regardless. Life^2 regardless. All that's worth a bug's fart where my idiot crush is concerned. My cheeks heat. My heart absconds. *Pop!* Gone. Not in small part because there is a zero percent chance he's here—dressed like that— alone. And sure enough.

Aran's next, catching up with Bode, reusable bag hung on his wrist. Then Finn and their boyfriend, Matt. Then Louise.

Then Cass.

All of them, clumping up to face me in the entryway, other customers coming in and going out, circumnavigating our awkward wad.

"Hey," I say with a wave.

"Hey," Cass echoes back. Like Bode, they're all dressed up. Different, but similar. Face paint, lots of colorful flair. Aran has a glittery temporary American flag tattoo on one cheek and the Indian flag on the other. Cass has dyed the ends of her Mohawk bright red and wears a matte cherry lipstick to match. Louise's hair is dyed like a pastel rainbow. I can still feel sweat cooling in mine.

"You all look . . ."

"Amazing?" Aran supplies.

I grin. "What are you doing in Aurora?"

"Pit stop," he answers. "You?"

"My dad lives here."

"Nice."

Matt pushes between Finn and Louise, smiles at me, says, "We should go. Good to see you, Lucille," and heads for the doors. It feels like mercy.

Finn goes next, then Louise and Aran and Bode—with a quick wave—leaving only Cass. Cass, whom I haven't seen or talked to since that night in the park three eons ago. Just looking at her, I feel all of it—Dad's new life, Marco, my *midgrowth clone*—gurgling up my throat. Everything I've been doing alone, without her, crowding together at the back of my tongue.

I could gag.

"So," she says, "how are you?"

"Oh, you know." I look at my feet and laugh.

"Obviously, I don't."

"I didn't mean it like that. I mean—" I shake my head. "Busy. Doing that internship I told you about. SAT prep."

"The works."

"Yep." I pull out my ponytail and fluff my sweaty hair. "You?"

"Good. Busy, too. We're shooting scenes today for a short

film Louise and Finn wrote and we're all working to put together. That's why we're dressed up." She shrugs. "It's fun."

"Awesome."

"Yeah."

We stand, awkward. Quiet.

Then she says, "Better go. We were filming down at—"

"Doesn't matter."

She frowns.

"Sorry," I say. "That was rude. I just . . . Forget it."

"Okay," she says. "Well." And turns to go.

When she's almost to the doors, I call, "Hey."

She stops, looks back.

"Does my dad talk to yours much lately?"

"I don't know. Why?"

I purse my lips. "I know we haven't been, well, much of anything lately. And it probably won't come up. But."

"Spit it out, Lucille."

"My dad thinks I'm spending tomorrow with you. So, in the one-in-a-million chance it comes up . . ."

"You want me to cover for you?"

"I've done it plenty for you." Like every single time she and Aran went out before she turned sixteen.

"I know." She looks at me. Close this time, up and down. "Are you . . ."

I roll my eyes. "I'm fine."

And she nods. "Okay."

It's quiet.

Cold.

My head hurts.

I open my eyes. The room's dim. A silhouette stands in the open doorway, backed by blinding white light.

"Cold," I say, rasp it. Throat aching.

The figure moves. Sleek bun, careful movements, Isobel pulls a second blanket up from the foot of the bed to cover me, tucking it around my shoulders, leaning down, reaching across me to secure the far side, and her face. Her beautiful, perfect face isn't plastic or blank.

It's crumpled as, silently, she weeps.

I wake again, and the room's bright. I reach a hand up to shield my eyes, dragging IV tubes with it.

"Lucille?"

I blink until my eyes adjust and look up to see Dr. Thompson standing beside my bed. Some of the others are here, too. Dr. Kim at the foot of the bed. Dr. Adebayo at my right. Isobel, watching from the doorway.

"Lucille," Thompson says again. "Can you tell us the date and where you are?"

I try to swallow. Dr. Adebayo hands me a cup of water, and I take a long drink through the cold metal straw.

"Sunday, July twelfth," I answer, voice like sandpaper. "Inside god's shiny white asshole."

A pause.

Then Adebayo laughs.

Thompson and Kim smile, exhale.

"So." I try clearing my throat, but that only makes it worse. "Did it work?"

Dr. Thompson smiles down at me. It's the most genuine I've ever seen her look. "Yes, it did."

CHAPTER FIVE

Clothes in the closet. Shampoo and makeup in the bathroom. Fresh sheets on the bed. An oversized dry-erase board hung on the wall, the grid of a calendar on one side with bright red X's marking off the days. Eighteen since the Mimeo. Ten since they moved her to the final incubation pod. The one I lay in for the body mold. The one where they assembled her, piece by vital piece, then set the ITOP to print her skin.

My phone dings on the kitchenette's counter, and my heart leaps. But it's Mom, texting that she'll be home late. I type out a quick reply, then set my phone back down next to the journal I've been keeping since the Mimeo, half-full and with her name—suggested by Thompson, for "ease"—on the inside cover. I open it and trace the letters with a finger. Mine but not mine.

Twelve days until the end of Reach the Sky. Eighteen until the start of junior year. New blackout drapes on the windows. Door and cabinet hinges oiled. Non-creaky, safe-to-step spots on the floor marked with painter's tape. Squeaky bed frame dismantled, mattress and box spring laid directly on the floor.

I grab the TV remote off the coffee table, turn the volume up to twelve—like the note I put on the screen says not to exceed—then go down to the garage, stand next to my car, close my eyes, and listen.

Nothing. Like the half dozen times I've checked before.

Boris joins me, nails clicking on the concrete, and touches his nose to my hand. I pet the spot between his eyes like he likes. He leans his heavy body against my leg, tips his nose up, and closes his eyes, serene. She'll meet him first. Then, Mom.

Single set of keys. Color-coded calendar. Daily continuity briefings. Regular reports to Life² on top of the Body Area Network and GPS implants to track her vitals and location. And my swelling sense of *almost*.

"What do you think, Bobo? Ready for a second me?" The tight curl at the end of his tail wags against the concrete floor.

Upstairs in the apartment, a phone rings. I sprint, answer, "Yes?"

On the other end, Dr. Thompson says, "Time to wake her up."

CHAPTER SIX

t's quiet.

Warm.

And bright.

I squeeze my eyes shut.

I'm . . . Recovery. The recovery room?

Inhale.

Air (nitrogen, oxygen, argon, carbon dioxide) pulled in through my mouth (incubation pod with a half-grown tongue, her tongue, *my* tongue), down my trachea, bronchi, pleurae, left lung, right lung, alveoli, diaphragm, and the muscles in my neck.

Exhale.

Gas exchange.

But close. Confined.

I swallow. My throat and tongue are dry. I remember (*I remember, I remember . . . Cass at Target, dinner with Dad, mask on my nose, count back from ten, nine, eight . . .*) choking. Blue gel. (Everywhere. Eyes, ears, up my nose. *Naked, twitch, inhale, choke, choke, cho-oh-oh-oh-oh— GET IT OUT!*) No. No, that was, wasn't, wasn't this . . . *this* is from the intubation for the Mimeo. Plastic tube shoved down my throat to make me breathe. Screws through my scalp to keep my head still. My head and eyes hurt. Why do my eyes hurt? Why's the room so bright? I lift a hand (heavy hand, heavy fingers, heavy arm) to block it, but—

My hand hits something. Tight above me. A few inches, maybe six.

Then, the beeping. Fades in like my ears are waking up. Muffled, separate, outside. But increasing. Mirroring my heart rate, because—

"Stay calm," a voice says near my ear. Dr. Thompson, through a speaker, somewhere up by my head.

I try to open my eyes.

"Too bright," I say. My voice cracks. The lights dim.

"Lucy," she says. Not Lucy, *Lucille*. She's never made that mistake before.

I blink.

Everything's blurry. *Where are my contacts?*

Again.

My vision clears.

"Take it slow." Thompson stands (outside) beside me, distorted by the curve of glass. "Would you like me to open the capsule?"

Capsule.

The pace of the beeping spikes.

This is not the recovery room. Back a pace, over by Drs. Kim and Patel and Adebayo and Karlsson, is . . .

Me.

But not me.

Lucille.

Because *I'm the clone.*

LUCILLE

It faints.

She faints.

It, she. I, her.

She's me.

Her face, her hair, her voice, her eyes, tongue, elbows, shins, ankles, toenails, everything. They're mine.

Almost.

Dr. Thompson presses a button and the dome of the capsule lifts. The others crowd in and I step closer, watching between their shoulders as they volley questions and data between each other.

She's pale. And pinkish. Skin like velvet. Like . . . *new*. Resting on the bed of the capsule by her hospital-gown-clothed thigh, her hand twitches, fingers curling in toward her palm. Except for a series of lines—pink, healing, freshly made—on her palm and inside each knuckle, it's smooth.

I look at hers, look at mine. Hers, mine. Hers. Then lean forward, peering around Dr. Adebayo—who's removing a series of sensors from her scalp—to look at her right temple. It's there. Half an inch long and already scabbing. I touch my own scar—long-healed, barely visible—and remember flying over the handlebars of my purple-and-white bike as my tires skidded out from under me.

SemblanceSync. To make our imperfections match.

Her hand flinches again. Her eyelids flutter.

"Refresh her sedation," Thompson says, "then let's move her."

Patel nods and reaches for a syringe from a rolling tray off to the side of the capsule, plunging its contents into her IV's injection port. He waits, watching her vitals on the screen mounted above the capsule, then unplugs the IV's tube from the port in her hand.

Drs. Kim and Karlsson bring over a gurney from the far wall and four of them lift the capsule's entire platform onto the gurney, clicking it into place.

It's the weirdest thing, watching someone move your unconscious Facsimile. Watching Patel shift her arm, Adebayo steady her head, Kim reposition her legs. Like when your hand or leg or arm falls asleep and you brush it with your feeling hand. They're both your appendages, but the sensation's one-sided.

With the platform secured in place, Kim and Karlsson push the gurney out of the room and into the hall. I follow a pace behind, staring at her feet. Bare, so pink and clean and perfect. Because she's never had a blister, never worn uncomfortable shoes.

Never stood.

Never walked.

It's all the weirdest thing.

LUCY

I wake up alone.

At least, by appearances. I'm the only one in the room, lying on my back on a bed. Heavy, dead weight. Like a carcass, though I'm (alive) conscious.

I can feel them (her) watching. She has to be.

It's all white. Walls, floor, ceiling. Twin bed and single chair, pressed up against the wall. Doors, one normal, one sci-fi, its outlines barely visible. White ambient light, no windows. White and even more fucking whi—

No.

In the corner of my (*her, her, her*) eye. On the white bedside table.

An orange vase with a single orange flower.

LUCILLE

We watch through an observation window in an adjoining room. One way. So we can see her, but she can't see us.

Our room's dark. Hers glows with Life^2's incessant bright light. Stark, sterile, white. Except, on the bedside table, a speck of color. Like a single drop of paint. An orange flower in an orange vase.

Lucy opens her eyes, blinks, rolls her—*my*—head to the side, and Dr. Thompson leaves her place at the observation window, striding across the dark room toward the open door. I turn to watch her go, and see Isobel standing in the doorway. A silhouette against the hallway's blinding light.

Dr. Thompson breezes past her as she takes one smooth side step out of the way.

LUCY

Down past my feet, the sci-fi door slides open, and Dr. Thompson comes in. I—

I, I, I. I'm an *I*.

But I'm not me.

Not Lucille.

Looking at the flower, I try it out. Whispering, so low there's no real sound, only differently shaped air. "I'm not Lucille."

It doesn't help.

I try to sit up. Doesn't work. My muscles are . . . (all those muscles in all those pods, suspended in blue gel, living meat) *bio-goop*. That's what I am, right?

Printed.

Extruded.

Grown.

I try to move again. Fail. And my right hand starts to shake, vibrating on the mattress by my side.

Dr. Thompson pulls the chair over to my bedside and sits. "Hello, Lucy."

I watch her with my head still turned toward the flower since I can't turn it back. Her expression is predatory. Her eyes a-fucking-light. Like she's waiting for a miracle. Like she's *owed* one.

"Do you mind if I call you Lucy?" Her tone grates. It's alien. Singsong sweet like she's talking to a beloved pet, and it makes me feel like I'm, I'm, I'm . . . *"I'm going to choke," I say, watching Cass unwrap another Starburst and shove it into her already full* mouth. *She chews, slowly, dramatically, two-thirds of the pack down, one-third to go. "Seriously, Cass . . ."*

My hand shakes.

". . . I don't know the Heimlich."

And she smiles wide, Starburst juice on her teeth. "Yesh you oo." Then leans over and spits the wad out onto the grass.

I grin at her, triumphant. "Told you you couldn't do the whole pack."

Laughing, she shoves my shoulder. "Not my fault your enormous mouth gave you an advantage. Next time I'll—"

"No," I say. My sixth word. *Too. Bright. I'm. Not. Lucille. No.* Feels significant.

She nods. Her eyes shift to my hand. I try to move (hide) it. Can't.

"The muscle spasms are normal," she says. "Your nervous system is rebooting. Essentially. It will take time for the connections to solidify."

I try again. One more time.

My hand moves. Jerkily. "Normal," I say. *Seven.*

Thompson nods, brow creasing. The light in her eyes dims. I (Lucille) know(s) that look. It's doubt.

Disappointment.

Resignation.

Her shoulders drop. She tips her chin up. Microgestures. But they say *Not again.*

She thinks it didn't work.

LUCILLE

When she moves, her hand jerking awkwardly at her side, I feel it. Not literally. But like that horror-movie gag where the subject and their reflection in a mirror move separately.

"Normal," she echoes Dr. Thompson. Her voice—mine, but not mine. Different. The way you sound strange to yourself in videos—comes through the speakers mounted somewhere above me on the wall.

I can feel the word inside my mouth.

I swallow, shift closer to the window.

The others are already packed in tight, noses nearly to the glass. Holding their breath.

Then she says, "How long are you going to sit there staring at me? Figure you got a good enough look when you were putting me together."

Around me, the others exhale. Ecstatic. There are whispered cheers, silent high fives.

And me?

I'm an amalgam. Shock and amazement and anticipation and relief. Watching her feels like seeing a new color for the first time. The impossible made possible. A living, breathing paradox. One that makes me not *just* me, not *only* me, but so much more.

LUCY

"How long are you going to sit there staring at me?" I say. *Eight, nine, ten, eleven . . . forget it.* "Figure you got a good enough look when you were putting me together."

She beams at me. Like a spotlight. I've (Lucille's) never seen her smile like that. I'd cringe, but *I can't move.* I feel helpless. Trapped. I can feel my body, but I'm a passenger in it. A trespasser.

"What are you thinking?"

My mouth fills with saliva. I concentrate and manage to swallow it down. "I can't move."

"Rebooting," Thompson repeats. "And your muscles are—"

"I'm aware. What I mean is, *I need help moving.*"

"Oh," she says, "of course." And glances at the wall to my right.

A second later, Kim and Adebayo come through the door.

Dr. Kim stops a foot back from me, hands up. "What do you . . ."

"I want to sit up."

They each take an arm and shift me, propping me up against the wall. "Good?" Adebayo asks.

I try to nod. My head lolls to one side. I manage to center it. "Thanks."

Thanks.

Thanks.Thanksthanksthanksthanksthanksthanksthanks thanksthanksthanksthanksthanksthanksthanksthanks . . .

"*Thaaaaaaaaaaaaaanks,*" he says.

Smells like . . . nothing. Plastic-wrapped, blister-packed, boxed, stacked, and sealed, nothing. The quiet sound track of decade-old pop music. The glare of fluorescent lights and dingy linoleum.

Sweat in my hair. On my lip.

Shame in my stomach. Dread like a living thing, as deep as my—

Bones.

It's bones. Bode's T-shirt. An American flag. The Stars and Stripes. They're all made of (femurs, mandible, clavicle, twenty-seven for each hand, separated, splayed, encased in blue goo) bones.

It's gross. Disturbing.

Beautif—

"What happened?" Thompson asks. Eyes wide. Perched forward on the edge of her chair.

"Memory."

The room, beyond my breathing, my heartbeat, the *tick, tick, tick* of the second hand on Adebayo's watch, is silent.

"Of?"

"Target," I say. "Yester—" No, not yesterday. "What day is it?"

"Thursday," Thompson says, "July thirtieth."

I'd lost two and a half weeks.

"Are you . . ." Thompson trails off. I've never seen her stumble. "Can you describe it? The memory? What does it feel like to experience one that isn't yours?"

"Not mine," I say, and roll my head to face the wall to my right. "How is it not mine?"

CHAPTER SEVEN

LUCY

Still propped up in the little white bed, alive for, I don't know, an hour or two, I listen to Dr. Kim detail my Facsimilate schedule: daily doses of four sessions for the next two weeks to "facilitate your integration into—"

"Life?"

"Your Original's life, yes."

While he talks, I stare at the ceiling past his ear because I can't turn my head and I'm sick of looking at his face. "Where is she?"

"Lucille?"

"No, Taylor Swift."

He blinks at me like I'm an appliance that up and decided to talk. A muscle twitches in my jaw. I say, "Hard to think of me as a person capable of autonomous thought when you helped grow and assemble my organs, yeah?"

Dr. Thompson, standing behind Kim near the foot of the bed, breathes a satisfied laugh and says, "Your cognitive level is . . ."

"Unnerving," Kim supplies, eyes back on his tablet, where he reads my vitals for the third time in an hour.

". . . impressive," Thompson finishes. "Lucille went home."

"Why?"

I wish for a buzz, a hum, a drizzle, *something*. I'd take a dripping faucet. The faint soprano keen of hydrogen lights. Anything but this room's perfect silence. So flat and stark I can hear the saliva in Thompson's mouth when she opens it to say, "We believe separation is preferable at this stage, so the Facsimile can present its best self at the moment of introduction."

I stare at her, try to lift my head. Fail. Close my eyes and think, *Its best self, its, its, it's . . .* "It's not anyone's fault," she says. "It just happened."

I rub Boris's ear, and he groans happily, head pushing into my hip. "Okay."

I hear Mom sigh. "I only want you to understand that your dad and I still care about each other," she says, "that it wasn't about either of us screwing up."

Eyes down, petting Boris, sour crimp of hurt in my chest. "Which is . . . better?"

A pause. "Isn't it?"

Look up. Look up!

LOOK UP!

Isobel stands in the doorway, back straight, hands clasped. Eyes on me. *How long has she been there?* I open my mouth to say something, but she says, "Dr. Thompson. Phone call."

Thompson nods and follows her out of the room.

I close my eyes again. "So, Facsimilate. Which one's first?"

Mobilivate.

Twenty-five hours alive. Friday, and I should be at Reach the Sky. Except "I" already am. And I'm not "I." I'm not "me." *Me.* Two tiny letters, so small, yet enormous. Significant, complex. Because "me" implies self; "self" implies individual; "individual" means "single," "one," "original."

Which I am not. I'm . . .

It's the truth thing.

The sky is blue.

I'm Lucille Harper.

Lucy.

LH2010.2

I saw it on Kim's tablet, the label on my files. "LH2010.2."

Point two.

But which one's true? Am I Lucille because I have her (my?) memories? Her (my) DNA? Her (*my*) skin? Because lying on the bed in my bright white cell, I can feel the sour hollow of forgetting something, of knowing I'm supposed to be somewhere else, yet I'm in this secret nowhere. Being . . . not nothing. Something. I'm *something.* But not me.

"It's not a cell," Adebayo says, lifting me from the bed into a wheelchair.

I can't look at him. Not like I don't want to, like I can't turn my head. It just flops a bit to the left on the chair's headrest, then rolls back to the middle. "Oh? Am I allowed to leave? Could I up and walk—" I laugh. "Oh, right."

He pushes me down the hall. "Your body's functionality will improve quickly."

I don't say anything. Not because words still feel precious, but because I'm learning there's power in my silence. My voice is, quite literally, the only thing I control.

Adebayo pauses in the hallway, presses his hand to a near-invisible panel in the wall, and pushes me into a blinding room. I lift my hand to shield my eyes.

I lift my hand to shield my eyes!

"Lucy!" Thompson cheers from somewhere ahead of me. "That's wonderful!" Footsteps, and her voice nears. "Did you have to focus? Or was the movement subconscious?" I'm, I'm, I'm . . . *I'm going to throw up. The light's so bright, so hot. Heavy, constricting. And they're all watching. Phones up in the dark beyond the stage. Recording, waiting.*

The music starts. Cass at my left, a dancer whose name I can't remember at my right, sequins glinting. They move with the beat, starting the choreography. While I, while she . . .

The room dims. Screens roll down to cover the windows and cut the glare. I lower my arm, muscles twitching, arrhythmic. "Subconscious," I answer. But I know there was a lag, from the way Thompson and Karlsson look at me.

"That's fantastic, Lucy," Thompson says, praising her pet for successfully performing a trick. "And after?"

I blink as my eyes adjust. "Memory. Dance recital when I— when she was six."

Thompson's brow rises. "Interesting." She looks to Karlsson, who writes something on her tablet with a stylus. "Self-correction and disassociation with the Original at"—she checks her smartwatch—"twenty-five hours and thirty-nine minutes."

I clear my throat. The pinky finger on my right hand twitches. Thompson's attention returns to me, pausing on my hand, then lifting to my eyes, and I ask, "What are you talking about?"

"Your recognition of your status. It took OM2009—"

"Isobel." Her voice comes from behind me. All three doctors shift their attention to its source. "My name is Isobel."

Expression flat apart from a tightening around her eyes, Dr. Thompson says, "Of course. Do you need something, Isobel?"

Turn, turn, TURN YOUR DAMN HEAD!

But I can't.

"You've received a delivery from New York. Would you like me to leave it in your office?"

"Is it marked urgent?"

"No."

"Then, yes. Put it on my desk."

I hear Isobel's footsteps, followed by the sound of the door sliding closed.

Thompson lets go a long, slow breath out her nose and turns back to me. "Let's get started."

With Dr. Adebayo monitoring my brain activity, Thompson monitoring everything, and Karlsson on "poking and prodding" duty, I spend the next two hours wiggling my fingers, flexing my toes, rolling my ankles, practicing using my facial muscles, and lifting my arms. Once I can bring my index finger to my nose, five times in a row, using both hands, without gouging out an (infant, aftermarket) eye, Thompson has Adebayo lift me onto a table where Karlsson presses pads to my skin, then uses a machine to deliver small electric shocks through them to tone my muscle goop.

Thompson explains, "Your inability to control your body is both neural and muscular. Your nerves are growing rapidly, filling the gaps left by the RapidReplicate and assemblage processes, and your muscles have never been used. Both need directed intervention to ensure your success as a life surrogate."

Life surrogate.

It. Facsimile. Life surrogate. Point two.

I stare at the ceiling until we're done. Karlsson pulls the pads off one by one. Adebayo removes the sensor headset, helps me sit up, then shifts me to the chair.

"Now what?"

BodyProg.

During which Dr. Kim checks things like urine output and glucose levels and the composition of my various bodily fluids and secretions while he avoids my eye (*look at me, look at me, look!*) and asks things like if I'm experiencing any pain (no) or discomfort (I'm a meat robot with a glitching operating system, what do you think?), then calls for Patel to help load me onto the gurney for the body scanner.

"Remember how this goes?" he asks, voice in my earphones.

"Yes." I close my (her) eyes. The platform retracts into the machine. The mechanisms kick on. *Isobel's orange earrings. Isobel, Is, Is, Is, Is, Is . . .* "Is it conscious?" *someone shouts. Muffled. Distant. While thump . . . thump . . . thump . . .*

Blue.

In my eyes. My nose.

My throat. Choke, choke, choking—

The capsule's lid lifts.

"What the fuck?!" *Kim screams. Louder, closer.*

Then.

"Get it out!" *Thompson this time.* "GET IT OUT!"

And the blue (in my ears, my lungs) moves. Chunks of it.
Handfuls.

While my heart thump, thump, thump, thumpthumpthumps—

"Lucy?"

The machine stops.

Quiets.

Platform moves.

Heart pounding, breath burning, in and out, in and out (*in, one, two, three, out, one, two, three, helps with the panic*). Kim takes off my earphones. "Lucy. What—" He stops himself, shakes his head. Doesn't think I can answer or doesn't want to know.

"I woke up."

"You weren't sleeping."

"Not now. Before. In the capsule, the blue goop. I woke up."

He pales. "No. You can't remember that. You weren't— You remember that?"

I guess I do.

SyncroMem.

Dr. Adebayo sits back in the rolling desk chair positioned

between me and a desk set up with three large computer screens. He points to the monitor nearest to me; on it is the 3-D image of a brain, *my* brain, with various areas alit. "This is your current brain map." Next, he points to the central monitor. The image is far more complete than the active, semi-translucent map of mine, transmitted in real time by the sensor halo I'm wearing.

"Is that her, *our*, connectome?"

"Yes." He smiles. "And we hope so."

"Hope what?"

"That it is your connectome as well. Your cognitive level makes me very optimistic."

I cough a laugh. "What happened to the ninety-eight percent"—*Ninety-freaking-eight! He did his whole paper in verse*—"success rate?"

He focuses on the third and farthest screen, scrolling with a finger down a list of data that I can't read from here. He taps a line to highlight it. "Two percent is consequential when you're discussing the brain."

My nose itches. I lift a hand to scratch it and smack myself in the face. I try again. Succeed. Lights flash on my brain map as I do it.

"Ready?" he asks.

I nod. *Successfully! On the first try!*

Focusing back on the screens, he says, "We'll start with word association. I'll say a word, and you respond with the next word you think of. Okay?"

"Okay."

"Green."

"Grass," I say.

"Animal."

"Bear."

"Square."

"Peg."

As we volley, I watch the center and closest screens, with their synchronized pinpricks of light.

"School," he says.

"Bus."

"Honor."

"Code."

"First." *First, first . . . "First time, Saturday." Cass grins. She leans back against the wall between Louise and me on the bench in the sophomore lobby.*

"And?" Louise asks.

Cass rolls her head to look at Louise. I can't see her face, but I imagine that besides the blush in her cheeks she's arched a coy eyebrow. "And what?"

"Details! The ins and outs!" Louise laughs. Cass gives her a playful shove with her shoulder. My skin feels sour. That twinge you get in the back of your mouth when you think of lemons, but—everywhere. I wonder if my cheeks are too pale or too pink, knowing they are one or the other but not sure which. Just too.

Louise shifts on the bench, squaring her shoulders to face Cass. It makes them separate. Together yet alone. "At least, tell me if it was good."

Still facing Louise, Cass looks at me. Not a conversation-in-a-glance like we used to share, but a check-if-you're-listening one.

Louise notices and says, "Or wait and tell me later." She winks, then looks around Cass to me. "Wouldn't want to make Luce uncomfort—"

"Last," I say.

And Adebayo pauses, looking between the screens and scribbling notes, because this time, the pinpricks in Lucille's and my brain, indicating our answers, are different.

I meet with Dr. Thompson for EQuivalence in her office.

Sitting in a stiff white chair across from her, I weave my fingers together in my lap. I can do that now. Bend my arms, move my fingers, link them together, rest them, palms up, atop my thighs.

The lines on my hands are still too pink. Too pink, too few. You never think about how many lines there actually are on your hands. Not just fingerprints and knuckle creases and the ones when you cup your palms. But hundreds of others. Thousands of tiny lines. A lifetime of texture.

And mine are like a doll's.

"How are you feeling?" Dr. Thompson asks.

It's how she's started every one of these, even though she has instant access to all of my vitals, even though she trails me from session to session.

Four and a third days of life, fourth day of existence training, and my whole body hurts. Every one of my printed, extruded, layered, assembled muscles is sore. But I can hold my head up for over an hour. Can shift myself in this chair. Can stand for twenty seconds before my knees buckle. And this morning I sat in the shower and washed my own hair for the first time in my life.

A hundred and four hours. Six thousand two hundred and forty minutes, give or take, of being this. Whatever this is. Of being me. Whoever I am. And every single one (waking and asleep) has felt like trying to remember something I'm not sure I forgot.

How am I feeling?

"Thirsty," I say, and I see it.

The flicker. Annoyance. Suspicion. Beneath her Proud Pet Parent veneer. She grins, sharp and perfunctory, then taps the screen of her smartwatch.

"It's the wrong name," I say.

"Sorry?"

"Equivalence. You should call this one something else."

Her face changes. I've surprised her. "Why is that?"

"Equivalent means the same. Equal."

"And?"

"You ask how I'm feeling. What I'm thinking. Tell me"—*me, self, individual*—"this session is about helping me adjust to the mental and emotional aspects of being a Facsimile, of doing all that I'm required as my Original's counterpart. But that means I'm—"

The door slides open in the wall to my left. I watch Isobel enter, holding a tray with a pitcher of water and two empty glasses. She moves to set them on the coffee table, and I say, "I'm not equal."

Isobel stills. Only the barest pause. Fills one glass, then the second, while I continue, "I'm a substitute."

"Yes," Thompson says, "you are the sum of your purpose."

I lean forward, reaching for a glass. But my hand starts to shake and I can't, can't, *can't-can't-can't-c-c-c-c* . . .

Isobel touches my shoulder, urging me to sit back in the chair, then hands me the glass. Slowly, carefully, waiting until I can hold it steady in my grip.

"Thank you," I whisper.

She nods.

Dr. Thompson watches.

Two weeks of this.

Mobilivate until I can sit, stand, walk, run. Until my body answers my asks before I know I asked them.

BodyProg until Kim's sure my blood won't turn acidic and I'm not going to shit out my spleen.

SyncroMem until Adebayo's certain the Mimeo worked. "Ninety-eight percent?" I ask, and shaking his head, he smiles. "Better."

EQuivalence until . . .

"Last day," Thompson says.

I mirror her posture (legs crossed, hands clasped in my lap, head tilted to the side) and reflect her placid smile back at her. "Last day."

"It's an understatement to say you've excelled, Lucy. You have exceeded every expectation."

Thanks? "I'm glad."

Her focus ticks from my head to my smile to my hands to my crossed legs. Like she's making a list. Still staring, she shifts, uncrossing then recrossing her legs and resting her elbows on the chair's arms. It feels like winning a game of chicken.

"Do you feel prepared for your field trial?"

EQuivalence until I can look at the woman in charge of my creation, the woman who gave me life yet calls me "it," stretch my plastic smile, and say, "Absolutely. I'm excited to finally take my place as Lucille's Facsimile," while hating her so deeply it's cellular.

Thompson runs through the protocol for my release (daily check-ins via phone, at least one in-person appointment each week or immediately at the first sign of "malfunction," the BAN chip integrated into my neck behind my right ear for remote monitoring of my vitals, the GPS chip in the same place on the left) and I let my smile relax, tighten my brow, shifting my expression from "benevolent glee" to "focused attention" while I tend to that hate, my rage, knowing that with proper care, it could sustain me. All tight and hot and roiling. My own personal nuclear reactor, cradled inside my chest.

It makes me wonder if they did their job too well. If I'm really what they intended. They, by definition, by *practice*, don't want an individual. They want a product. A doll with a pulse and a preprogrammed Lucille lexicon. While I'm . . .

What am I?

"And after?" I ask, concentrating on keeping my tone light. "Lucille never— I don't have a memory of you explaining what happens to me when the trial's over."

Thompson checks her smartwatch, too far away for me to see its display. "You will serve as our prototype," she says, looking up again. "I'll present you to the Board as proof of our branch's success, then to other investors and clients as is necessary."

"Like a floor model."

She smiles. "Precisely. And Life Squared will keep you on hand as an example for future clients."

"So I'll live here. A sentient brochure. Forever."

"For as long as you continue to serve your purpose."

There's no banquet. No party with a "Bon Voyage" (or better, "See You Soon!") cake. Just dinner in my room like every night. Balanced meal, nutritious, bland, on a segmented white cafeteria tray. Alone.

Tray on my lap, I chew a bite of brown rice and eye the notebook next to me on the bed. I don't recognize it. Yet, I do. Not like I've seen it before, but like I can feel her seeing it on the shelf and picking it out, the flat black cover that feels like fabric, with a geometric pattern visible only when it catches the light. I know that inside I'll see my (her) handwriting, detailing all the things she's done for the past few weeks that she thinks I'll need to know in order to live her life.

Thompson gave it to me at the end of our session today, saying Lucille had dropped it by this morning. I picture her writing the final entry. Tucking it into her bag. Driving here. Waiting for

Isobel to open the gate. Then passing through the doors until she's in the lobby and we're both occupying the same building, the same space.

It's all in first person when I imagine it. I see her (my) hands doing the writing, gripping the steering wheel. Hear her (my) voice as she hums along with a song on the radio. Feel the surge in her (my) heart rate as she passes through the gate and both doors.

I try. But I can't see her from the outside.

A knock.

I wait, but no one enters, so I call, "Come in."

The door slides open. Isobel stands in the hallway, alone. She steps into my room and presses the pad on the wall to close the door behind her.

"Do they need me for something?" I ask.

Stiff shoulders, perfect posture, hands clasped lightly in front of her hips, she stops midway between the door and me on the bed. A crease appears between her perfect eyebrows, the only shift in her otherwise vacant expression. "I can't decide if I hate you."

"Hate me?"

She blinks, and the crease is gone, replaced by a plastic smile. "Are you finished with that?" she asks, gesturing to my tray.

No. "Sure."

I stand to hand it to her. When she reaches for it, she grabs my hand.

Subtly.

Secretly.

And pushes something hard and plastic into my palm as she takes the tray. Her eyes flash to the hidden observation window in the wall, then back to mine. A warning.

"Thanks," I say, and take a step back, crossing my arms to conceal whatever she put in my palm.

She nods, then turns toward the door. When she presses the pad to open it, she says, "Good luck," but doesn't look back.

I wait for a count of ten, then close myself in the bathroom, open my palm, and find a flash drive.

CHAPTER EIGHT

LUCILLE

I roll to a stop at the curb outside Life^2, turn off the car, climb out, and stare.

I was here yesterday, dropping off the notebook and a set of clothes with Isobel, but today feels different. There's a fullness, one that's prickly and bright.

The video-com screen flicks on, and Isobel's face appears. *"Lucille?"*

I step up. "I'm here."

The gate opens.

She greets me in the lobby, wearing her usual stiff skirt suit and deliberate expression. I think of her weeping over me after the Mimeo, but it feels distant and surreal, like a dream. "Ready?" she asks.

I nod.

She leads me in the direction of the conference room. With every step, the knot in my chest goes tighter and tighter, until it's so taut it hums.

And then we're there.

Then *she's* there.

"Lucille," Dr. Thompson says, standing at the head of the table, "meet Lucy."

She sits in the chair next to Dr. Kim across the table from me, her back to the courtyard with its brilliant sun streaming in around her. It catches in her—*my*—hair, illuminating the flyaway strands like gold.

Her eyes meet mine. *My* eyes meet mine.

She leans forward, and her hair slips over her shoulder. I lift a hand to loop my own behind my ear and am legitimately unsettled when she doesn't lift her hand too.

"Sit," Thompson says. "Please."

I do, closing the distance between us to three feet.

She's wearing the clothes I brought for her—loose white T-shirt, jean shorts, my extra pair of tennis shoes—and the notebook sits on the table in front of her. I wonder what she thought of it.

I wonder if she thinks. Are the things that pass through her head . . . mine? Not mine, as in an echo of what I'm thinking *right now*. But mine as in what I would think if I shared the same advent.

I stare.

She stares back.

I narrow my eyes.

She narrows hers.

I tip my head.

She tips—

"Lucy."

She looks to Dr. Thompson, and her expression flips to an innocent grin. "Yes?"

My voice. Out of her mouth.

Thompson holds her eye for a moment, and there's something

there. An uncertainty. She takes the seat at the head of the table and turns to me. "Lucille. How are you feeling?"

"A little sick," I say, then smile. "But don't worry, I won't make a mess on the floor again."

She grins. "Good."

Lucy huffs a breath out her nose. Is she remembering it?

I glance at her and away.

Thompson laces her fingers together on the tabletop. "Let's get started."

We stand in the lobby, half an hour of detailed protocol later. Thompson, Kim, Lucy, me. And Isobel, back a pace.

"Well," Lucy says. "What are we waiting for?"

I swallow. My saliva, throat, the air, everything's thick. Like a dream where it's too hard to move. Like the SUV, pressing down around—

No.

I shake my head. Take a deep breath. Feeling weird is normal, right? This is weird. I should feel weird. "Nothing," I answer. "Got everything?"

She holds up my notebook and the phone Thompson gave her for check-ins—literally the only things she owns—while giving me a blank-faced look.

"Right. Silly question."

"Remember, first appointment is Sunday," Thompson says.

We nod. At the exact same moment. In the exact same way.

And I think, *Deep breaths.* That's all. Deep breaths and the plan. Protocol. Daily check-ins by phone, weekly check-ups in person. The BAN—for monitoring vitals—and GPS chips in her neck. Call or get to Life^2 immediately if someone suspects, if something goes wrong, with her body or otherwise. Plus the calendar filled out on the wall at home.

Just a month.

A whole month.

And like that, it's gone. The tension, the fear. I walk out the door, Lucy a step behind, feeling buoyant.

"Good luck."

I—*we*—pause, turn back. Mirrored movements. Duplicated like déjà vu. A glitch.

Isobel stands in the doorway wearing her impassive face, then as I watch, her gaze slides from me to Lucy.

They share a look.

Lucy nods.

Isobel steps back and lets the door close.

Enclosed in the tiny entryway, that nowhere gap between the real world and whatever Life^2 is, Lucy turns to me, or, to the door, waiting for me to push it open.

She's so real. So solid. So much more than a figment. So much more than parts.

She meets my eye, and I turn away.

LUCY

I'm raw. Squishy and bare. Like a mollusk ripped from its shell.

(Fun fact: When you de-shell a mollusk, it dies.)

We pull away from the curb, Lucille navigating with so much care and consideration it feels like riding in a marshmallow. Still, my heart races. I reach forward, turn on the radio, pick the preset for Dad's favorite rock station, catch Lucille's pinched expression, then settle back and close my eyes.

"How do you feel about meeting Lucille's mother?" Thompson asked a few days ago. "Living with her?"

Blank-faced, I'd stared at my hand, resting palm-down on my thigh. I stretched my fingers, again and again. Stretch, hold, relax. Stretch, hold, relax. And wondered, was the blood running through those thin blue veins mine yet? Just mine, not Lucille's. The heart pumps around two thousand gallons of blood each day. Kim told me that. Two thousand gallons per day, eighty-three gallons an hour, about a minute for a denoted drop to make its cycle through the body back to the heart. Which meant that on that day, the fourteenth day of my life, the blood they'd made for me had cycled through my conscious body something like fifteen thousand times.

Was that enough? Fifteen thousand passes through my self-aware heart?

"I suppose I feel . . ." I'd taken a deliberate breath. "Anxious? That she'll be able to tell I'm not"—I couldn't help it. A pause. But, a small one—"her daughter."

A Rage Against the Machine song comes on the radio and, eyes closed, I whisper along with Zack de la Rocha.

Lucille breathes a laugh. "Who'd have thought that, of every-thing, the lyrics to 'Bulls on Parade' would stick."

Her (my) voice still sounds so odd outside my head. "Right?"

"I remember Mom getting pissed that Dad listened to it with me in the car when I was little."

Me too. "Probably why we remember," I say, then open my eyes and meet hers for the briefest second before she looks back out at the road.

She swallows thickly. I watch her throat move, identical to mine, then turn to the window. Car, car, car, truck, car, truck, truck, semi, semi-my-my-my . . . *"My head hurts," I admit. "Admit." What a loaded word. Like telling a secret, confessing a crime or weak-ness instead of answering a direct question.*

"Right now?" Kim asks.

"Yes." I'd have nodded, but this is day two and I can't do that reli-ably yet.

"How much? Scale of one to ten."

"I don't know. A three?"

And the whole room relaxes.

"What?" I ask. "Would an eight mean my brain is melting back into goo-oooooooooo—"

Stress. That's what this is. Overstimulation making me slip, making me relapse, making my thoughts skip-*skip-skipskipskiiiiiip.*

White floors, ceilings, and halls. Smooth, slick, unblemished.

Ironic, maybe, thinking of Life^2, but it works. My pulse slows. My head stills. The sound of the radio fades back in.

We exit the interstate, and it's like looking through layers of tracing paper. A flip-book of inconsequential memories, of the hundreds of times Lucille has followed these streets, rounded these turns, all laminating together, one after the other, beneath this. Now.

I fight the urge to close my eyes again. Not because I don't want to see. But because seeing all of this (again) for the first time . . . hurts. The gas station we (they: Lucille, Mom, Dad) always go to. The turn to the hospital, the one for school. The giant lilac bush eight blocks from the house that Lucille loves to cut blooms from when she walks Boris. The spot two streets over where she flipped over the handlebars of her purple-and-white bike when its tires lost traction in the gravel.

I reach up and touch the healing (still pink, still new) scar on my temple where one of the doctors used a scalpel to carve Lucille's imperfection into my perfect (still pink, still new) skin.

Mine, but not mine.

All of it.

All of me.

You are the sum of your purpose.

Lucille slows and flicks on her blinker to turn toward home. I can feel it. Lifting my hand to flip on the blinker. Moving my foot to press the brake. My muscles twitch, nerves alit, ready to go through the motions even though my limbs don't move and I've never actually driven a car.

She turns into the driveway and hits the button to open the garage door, pulls into the stall, turns off the engine, and clicks the button to close the door behind us. It's too quiet. No music, no engine, just us.

Us.

We turn to look at each other, at the same time, sitting in the same positions. Each leaning an elbow on our door's armrest, hands in our laps. I didn't even do it on purpose. Only our expressions don't match. Hers is . . .

Curious. *Beatific.* And mine?

LUCILLE

She's . . . Clear. Appraising. *Present.* There's a brightness in her—my—eyes that's freaking *invigorating.* Sitting here—in a quiet interrupted only by our breathing and the muted clicks of my car's cooling engine—I feel ready.

"Want to go meet Boris?"

Her brow tightens for the barest blink, obvious thanks to her otherwise impassive expression. Then she opens the door and climbs out of the car.

I go first, walking into the kitchen to the sound track of Boris's delighted oh-my-god-you're-home dance. He whines, picking up his front feet and wiggling his massive body. I pet his head, rub his ears. Then he sees her. He barks, loud and authoritative, and lunges.

I grab for him, missing his collar.

She brings her hands up and says, "It's okay, Bobo." In my voice.

And he stops, a pace back, whining again but different, tail tucked and anxious. "It's okay," she says. "It's okay." Again and again, soft and calm, approaching him slowly, one hand out. He sniffs her. She steps closer, leans down. I hear her murmuring as she rubs the space between his eyes. He calms.

"Let's hope it all goes that well, right?"

She glances up at me, then focuses back on Boris. "He thought I was a stranger at first."

"True." I purse my lips. "Do you want to see the garage apartment?"

We cross back through the garage. "The tape's where the stairs don't creak," I say as we climb, pointing at the blue painter's tape X's marking half the stairs. "In case you don't remember. I know it's been a while since you've—since I'd been up here. Probably should've done this before the Mimeo." I laugh a little. She doesn't.

I push open the door—silent on freshly greased hinges—at the top. "Same in here." More X's dot the floor, randomly and in paths from the door to the kitchenette, kitchenette to the bathroom, bathroom to the bed, bed to the love seat. "So you can move around when Mom's home."

I watch her study the floor, the room. Her face reveals nothing.

"I tested the volume of the TV." I wave at the note taped to it. "Don't turn it up past twelve and you should be fine. Well, I wrote it all down." I cross to the counter, where I left the instructions I wrote out on a piece of paper. "They're in the notebook, too, but better safe than caught, right?"

Nothing.

I clear my throat. "Anyway. Only shower and flush the toilet when Mom's gone. Leave the drapes on the driveway side closed at all times, but the ones on this wall"—I gesture to the windows framing the bed, both open to let fresh air in with the drapes pulled back—"are fine, at least while the tree's . . ."

She looks to me, noticing my pause. "While the tree's full?"

"Yeah."

We both know she won't be here when the leaves change and fall.

I turn toward the bathroom, opening the door to the closet that separates it from the kitchenette. "Clothes in here." I close the door. "Shampoo, toothbrush, makeup, et cetera in the bathroom."

"Sheets on the bed?" she asks.

"Yeah, of—" I catch her expression and breathe a laugh. "Sorry."

"This is weird."

I laugh again. "Really weird."

She smiles. Not an Isobel Smile™ but one that's quick and real—I think—then sets the notebook and phone on the counter. She walks into the apartment, going slowly, stepping from one taped X to the next, testing a blank space of floor and listening to the creak.

I move to the front door, and watch, wishing I could hear what she's thinking.

Is she remembering the last time I was in this room before the Mimeo? Or something else? The last time Grandma visited? The times Cass and I had sleepovers up here, pretending we were grown-up, moved out, and living on our own? Eating ice cream, watching the first halves of scary movies before freaking ourselves out and swapping them for comedies. Gossiping about crushes. Wondering what it feels like to kiss. "Spit is not sexy," Cass said one night while we were watching *The Vampire Diaries.*

A phone dings. Not mine, hers, on the counter atop the notebook. I hesitate. It's hers, but does that mean it's also mine? Is there such a thing as privacy between an Original and their Facsimile? I pick it up and read the text: *Elevated BP 12:42 p.m., LH2010.2 pls respond.*

At 12:42 we would've still been in the car.

"Life Squared texted you," I say, and Lucy turns from the window. She walks toward me and I hold out the phone.

So many things I've never thought of. Never *thought* to think of. Like my shoulders. I never bothered to really consider my shoulders before. But now I see how they swoop up a bit. And the mole on her neck, the way it moves when she swallows.

She takes the phone. Her hand brushes mine. Skin on skin. And I flinch.

Our eyes meet.

I grin, embarrassed.

She reads the message, types out a reply, then sets the phone back on the counter.

"Are you . . . okay?"

The faintest crease appears in her brow. "Yes. Traffic," she says. "Must've made me nervous."

I nod, and she smooths her expression. "What now?"

I turn to the whiteboard calendar hung on the wall by the door. She joins me, echoing my posture—arms crossed, weight shifted to our left hips—and I honestly can't tell if she's doing it on purpose or not.

"So," I say. "This is the plan."

Silently she studies it, the legend denoting her purple and me blue, the color-coded blocks of time dividing a single life between two selves. I stare at her neck, just visible with her hair behind her ear. There are no scars from the BAN and GPS chips, though Thompson said they're both implanted in the back of her neck. . . .

Not "implanted." Incorporated. That's the word she used. "The chips were *incorporated* into the back of her neck at the base of her skull." Built-in.

"Dinner with Mom," Lucy reads in the purple section for tomorrow night. She looks at me. "Where will you be?"

I can't help it. My smile. My blush. "My first date with Marco."

LUCY

She wants me to ask about it, I can tell. She wants someone to share this news with. She wants (*she wants, she wants, she wants*) what she promised herself she'd get at the end of this countdown: to be *more, enough, no longer alone*.

But it's partial. She wants me to *want* to ask about Marco. She wants *anyone* to share this news with. But he isn't in the notebook, which means she doesn't care to actually share him, this, what she really feels, with me. It's conditional. *I* am conditional. The sum of my purpose.

So after an awkward beat I say, "I'm tired."

And she says, "Right. Of course." Then smiles, tells me to text her if I need anything, and leaves.

I stand in the same spot, as the sun moves and the apartment dims, for as long as I can, waiting. Finally, I hear her SUV in the driveway, the mechanism opening the garage door. And she's here. A murmur through the walls and hollows, a dozen yards away.

Mom.

Moving up to press my ear to the apartment door, I feel my mouth go dry. On the counter, the Life[2] phone buzzes. I ignore it. Follow the blue X's into the kitchenette and open the mini-fridge's door. *Careful! Don't slam!* reads the hot-pink note taped to the handle. She's even removed all the condiments from the door so the bottles can't rattle. I grab the Nalgene (full of water since I'm not allowed to use the faucet while Mom's home), unscrew the lid, and take a long drink.

Even after, my tongue feels fat, my spit-it-it-it-it . . . *"is not sexy,"* Cass says. *"That's why TV treats it like going to the bathroom or brushing your teeth. It's there but not there."* On the show, Elena *gets out of bed, leaves the hotel room, and ends up making out with Damon outside.*

"Assumed hygiene."

She laughs. "Right? No one has bad breath on TV."

"Nope. Everyone tastes like mint or a cool mountain breeze."

Blink, inhale, shake my head.

Staring at the love seat in the dim (no lights on after dark in case the neighbors notice), I can picture their heads above the back.

I could text her. I know her number. I wonder if Lucille's talked to her at all since that day in Target. If she has, it isn't in the notebook.

The truth is that I wouldn't know what to say. Missing someone you've never met is the strangest feeling. Mom, Dad, Cass. They're mine but not mine, same as my body, my memories. My everything. So, I don't call. Instead, I sit at the counter, text Life^2 back, then download Instagram, Snapchat, and the rest onto the phone, log into all of Lucille's accounts, and delete the "log-in from a new device" notifications from her email.

CHAPTER NINE

LUCILLE

"What do you think?" I ask, twirling so the skirt of my new dress flares.

Sitting on the edge of my bed, Lucy watches, expression blank. "It's nice."

I turn away to face the full-length mirror mounted on my closet door. I'm honestly not sure what I want from her. Enthusiasm? Interest? A cure for the brittle vacuum. A brand-new color. But while I can feel her behind me, warm and alive and—me?—taking up space, she's . . . Not vacant. It isn't emptiness, it's *distance*.

Which is antithetical, right? My body, my memories . . . yet. I thought it'd be like having my diary brought to life, one with an answer key in the back. Lucille Harper, Decoded. Maybe we just need time.

Or maybe this is all she is.

I smooth my hands down my dress. Hair curled, makeup done, kaleidoscope of butterflies in my stomach. Looking myself in the eye in the mirror, and I can still barely believe this is real. No more compromising. No more picking one or the other. I get to be a good, present daughter *and* go on my first date. I get to pick my mom *and* myself. I get to be both.

My phone buzzes in my pocket. I pull it out and glimpse Lucy in the mirror. She looks up from the floor in the same moment, and meets my eye. I roll my shoulders back and lift my chin, uncurling, realizing I've hunched in on myself like I'm bracing against a gust of wind. "Mom's on her way," I say to our reflections. "Said she's bringing Thai for dinner."

Lucy nods. I "like" Mom's message, then grab my stuff and head toward the door. "Have fun?" My voice tips up, turning it into a question. One that drips with nerves and doubt.

"Yeah," she says. "You too."

I hesitate in the doorway. "Should I—"

She arches a brow.

"Should I wait? Make sure . . ."

"She doesn't notice I'm not you and attack me with a kitchen knife?"

Do I laugh? Is that a joke? Then she smiles and says, "It'll be fine. Enjoy your date." So I go.

I wait by the garage outside, bag with blanket and snacks on my arm. After ten minutes, Mom pulls up. I hold my breath, waiting. But, nothing. No screams. No panic. Five more minutes and Marco's here, rolling to a stop at the curb instead of pulling into the driveway like I told him to. I hurry down the lawn and climb in the passenger side before he can cut the engine. "Hi," I say, sliding in.

He jumps. "Uh, hi." He recovers with a wide smile. "You look ridiculous."

"Eyelashes ridiculous?"

"Absolutely."

"Well, you too." Nice jeans, button-up shirt, and a tie. "What is that?"

"This?" He lifts his tie, printed with a blurry, sepia-toned image of a supremely creepy guy holding a chain saw. "Are you trying to tell me you don't know who this is?"

I glance out the window, up the sloping drive to the front door.

"I do not. Is he a friend of yours?"

"Very funny."

I give him a toothy grin.

"You don't want to introduce me to your mom? Promise I won't embarrass you."

"She's not here."

"Oh, then who's . . ." He ducks down to look through the passenger window.

I turn my body to block his view. "Next time."

He shrugs and shifts the car into drive. I look out the back window as he pulls into the street and does a U-turn.

Standing at the window beside the front door, Lucy lifts a hand and waves.

LUCY

I watch her go. Boris's nails click on the tile as he plods up to join me at the window. Upstairs, Mom's shower turns off.

I haven't seen her yet. I stayed in Lucille's room when she got home, yelled, "Hi! I'm a mess! Food's on the counter!" at the door, and hurried into the master.

I didn't answer.

I'm honestly not sure what I thought this would be like. Being here, in (not) my house. Living (not) my life. Knowing every second that ticks by is another grain of sand through the hourglass. It's like living inside a perpetual moment of déjà vu. Except it wasn't *me* who sat on that couch while Mom and Dad said they were getting a divorce. It wasn't *me* who helped Boris learn to climb the stairs when he was a puppy. Wasn't *me* who camped out in the backyard with Cass every summer till this one.

"Hey. What're you looking at?"

She comes up behind me, closer, closer. Leaning down to rest her chin on my shoulder and gaze out the window with me. With her warmth at my back and her wet hair cool against my cheek, temple, neck, I let go a slow breath and *relax*. Truly. For the width of a moment, my bones feel less fake. I lean into it. Into her.

"Nothing."

LUCILLE

"It's relative," I say. "Your truth isn't necessarily mine, or, like, that guy's." I wave at a guy in the next lane over—stuck in the same Friday-evening traffic we are, his window almost even with mine—eating a massive meatball sandwich with both hands.

Marco leans over to get a better view of Meatball Guy right as a saucy ball drops out the end of his sandwich and rolls down his steering wheel into his lap. "Well, no. Obviously, not like that guy's."

The truck ahead of us rolls forward. We follow for three hopeful car lengths, then stop again. "But it's lots of things. From the little stuff like how cilantro tastes to bigger stuff like . . ." *How I have a clone at home?* "I don't know. If you're a flat-earther or something."

"Lucille." His tone is serious. "This is going to blow your mind, but. The earth is *round*."

I roll my eyes. "I mean, there's all this *stuff*. General consensus, culture, beliefs, your family and friends and whoever else. Like a rubber-band ball. Every rubber band is some other facet of your reality, some truth. And you're in the middle of it. Wadded up."

From the cup holder where I set my phone, the GPS lady warns Marco that the exit for I-76 is in two miles. We crawl forward another dozen feet, and, dutifully, he watches for a gap to merge right. I haven't told him where we're going yet—it's a surprise. I asked him out, so I planned—just plugged the address into my maps app and told him to follow along.

I keep waiting for the call. The panicked *"Who the hell is this, she's definitely not my daughter"* call, but it doesn't come. And the more time ticks past, the more I relax. It's going to work. It's already working.

"So. What you're saying is that everyone is mashed inside their own little reality."

"Yeah."

"And because of that, because of all those rubber bands, your decisions don't matter."

"No!" He's misunderstanding on purpose. I can tell from his

grin, wide and inciting as he checks his blind spot and makes a quick shift into the right-hand lane behind Meatball Guy. "What I'm saying is that— Okay. Take me. Super-studious, go-getter me, right?"

"What do you mean?"

"My brand. I've always been Lucille Harper, Overachiever, to people."

"To what people?"

I shrug. "Everyone. Kids at school. Teachers. My parents. Friends."

Friends. Do I still have any of those?

"Okay," he drawls.

"But it's chicken and egg. Like, I don't even know when it started. Elementary school? At some point, I tried hard. Then people expected me to try hard. Which pushed me to keep trying hard to keep up with their expectations. But when you meet people's expectations a few times, they have this nasty habit of raising them. Like, wow, you did awesome. But the next time, 'awesome' isn't special anymore, it's normal. Then pretty soon 'normal' starts feeling like 'not enough' because it isn't 'awesome.'

"So you end up, like, running on a treadmill that, every time you finally hit your stride, kicks up a notch. Increasing the speed or the incline or both. Until you're constantly trying, and failing, to catch up.

"And the best part is, I don't really know why I'm running on the treadmill at all." I take a deep breath. Marco, quiet, merges right a final time, then peels off at our exit. "So what I mean is, do I want what I want—college or whatever—because *I* want it? Or because a bunch of people have spent years expecting me to? And if it's the second one, am I really in control?"

"That's . . . bleak."

"It's not bleak. It's realistic."

"*Or*," he says, shooting me a sideways glance, "since we're getting all existential here. It's convenient."

"Convenient?"

"Yeah. A cop-out. Because if you say you don't control who you are or what you do, aren't you really saying that stuff can't be your fault?"

I make an uncertain sound in my throat. "Clarify."

He checks his mirrors and blind spot as he merges onto I-76. "Okay. Take Leatherface." He smooths a hand down his tie. "He's a murderous psychopath who wears his victims' faces."

"Apt comparison. Very flattering."

"Stay with me! I'm making a point. Swear."

I wave a hand for him to continue.

"His whole psychopath family supports his murdering, right? Funneling lost coeds his way. *Enabling* him. Basically being, like, 'Yeah! Go, Leatherface, go!' They're his ball of rubber bands. Does that mean it's not his fault?"

I breathe a laugh. "Guess I should be glad my rubber-band ball shaped me into an overachiever instead of a chain-saw-wielding maniac."

"Victim-face-wearing, chain-saw-wielding maniac."

"That's a mouthful."

"But that's not really what I mean. I think what I mean is that of course it's his fault. Someone can yell at you every day to pick up the chain saw and do some human-hunting, but he's the one who said, 'Sure, cool, I'll do that.' But, you know, mutely. Since he doesn't talk."

"Yeah, but . . . not like a murderous rampage and getting into an Ivy League school are comparable goals."

"I know. I just mean, if you don't want to be . . . *that*"—he shrugs—"then don't."

He makes it sound so easy. And maybe it is for him? But I can't remember a single time in my life where I wasn't stuck inside my own head. Where I wasn't thinking about how what I said or did looked from the outside, if it fit into how I wanted people to see me, to think of me. If it fit inside whatever shape I thought I was supposed to take. Smart, pretty, fun, interesting, thoughtful, easygoing, determined, cool. All of it, all at once. Rounding out the edges of the Perfect Girl.

Because that's what I'm supposed to be, isn't it? Everything?

Watching out the window as the GPS lady announces the last mile till we exit I-76, as my phone stays free of terrified texts and calls, as I settle into my first night of being both, I smile. Because that's what Life^2 gave me. Everything. And after a month of that, I feel confident I'll be able to figure anything out.

"That, uh, took a turn," Marco says. "Have I told you yet how very pretty you are? How special and shiny and bright?"

I look back at him. "And I smell good, too?"

"Like sunshine and puppy hugs."

I laugh.

He grins, then flips on his blinker to follow the GPS's directive to exit right. "Okay, your turn. Shower me with compliments. *Seduce* me."

"All right." I twist in my seat to face him, looking him up and down, forcing my smile flat. We slow to a stop at the end of a long line of cars waiting at the off-ramp's stoplight. "Your tie is appropriate."

He slouches dramatically in his seat, worming down till his back's almost on the bottom. "My loins, Lucille dash Beautiful Smile. They're melting."

"I will pay you real money, like, five whole dollars, to never say the word 'loins' in my presence ever again."

"Loins," he says, still melted. "Loins, loins, loiny loin loooooooiiiins."

"You should have to pay *me* for that. Like, a dollar each mention. *At least.*"

Grinning, he sits up. "I'll owe you."

The light changes, and the cars ahead of us inch forward. GPS lady says, *"In one hundred feet, turn right."*

"So," he says, "why's my tie appropriate? Unless this 'date' "— he does the air quotes—"is all part of your plan to deliver me to a chain-saw-wielding maniac, in which case I have some objections."

"Hardly," I say. "That would be a waste of your ridiculous lashes."

"Not if he—"

"Don't—"

"Two words."

"Nope."

"Lashes Face."

"That doesn't even—"

"Okay, okay, I've got it: *Marco Mask.*"

"Dear god."

"What? My face would make a great ma—"

"Stop. Now."

He grins. The GPS lady gives her last direction, and he turns into the parking lot.

"Behold," I say, "the reason for your tie's appropriateness: a shitty old slasher film at a drive-in!"

"No way! *I Know What You Did Last Summer*?" he says, reading the marquee. His expression turns into a legit emoji, that one with the wide-open smile and too-big eyes. He pulls up to the booth to get our tickets, then, focusing on navigating the parking lot, looking for a good spot, says, "First, this is amazing. *You* are amazing."

He pulls into a space in the middle, halfway back from the screen. I reach for the bag of snacks and blanket I left in the backseat, avoiding his eyes thanks to all the delighted blushing, and take three seconds to check my phone. But there's still nothing. Forty-three whole minutes, and nothing. I send the Life^2 number a quick how's-it-going text and slip my phone into the pocket of my dress.

Outside, Marco helps me spread the blanket on the still-warm hood of the car. "Second?" I ask, climbing up.

"Second." He sits beside me. "Did I hear you suggest that *Texas Chainsaw Massacre* is shitty?"

"Um, maybe?" I smooth the skirt of my dress around me. "I've never seen *Texas Chainsaw Massacre* and so cannot declare it either shitty or good."

He shifts closer, so we're hip to hip. "Disturbing."

"What is? Me never seeing *Texas Chain*— Okay, I don't feel like saying that whole title again. Why didn't they just name it *Leatherface*?"

"No, no no no no." He shakes his head emphatically. "*Texas Chainsaw Massacre* is neither good nor shitty, it is disturbing. Start to finish, *forked-up*. The original, of course. The other ones range from whatever to meh, but the original is a solid *eeeeeeeee*."

I laugh. "What does *eeeeeeeee* mean?"

"That you kind of hate what you're watching but respect it for making you hate it? Hate, like, *dear god this is going to haunt me for weeks it's perfect*."

"Sounds awful."

"It is. Also, awesome. And I'm totally going to make you watch it someday."

"No thanks."

"You can cover your eyes if you want."

"But then how will I plug my ears to avoid hearing the shrieking? I assume there's shrieking."

"Of course. And, I'll help you."

"Cover my ears?" I can barely believe how good it feels, sitting this close to him, feeling his body heat mingle with mine. Feeling, *knowing*, that I'm wanted. And not even just in a general sense, but by a guy like him.

"Sure." He smiles at me, face lit by the last of the sunset and the glow from the screen, which is playing a rotation of ads. "Or I'll build you a blanket fort to hide in."

"Or we could just not watch it."

"No way. Blanket fort."

"It's not fair," I say. "I don't have anything to inflict on you."

He brings his knees up, resting his elbows on top with his hands clasped between, and the nonchalance of it—the way his shoulder rests against mine, the way his arm overlaps my personal space—wrecks me. At least three points of contact between us, and it's . . . *normal*. "What," he says, "no sexist stereotypical love of rom-coms?"

I shake my head. "Honestly? I'm not sure what I like."

"Other than me."

"Funny."

"But true."

"Yes. Anyway. I blame the rubber-band ball of expectations. It's made me a little one-note."

He laughs.

"What?"

"You are so not one-note."

"How so?"

"Oh, I don't know. Let's discuss the internal and external cyclical validation of identity some more, and I'll see if I can figure it out."

Even though my phone didn't buzz, I reach into my pocket to check the screen for a reply. "Just wait till you hear me talk about parthenogenesis, biodegradable polymers, and the G-zero cell phase."

"Um, *what?*"

I laugh. "Okay, so I have at least three notes. Academic ambition, existential ramblings, and an ability to spout random scientific jargon."

"Right," he says, rolling his eyes. "Just three." He stretches his legs out and leans back against the windshield. "Let's play a game."

"A game." The sky's nearly dark. Or, as dark as the sky gets in the middle of a metropolis that's home to a few million people. Cars have filtered in around us, some people backing in to watch through the open hatchbacks of their SUVs, others sitting outside like us, a few blasting their music while we wait for the preview to start. My phone buzzes against my thigh, a text from Lucy: *Good, watching a movie.*

I breathe deep and lean back on the windshield beside Marco, feeling like I could float straight up into the sky. "Like Truth or Dare?"

"No. Sort of. More like, I'll say a word and you tell me something about yourself that you associate with it."

"What?"

He pushes himself up onto one elbow and looks down at me. A spot down low in my stomach squeezes. "Like, I say 'water,' and you tell me that you're a championship swimmer or how you fought off a man-eating shark one time. Or whatever, really. The rules are fluid."

"Nice pun."

He smiles wide and gorgeous, still hovering barely six inches above me.

"Okay," I say. "I'll play."

"Awesome." He lies back down and reaches for my hand, lacing his fingers with mine. "But that's not the word, so save your 'awesome' association. How about . . . dog."

"Too easy. My Great Pyrenees, Boris."

"Those huge white slobbery dogs?"

"Yep."

"Ari's going to be so jealous when I tell her. She's been asking for a dog since she could talk, but my mom won't let her have one. You'll have to text me some pictures."

"Will do."

The screen turns green and a preview starts, but neither of us moves.

"My turn?" I ask. He nods, and I think for a second. "Macaroni."

He squeezes my hand. "Good one." I turn my head to look at him. Staring up at the sky, he says, "Backpacking with my dad. You have to be careful about weight, so he'd buy this awful just-add-water dehydrated stuff. Worse than Kraft, even, since at least you use milk and butter in that. But the fun thing is that we'd always have it our first night, and I'd be so tired and hungry from hiking in that it'd taste like the best meal I'd ever had."

"You still go with him a lot?"

He shakes his head. "I see him maybe twice a year."

"That . . . sucks."

He shrugs against the windshield. "It's one of those things, you know? Like how you get used to a smell and then can't smell it anymore? Normal."

I think of my dad's apartment. The weeks it took after he moved out to stop listening for him to get home in the evenings, for Boris to stop waiting by the garage door. I want to ask him how long that took, for it to feel normal. But I also don't want to know.

"Okay, now me," he says. "Chemistry."

I lean up to give him a look, like, *really?* Then laugh when my answer pops into my head. "Oh no. Your bubble of me is going to burst."

Marco's eyes go wide. "Why?" He shifts up too, turning onto his side and dropping my hand to prop his head up on his palm before immediately reaching for my other. I mirror him so we're lying at an angle on the windshield, facing each other. "Did you lure me here under false pretenses after all?"

"Not chemistry like . . . romantic sparks." I can smell his deodorant or cologne or shampoo or whatever mixture of those he uses. I purse my lips to keep from smiling too wide. "Chemistry like bases and acids and compounds."

"Oh, good. Proceed."

"Okay." I take an exaggerated breath. "I took chem two last spring and . . . cheated on every single test."

"Ha! Really?"

I give him a slow nod. "Yup. I'm shit at memorizing formulas. And I have no intention of studying it in college, so I wasn't about to let that grade eff up my whole average."

He's rapt. "How'd you do it?"

I shrug a shoulder. "Snuck in a cheat sheet in my shoe. When you're the perpetual overachiever, teachers stop looking very close."

"Damn."

The screen goes black in the space between one preview and the next. Around us, people mutter and eat quietly. "My turn," I say. "Blue."

"*Aw!*" Marco rolls back, away from me, pulling our linked hands with him. "Mr. Blubbers!"

"Oh no. What is a Mr. Blubbers?"

"Only a stuffed blue whale and my most prized possession of all time. Well, I don't know if he was actually a blue whale, but he was a whale that was blue."

"Was?"

"Yes, *was!*" he says, indignant. "My mom washed it once when we lived in our old apartment and *someone stole it out of the dryer.*" He sits up, twisting back to look at me, incensed. "I mean, *who does that?* Steals a ratty old stuffed toy out of someone's dryer?"

"Someone who's going to spend eternity trekking, barefoot, across an endless field of thumbtacks."

"Hell yeah, they are."

"Why 'Blubbers'?"

"Because of whale blubber. Which, at five, I thought had something to do with whales chewing giant wads of gum. And *oh* was I sorely disappointed when I got older and actually googled it."

"Rough."

"Yeah. And I clicked images."

"*Eeeeeeee.*"

"Precisely."

The preview stops, the opening credits for *I Know What You Did Last Summer* roll, and Marco cheers. He drops my hand to fist-pump and whoop when the title appears on the screen, and he's not alone. He reaches back for me, grabbing my hand again and pulling me to sit up beside him. Then he leans in close and whispers over the opening song, "Okay, last one. Don't kick me."

I laugh, and he says, "Kiss."

I roll my eyes even as my cheeks heat.

"And no cop-outs. Like grandma kisses or anything."

I swallow. He's so close. And I like it. But also. "In that case, I don't have one."

"Really?"

"Yes, really," I say, not whispering. "And yes, I'm embarrassed about it."

"Why?"

In the light from the screen, I give him a look. A *What are you talking about, of course it's embarrassing* look. Then word vomit: "Because I'm sixteen and have never been kissed. Because this is my first real date. Because this is my first *any kind* of date. Because kissing people is the normal thing to do."

"If you're allo, maybe," he says. "Or not. What's normal, anyway? Does not wanting to kiss anybody make you abnormal?"

"Of course not, but—"

"But then you're embarrassed only because you think I'll judge you for never having kissed someone?"

I don't know what makes me want to be honest, to lay all my insecurities bare. The dark, maybe, interrupted only by the screen's shifting light. Or the other people, quietly watching the movie, apart but together. "No," I say, whispering again. "I'm not embarrassed because I've never kissed anyone. I'm embarrassed because no one's ever *wanted* to kiss me."

"I want to kiss you." Smiling, he shifts even closer, his face barely an inch from mine. "If you couldn't already tell, thanks to my impossibly subtle word choice."

"Okay." I barely breathe it.

But, this close, he hears me.

And brushes his lips against mine.

I lift my chin, and kiss him back.

"Speaking of backpacking," Marco says.

"Backpacking?" Sitting in the dark, parked at the curb in front of my house, everything above a whisper feels too loud. We lean against each other over the center console, neither of us in a hurry to move. No curfew, no need. I could stay out here all night if I wanted to. Go anywhere, do anything.

With his head resting on mine, I can feel Marco's jaw move. "Yeah. Macaroni. Backpacking with my dad. Keep up."

I breathe a laugh. "Got it."

"When does your school start again?"

"Why?"

"Well, for the past few summers my friends Taylor and Remi and I have gone backpacking the week before school starts. Meaning next week. And, well." He takes a deep breath. "Do you want to come?"

My lips still feel swollen, almost sore. I used to think that was fake, that you can feel kisses lingering on your lips. Turning to look out the window at my darkened house, I lift a hand to touch them.

No fires.

No pitchforks.

Not a single text or call.

She's in there right now. *I'm* in there, as far as my mom's concerned. School starts Monday, but "I" can still be there. I can go backpacking, be with Marco, and still do exactly what I'm supposed to do. I can be everything, have it all. And no one even has to know that it's not all me.

So I turn back, meet Marco's eyes, and say, "Sure, I'll come." Because I can.

CHAPTER TEN

LUCY

I pull the handle, half open the car door, and pause.

"You'll be fine," Lucille says in the driver's seat. "It'll be good."

I take a slow breath (*in, one, two, three, out, one, two, three*) and finish opening the door. Out on the sidewalk, I turn back, bend down. She's wearing sunglasses and a baseball cap. Lucille Harper, Off Duty. "Will you pick me up, or should I walk?"

"It'll be too busy after school, so walk? Or I could pick you up a few blocks away?"

"I'll walk." I step back and close the door. Lucille waves as she pulls away from the curb. She's trying so hard. And I get it. I *literally* feel it. But beside her urge to say and do the "right" thing with me is the ticking clock, and her utter indifference about what it means for me. I'm like a Band-Aid for her. There when you need it to cover a wound, easy to discard once you're healed.

The Life^2 phone buzzes in my (her) messenger bag, and I wonder which chemical concoction my emotions have triggered for the BAN this time. "You planning to check in with me every time I hiccup?" I'd asked at the Facsimilate appointment yesterday, and Thompson had smiled humorlessly and said only, "Yes."

I pull the phone out. *Status?* the text reads. I write back, *First day of school.*

It's gone before I think to reword it. To wonder if the fall semester at DU has even started yet. But no one replies, which is just more proof they don't care. Lucille's age is like this open lie we're all in on. Thompson explicitly, with the others following her lead. As long as my skin's not sloughing off and I haven't gotten caught, right?

I watch her brake at the parking lot's exit, blinker on, turning left. Away from home. Once she's out of sight, I turn to the building. I'm more than half an hour early. Early enough that I wonder if the doors are unlocked. I reach in the bag and dig out a pair of earbuds I found in Lucille's desk.

I thought about it. A lot. When Lucille left Friday night, when Mom was in the shower, when the movie ended and Mom woke up (she'd fallen asleep halfway through) and shifted her blurry self upstairs to bed. I could've done it right then. Climbed the stairs, sat at the desk, opened the computer, and plugged in Isobel's flash drive. I'd had it in my pocket all night. I even got as far as holding it poised beside the USB slot.

Then I pulled the Life^2 phone out of my back pocket and downloaded a bunch of music onto it instead. Because I (*I—I—I—I—I*) wanted to.

And because there are some questions I don't want answers to. Questions like: Did Thompson tell the truth about what happens when the trial's over? If so, what happens if I stop serving "my purpose"? Or when a newer model comes along? Will I get scrapped for parts? Clean Life^2 bathrooms? What the fuck does "decommissioned" even mean? *The asset returns to us, to be decommissioned or repurposed as we see fit.* That's a good one, memories-wise. One that's so bland and unimportant in Lucille's mind that it's mostly blurred. In my head, it's lit like a fuse.

But that's the B team. The first-string questions are even better: Am I an abomination? Am I even human? Do I have a soul?

The truth is, I don't know why Isobel gave it to me. Sure, knowing what's on it would probably help clear that up. But answers or a warning, does it matter? What difference could it possibly make? Knowing won't suddenly make me *not* a clone. *Not* an "asset." Plus, there's something terrifying about knowing. About not knowing, too, I guess. But right now I have my knowns. Four weeks to prove to Life^2 that I'm a success and can be Lucille, refrain from melting into a pile of exceedingly expensive, manufactured bio-goop, and return whole and seasoned and ready to do my duty as a living prop. All so Life^2 can take RapidReplicate to market.

I control almost nothing, but at least with the drive I control what I know. Once I open it, that's it. No going back. As (not) my mom loves to say, "You can't put the toothpaste back in the tube." And I don't know if I want to squish this toothpaste out.

I couldn't look at Isobel yesterday. As omnipresent as ever (if not more so) and shadowing me through every diagnostic step. Silent, but with her expectation hanging in the air like exhaled breath.

Sorry, Isobel, but what I don't know can't hurt me, right?

I head inside, plugging the earbuds into the phone, into my ears, and cranking "Ænima," by Tool. All the flushing and fucking (not the biblical sort) really speaks to me right now. I wouldn't say being a clone makes me a nihilist, but that's only because I don't know what being a clone makes me. So, thanks, "Dad," for the easy access to all things nineties rock/metal/grunge, because it's . . . helping.

I click the volume a few ticks higher. So high I can't hear anything else. Not the few other students and teachers populating the halls at this ghastly hour. Not even my own footsteps as I walk to the library to hide until the warning bell.

We practiced for this. Lucille (always) had a plan: Study the notebook (which was the driest shit ever, filled with stuff like what she and Mom ate for dinner, what she and Dad watched on TV, and what they talked about—her class and Reach the Sky and SAT prep junk, avoiding all things "Marco" and "clone," like mentioning them might trigger some ancient curse). Rehearse talking points like what "I" did this summer. Be Lucille.

Easy, right?

I close my eyes and take three deep breaths through my nose.

Mom couldn't tell the difference.

I'd felt like a cinnamon roll, all warm and sweet and gooey. A trivializing simile, I know. But I don't know how to describe it in a way that'd do it justice. Sitting with her Friday night, wrapped up in the same blanket on the couch. The warmth, the calm and simple existence. And not just existing, but *belonging*. I fit. *I* fit. In all my Lucille-shaped, ersatz individuality.

It was the best moment of my life.

I open my eyes and sigh a laugh. "My life." All nineteen

conscious days of it, counting the fourteen spent on the Facsimilate hamster wheel.

The first bell rings, a ten-minute warning, and I push out of the chair, trying to wrap that cinnamon-roll feeling around me. But it flakes off with every step.

First up is AP calc. I pick a seat in the back and keep my head down while the other desks fill up around me. No one says hi to me. No one says anything. I can't decide if it makes me feel relieved or impressively, immaculately lone-, lone- . . .

"Lonely?"

"No," she says. "Why would I be lonely?"

Cass shakes her head. "Because you spend every lunch in the library like a fourteenth-century monk?"

"How specific," Lucille mutters flatly, but I feel the sting, a crystalline film between my muscles and skin.

"You know what I mean."

"Yeah. I do."

"So?"

Annoyance. Impatience. That's what Lucille heard. In the memory, I could *feel* her hear it, like anticipating a blow.

But.

Like with so many of my (her) memories, it's like looking through a filter. A heavy tinge of Lucille, her biases, her assumptions. Coloring Cass's stance and expression and tone until every flicker of genuine interest and concern had been tainted.

(Project much, Lucille?)

Someone kicks my desk, and I flinch.

I look to my right at a senior I recognize from pre-calc last spring. He points to the teacher at the front of the class, who asks, "Lucille Harper?"

"Yeah." It comes out more croak than word. I clear my throat. "Sorry, yeah. Here."

He nods and calls the next name, finishing out the list. Then class starts, and like every first class in the history of first classes, it's pointless. Books. Syllabus. Goals. Hopes. Dreams. Then thirty minutes of pre-calc refresher before the bell rings and we file out toward second period, which is art. Painting, specifically.

I duck into the art room, lean against the wall beside the door, rest my head back, and close my eyes. It smells like clay. Wet, heavy, cold . . . *beneath my bare feet, flip-flops discarded in the grass. "You sure your mom's not going to be mad we're digging a hole in your yard?" Cass asks.*

"It—It—It . . ." I shrug. "It's just dirt."

We're nine. With muddy hands and muddy toes, knee-deep in a fresh hole with full shovels and the summer sun so bright and hot in my hair—

"Lucille?"

I open my eyes.

It's Bode. Coming out of the connecting kiln room, arms full with a roll of canvas and lengths of wooden framing, wearing dark-rimmed glasses, a neon-pink T-shirt, black pants, and worn-out skate shoes.

I can feel them. A heat, an ache. A flip-book of strobing images, feelings, assumptions. Every single memory she had of Bode, peeling, cracking, bending. Shifting rapidly from hers to *mine, mine, miiiiiiiiii—*

"You okay?"

I blink.

"Yeah." *Take a breath, deep and slow.* "Yeah." I step forward, hands out. "Need help?"

"Sure," he says, and gestures for me to take the canvas roll.

I slide it out from where he's got it wedged under his arm and follow him toward a massive table set up by the slop sinks in the back corner of the room. Bode drops his armload of frame lengths onto it. I set the roll of canvas beside them.

"So," I say. He's the first external person to "meet" me as Lucille, and I feel like my guts are going to writhe their way out of my abdomen. *Maybe this is it. What they've been so diligently testing for. Day nineteen, and it starts with my intestines. IntestinalAbsconding.*

No.

It's nerves. Regular-ass nerves.

"You're in this class?" I ask.

Arranging the lengths of framing by size, Bode smiles. It's one Lucille's seen before. Close-lipped, eyes averted. In her memory, it's tinged with polite indifference. But now I think he just looks shy.

"Sort of," he says. "First period is my independent study. And right now I'm technically in life studies, but I'm helping Mx. Frank out as their TA for it."

"Wow. You get to spend all morning in here?"

He smiles again, looking up and making quick eye contact this time. "Yep."

"I'm jealous."

He breathes a laugh. "Really?"

It's so strange, because I can hear it the way Lucille would hear it. With a bite of condescension. But I also hear it my own way. With straight disbelief.

I laugh back, just as breathy. "Obviously." I gesture to the windows, the colors, the smells. Can you feel nostalgic for a place you've never been? Can I feel nostalgia at all?

"I didn't think you liked art." He shifts the roll of canvas on the table, making sure it's parallel to his sorted lengths of framing. "I remember in junior high how much you hated that papier-mâché mask project we did. And, well"—he glances at me, sidelong—"really, every project."

"Huh." I cross my arms. I can't find those memories. Not even a whiff. "I don't remember that."

He shrugs.

It's uncomfortable. Not being able to recall those memories makes me feel partial. Is it because Lucille doesn't remember? Or because the Mimeo's flawed?

I shake my head. "Well, I'm excited to be in this class."

A pair of students walk into the room, talking to each other, oblivious to us. Bode looks at them, then back at me, fidgeting with the placement of the canvas roll again. "Yeah?"

"Yeah. Luc—" I catch myself. "I was dreading the art credit, but now that I'm here? I'm, um . . . excited?"

"That's, um . . . good?"

A hot little ball of hurt forms in my gut.

Then he grins. He's teasing. I grin back.

The warning bell rings, and people file in quicker now. As the final bell sounds, Mx. Frank walks in through the kiln room that connects to the pottery-drying room, supply closets, and their office, and tells us to circle around the massive table for a demonstration on making our own canvases. Except for when he's helping with the demonstration, Bode stands with me for the whole class. When the bell rings, he asks, "Coming?"

I nod and follow him into the hall.

Lunch. Her memories all wear a brittle Lucille Harper, Overachiever, veneer of Necessity and Productivity. But beneath that sits the tarlike puddle of rejection. Syrupy, viscous. And even though this is what I'm supposed to do (*Your goal for the trial is full immersion, Lucy. Find the boundaries and test them*), I wonder what she'd think of this. Me, walking with Bode. Him, wondering aloud if there'll be any good vegetarian options this year, or "shitty iceberg salad with, like, two sad cherry tomatoes and a little crouton dust" like last year.

Me, thinking, Butterflies, just butterflies. From a crush. A normal-ass crush. Thanks to years of memories and feelings and his smile's so nice, not sections of my intestines going necrotic, necrosis, neurosis, neurotic-tic-tic-tic . . .

Him, saying, "It's not even because meat is murder. Though it is." He steps into the line in the cafeteria. "Technically. It's killing. Purposefully. Which is murder, right?"

Laugh. That'd be normal. He's joking, kind of. So, laugh, laugh, la-a-a-ahhhh . . . I squeeze my eyes shut tight and shake my head. The Life^2 phone vibrates in my bag. "Can't say I know *Webster's* official definition of 'murder' off the top of my head."

He grips the straps of his backpack, high up on his shoulders. "It's more the muscle part. I can't get over the fact that you're eating something's muscles." He sticks his tongue out and fake-gags.

"Mmmm, muscles," I say.

We reach the front, and he hands me a tray from the pile before grabbing one for himself. "Right? So gross."

"Muscles from a carcass."

"See? Yuck."

"Or a corpse."

He laughs. "Stop."

"Ooooh, *cadaver*."

"Okay, but for some reason that one doesn't gross me out."

"A *moist* cadaver."

"Fine. You got me. That's horrifying." He loads up his tray with a salad (spinach and arugula, no iceberg lettuce in sight), a banana, and a carton of chocolate milk.

I fill my own tray, and we pay. "Sure, no muscles, but gland secretions are okay?"

Walking a pace in front of me, weaving between the tables full of students eating, he glances back and smiles wide. "*Chocolate* gland secretions."

My stomach flips.

A crush. A real one, right? Not some residual imprint.

Cass, Aran, Louise, Finn, and Matt are already crowded around their table, eating and talking and laughing. Bode walks up with me, and they stop. Like in a movie. A cartoon where the characters blink with the accompanying *blink, blink* sound.

Cass says, "Hey!" And Aran grins, but with uncertain context. Louise's eyes go skeptically wide. Finn grins, takes a sip of their drink. Matt waves.

And I . . . stand there.

There's only one empty seat, Bode's, between Louise and Matt. But he sets his tray down, grabs a chair from a nearby table, and shoves it in next to his (on the Matt side), forcing everyone to shift over to make room.

"Hey, Lucille," Aran says.

I smile. "Hey."

"Long time no see," Finn says.

"Yeah. Long time."

Sitting across the round lunch table from me, Cass asks, "How was your summer?"

"Good." What else am I supposed to say? *It was awesome. Spent most of it piecemeal, growing in a series of high-tech pods before being assembled and gifted with life last month.* "Yours?"

"Same," she answers. "Good. Short."

"What happened to your face?" Aran asks.

"What?" *Brain matter oozing out my nose, cheekbones shifting, skull going concave.*

"The cut on your temple."

I reach to touch it, though I know what he means. The still-pink scar to mimic Lucille's. Cass narrows her eyes. "Isn't that from . . ."

"Bike wreck," I finish.

She keeps looking at me (*don't notice, don't see, don't don't doooo—*), then shakes her head. Aran shifts his focus to Bode, asking if he wants to go skate after school, and the mood settles. Cass takes her phone off the table, stares at it in her lap, then meets my eye with a small, significant grin. I look back and shrug a shoulder. She checks her lap again, frowns, sets her phone back on the table, and the moment's gone. Then Bode teases Matt for eating "ground-up moist cadaver," aka a hamburger, and lunch devolves into a gross-out contest with Aran winning by a landslide by bringing up the origins of "artificial vanilla flavoring," aka beaver anal glands.

Louise makes a face. "That can't be true."

"What I want to know," Cass says, "is where they get it all. Beaver farms?"

"No one google that," I say.

"Please," Bode adds. "For the love of ever having an appetite again. Don't."

"I'm doing it." Cass picks up her phone and taps in a search. "It's called castoreum. From the castor sacs of North American and European beavers." She reads for a few seconds and paraphrases, "The sacs are located by their anuses, and they use it to mark their territory and such. And"—she holds up a finger and quotes—" 'Though it's been used by humans in perfumes and foods for more than eighty years, it is too expensive and difficult to obtain to be found in many foods today.'" She sets her phone down. "There you have it, fools. Put your fears of eating beaver-butt discharge to rest. Though the article said you can buy it on Etsy if you're so inclined."

"I'm buying some," Aran announces.

"*No*," Bode and I intone. We smile at each other, and it feels like a real-life Moment. With the clicking and the sparks.

Then he turns to Aran. "Actually, do it. I dare you."

"Dude," Aran says, looking at his phone. "It's like twenty-five bucks for five milliliters. *Before* shipping."

"A steal!" I cheer. "For genuine beaver castor gland secretions?"

"Except also," Bode says, turning back to me, "a whole beaver probably died for it."

"As opposed to half a beaver."

The warning bell rings and we move. "Could you kill half a beaver while keeping the other half alive?" he asks.

"Jesus Christ, you guys are morbid," Louise complains.

I grin, half to myself, and say to Bode, "Sure you could. Scientists have started growing human organs for transplant. Seems like they'd be able to keep half a beaver alive, no problem."

The others file toward the trash cans and the door. Bode hangs back with me. "The front half or the back half?"

"Either?"

He laughs. We walk side by side, shoulder to shoulder. I dump my trash, then he dumps his. "Is that for real? The organ thing?"

"Yep."

"That's . . ."

"Gross," Finn says while Matt says, "Incredible."

We hover by the doors. "Like, using the recipient's DNA?" Cass asks.

"Yeah. Removes the threat of rejection."

Matt nods. "Like I said, incredible."

"Or a slippery slope," Bode says.

I frown. "Toward?"

Aran leans in and whispers theatrically, "*Clones.*" Then laughs.

(*Kidneys, lungs, liver, femur, skull, jaw, muscle, muscle, skin, skin, skin . . . Pod after pod. Full of them. Full of it. Full of me.*)

"Okay, shut up," Cass says, and waves her phone around at us. "First-day-of-junior-year group selfie!" She turns her back to us and crowds in between Aran and me. Aran wraps his arm around her shoulder and crouches down to fit in the frame. Bode shifts closer to me. Matt, Finn, and Louise mash in around us. Cass holds her phone up and says, "Smile!"

LUCILLE

"This is making my organizational heart very happy," I say, watching Marco lay out the intended contents of his pack on the floor in his room. The twins—school doesn't start for them and Marco until next week—are downstairs watching TV.

"In that case, you can be in charge of checking things off the list. Call it foreplay."

"Ha!"

Smiling, he turns from his project and loops his arms around my waist. "The PG-13 kind?"

I tip my chin up to meet his eye, arch one brow—all cute and coquettish and *who is this new Lucille, I like her*—and say, "That would be acceptable."

He leans down to kiss me. "Okay."

Downstairs, the volume of *Teen Titans* creeps up a dozen decibels. Marco pulls back, rolling his eyes. "Sam!" he shouts toward the hall. "Turn it down!" The volume quiets. He turns back to me right as my phone dings.

"It's a conspiracy!" he wails, melodramatic.

I laugh, reaching for my phone on his desk because, well, my clone's at school pretending to be me, and it could be any—

It's a text from Cass.

Cass, who I haven't talked to since I ran into her at Target the day before the Mimeo, saying, *It's really good to see you. We should hang out. Catch up.*

My first instinct is to text back, and I tap the message bar to bring up the keypad, undoubtedly summoning the pulsing ellipsis on her end, before I realize what the text means.

I swipe down, close out of messages, and check the time. Lunch. Smack dab in the middle of it. The knot yanks tight in my chest. But why? Jealousy? Of my clone, of *myself*? This is what we're supposed to be doing. This is what I *want* to be doing. But the thought of her spending time with Cass stings.

"Hey."

I look back.

Marco stands with his head tilted and brow curved with concern. "Everything okay?"

"Sorry, yeah." I smooth my expression, realizing I'd been glaring at my phone like I was trying to divine my future in a cup of tea leaves. "All's well." I put my phone facedown on his desk and join him in the center of the room.

A boy's room. With posters for movies like *I Know What You Did Last Summer*—clearly, I am clairvoyant—*Scream*, and *Invasion of the Body Snatchers* on his walls. With a hastily made bed, pile of dirty clothes in one corner, and a cheap bookcase against one wall filled with worn Vonnegut and Atwood paperbacks.

A boy whose taste I've become familiar with. Whose hands

feel welcome resting on my hips. Whose chest I lean into, pushing him back, step by step, until we're on his bed and I choose to forget about everything but lips and hands and him, him, him. . . .

The volume of *Teen Titans* balloons to eardrum-bursting levels again. We've rolled over so he's on top of me, his hips against my hips, my shirt inched up, exposing my waist to the bottom of my ribs. Propped up on his elbows above me, Marco groans, then drops his head into the space between my shoulder and neck, mashing his face into my hair. "Turds," he grumbles.

I laugh.

He kisses my neck three times, fast, then rolls off me and his bed. Standing, he takes an exaggerated deep breath, pulls his shirt—twisted and bunched up around his chest—straight, then runs his hands through his hair. I sit up, and he smiles at me like I'm the sun.

I give him the same smile back before he turns and stomps down the stairs, yelling, "Sam! I told you to turn that down!"

Downstairs, the volume quiets. I can hear murmuring, Sam and Ari arguing about something, Marco patiently mediating. I take my time combing my fingers through my hair, smoothing out the tangles, thinking about Marco. Sweet, funny Marco, who can list every way Jason Voorhees has died in all twelve *Friday the 13th* movies, in order. Marco, who is so unabashedly *himself.* Confident but not arrogant. Considerate but not self-conscious. Marco, who likes me, who wants me, even though when I think of myself, it's with a prevailing sense of fear.

Fear of inadequacy, of looking foolish, of being too much or too little. Fear of not doing something, anything, *everything* right.

I resent it. That omnipresent sense of judgment. Feeling like I could do it all "right" yet still be wrong. Be ambitious, but don't try too hard. Be capable, but not intimidating. Be attentive, but not clingy. Be aloof, but not unattainable. Be feminine, but not too girly. Be "one of the boys," but not better. Fast, but not faster. Smart, but not smarter. Funny, but not funniest. Be cute. Be sexy. Be fun. Be *likeable*.

Be needed. Be wanted. Be *desired*. Like how Life^2 needs me, how they *chose* me. And how Marco wants me.

That's the answer. Two of me now, here *and* there. Two of us to fill up one space. There should be more than enough. We should overflow. Lucy, there, fixing a friendship, keeping up with classes, my parents, and everything else I'll get to step back into. Me, here. All of it, knitting together. Yet when I tried to spend time with her this weekend, keep her company when we were home alone after my mom got called in, she claimed exhaustion and turned me away at the studio's door.

My phone dings again.

I get off of Marco's bed to grab it from his desk. Not a text this time, a notification from Instagram. Telling me that @KickassCass tagged me in a photo. I open it and see Lucy.

Lucy, standing with Cass, Aran, Finn, Matt, Bode, and Louise in the cafeteria. Lucy, smiling next to Cass, who's got her arm outstretched to snap the selfie. Lucy, scrunched up next to Bode, who isn't looking at Cass's phone but at me, at *her*, in a way that's only a few shades off from how Marco looks at me.

CHAPTER ELEVEN

LUCY

"Things must be pretty serious with Marco if you're willing to go camping with him," I say. "And not even camping. *Backpacking*."

"Yeah." She smiles, folding a third pair of shorts and adding them to her pile. She's deep in it, preparing, daydreaming, prying herself free from her life like it was a parasite. So deep she didn't even bother to ask me about my second day on Official Lucille Duty. "I mean, I think so. We haven't talked about it."

I'm guessing you haven't talked about a lot. But I don't say it. What good would that do? I'm temporary. All of this is *temporary*. Her month to do more, be more, while I keep her life warm.

"Sharing a tent in the middle of cell-serviceless nowhere seems pretty official."

Her smile widens. "I know, right?"

I spin on the bar stool at the kitchenette's counter, pushing myself back and forth as far as the springs will let me go in either direction. Left: Lucille, packing her frame backpack, dug out of Dad's old stuff in the crawl space. Right: the dry-erase calendar, purple for the rest of the week, from tonight on, updated after Marco asked her along on this trek last week. Middle: I let my eyes blur.

"What time should I head in?" I ask.

"Mom said she'd be home by six, so . . ."

"Okay."

Then quiet again. The light sounds of her packing. The buzz of a text on her phone. The lift of her lips as she reads it and smiles. So much smiling. *Cool, so happy for you, must be nice. To have your whole smile-filled future ahead of you instead of, like, twenty-five days.*

I wonder if she realizes that I know almost all of her thoughts. The fizzy sort of glee she gets knowing she's been invited to something. Twisting anticipation about being alone with Marco. Lingering jealousy from when she saw that picture of me with Cass and her friends on Monday. The stinging undercurrent of worry that we'll get caught, though that dulls with each passing day.

I wonder if she realizes (or cares) how little she knows of my thoughts.

Her phone buzzes again. "Mom's coming home early. You should probably head down."

"Okay."

I get up to go, grabbing the messenger bag off the back of the other stool.

"Lucy?" she calls when I'm at the door. I turn back. She watches me, brow creased, head tipped. I fight an urge to mimic her. Then she inhales, shakes her head a bit, and says, "I'll leave a note about where we're going on the counter. And my phone. Since it'd be weird if Mom and Dad couldn't get in touch with you. Me. Whatever."

"You won't need it?"

"I'll tell Marco I forgot it and use his. No service anyway, remember?"

I nod. Turn away. Pause. Turn back. "Have fun."

"Thanks," she says, and I leave.

LUCILLE

Marco texts that they're here at 6:02 the next morning. Dressed and waiting, I text back a winking kiss, then set my phone on the counter next to a printout of the directions for where we're going—just in case—grab my pack, and go, creeping down the stairs, out the garage's side door, and across the lawn to where Taylor's parked her older-model Toyota Highlander at the curb.

When I step onto the sidewalk, Marco opens the rear passenger door and climbs out to meet me. "Check you out," he says, smiling. "A regular mountain woman."

"Right?" I say, gripping my pack's straps. "Minus the coat made of animal pelts."

"And the smell."

"Plus Gore-Tex."

"So, really," he says, opening the SUV's hatch and taking my pack to stack it on the other three in the back, "just a young woman going backpacking and looking *impossibly* hot in her hiking gear." He closes the hatch and pulls me in close. "Oh, and you smell really nice too. Not at all like tanned animal hides."

"I like that you find hiking gear hot. Feels like a low bar to beat."

He smiles. "You'd be hot in a Snuggie."

"A Snuggie?"

"Yes, a Snuggie." He leans down and kisses me.

"Dear obnoxious couple!" Taylor calls out the driver's window. "Get your nauseating asses in the car."

Marco kisses me again, longer, deeper, until Taylor yells, "I'm counting to three, then laying on the horn!"

We climb in the car, both in the back. Taylor pulls away from the curb and Remi turns around in the passenger seat to offer me his hand. "Nice to finally meet you, Lucille."

We shake hands. "Nice to meet you too, Remi."

He lets go of my hand and rests his head against the side of his seat. "Marco hasn't shut up about you since your first day at Reach the Sky. It'd be cute if it wasn't the conversational equivalent of eating a five-gallon bucket of cotton candy. *Packed* cotton candy." He mimes it. "Really mashed down."

"So, like, a five-gallon bucket of hard blue sugar?"

"Yup."

"That's . . . gross."

Marco snorts. "You love cotton candy. Even that packaged garbage they sell at gas stations."

Turning around, Remi laughs. It's one of the best sounds I've ever heard, bubbling and contagious. "That's true," he says. "I do love it."

Taylor does a rolling stop at the end of my block before heading west, and I glance back at my house through the rear window. I imagine my mom's alarm going off, the five-minute gap, then her soft knock on my door to wake me—*her*—up.

Her, Lucy. In my bed. Being me. While I'm . . .

I face forward again, and Marco reaches for my hand across the middle seat. Remi scrolls through XM radio stations. Taylor dances in her seat to the snippets of songs as he flips past them. I smile at Marco in the dim.

I'm being me too.

LUCY

I wake in her bed.

Hers. Not mine. I don't even have a flicker of doubt. It all looks and feels familiar, but "familiar" in the way a Starbucks is because they're all the same design.

Mom knocks and calls for me to wake up. I call back that I already am and listen to her footsteps, followed by Boris's, continuing down the hall. Downstairs, the sliding glass door opens and a second later Boris is barking in the backyard.

I sit up, and let my (her) memories filter through reality. Her room. Her bed. Her closet. Her clothes. Her desk.

I left the flash drive next to Lucille's laptop last night after trying and failing again to summon the courage to open it. Six days with it, and it's begun to pulse in my periphery. An incessant irritation, like ringing in my ears. I both desperately want and do not want to know what's on it, and I have no clue how to reconcile the two.

Maybe it's every answer I could want. Proof I'm a person, that I'm whole, plus a step-by-step plan for getting me out.

Maybe it's graphic descriptions and images of my future as a "decommissioned asset" being scrapped for parts. Maybe it's cat videos.

What you have to remember, Lucy, is that there is no You. Not in an individuated sense. It is not your life. Those are not your clothes. We use pronouns for clarity and, because of our need for you to blend in, it'd be too incongruous to call you It.

Good thing I have plenty of reasons for optimism, right?

Lucille picked out my clothes for the next three days and hung them up in her closet in sets, each above a pair of corresponding shoes. I look at them for maybe eight seconds before I push them aside to go digging.

When I walk into the art room after calc, Bode's standing at a drafting table working on his laptop. He looks up, and I am not disappointed. His smile's so wide his cheeks shift his royal-blue glasses. "Kick-ass shirt."

"Thanks," I say, joining him at the table. "The narwhal is the unicorn of the sea."

He laughs. His gaze falls to my lips and stalls there. "You look . . ."

Like me. That's what I thought when I stood in front of the mirror this morning. Oversized graphic tank, black leggings, winged eyeliner, matte-red lips. I look—

"Like yourself," he says. And I die a little. "If that makes any sense at all."

"More than you know."

Today we're sketching, preparing for our first project this semester. And though I know he doesn't have to, though I know he has his own work to do, Bode sits next to me for the entire class. He settles in, his well-worn, half-filled sketchbook next to my virgin one, his arm brushing mine as he starts filling his page while I stare at my bright, white empty one.

I laughed (loud enough that half the class turned to look at me) when Mx. Frank said we'd be doing self-portraits. Because it's too perfect. Average and expected and so painfully appropriate for someone whose face isn't (is?) her own. "Use whatever method, whatever style, you feel like," they said. Abstract, surreal, impressionist, photo-realistic, illustrated. They don't care as long as it's a "true and moving expression of how you see yourself."

So, sitting next to Bode, settling into my (manufactured) bones and (bioprinted) muscles and (aftermarket) skin, I draw. We have mirrors, but I don't use mine, flipping it over to work from memory instead.

My memory.

Memories of my reflection inside the capsule's glass, clouded by (*naked, twitch, inhale, choke, choke, choking on*) blue gel.

Of Lucille's face looking down at me, eyes wide.

Of my visage in every slick white surface.

When the bell rings, I feel like I'm surfacing. Like I'm taking my first breath after spending the last hour underwater.

Bode glances over at my paper and gasps. "Holy shit, Lucille. That's amazing."

And I say, "Call me Lucy."

LUCILLE

We pull into the trailhead parking lot around eleven, after a four-hour drive and a stop at a grocery store. Taylor leaves our permit receipt on the dashboard, then locks her car. Marco snaps a bear bell onto his pack before handing me a second one. It's bright red.

"Cute," I say. "Think it'll still be cute after a bear eats me and shits it out?"

"Definitely. Bear-shit bling." He grins and kisses me on the cheek. "But, also, I have bear spray. And Taylor has an air horn."

"Good." I kiss him again.

"Okay," Taylor says. "Enough of that."

Marco laughs. "What, kissing?"

"Yes."

"Aw, come on," Remi says, hefting his pack onto his shoulders. "They're adorable."

"Remi, of all people, you should be on my side. You're the reason we have, well, *had* a moratorium on significant-other tagalongs in the first place." She glances at me. "No offense."

"None taken. I think." I shift my shoulders under my pack straps.

Behind me, Marco lifts my pack, taking the weight of it off me, and says, "Tighten the straps so it sits higher on your back."

I do and feel immediately more comfortable.

"One time!" Remi says. "I bring a boyfriend along *one time* and there's a 'moratorium'?"

"One time?" Taylor scoffs. "That 'one time' ended in us bailing on the whole trip before dawn on the second day because you and what's-his-name, Buck?"

Remi gives her a look. "Beck. Like you don't remember."

"Bickered literally nonstop." She looks at me. "Non. Stop. I don't think they even breathed. Or they'd mastered circular breathing."

"Circular bitching," Remi says with a grin.

She glares at him. "Funny."

We start for the trailhead. It's hot, the sun high above us, and I'm already sweating. My sunglasses slip a millimeter down my nose. Remi falls into step behind Taylor. Marco holds his hand out for mine and together we cross the parking lot.

"Well," Taylor says, glancing over her shoulder at me, "that circular bitching ended in Beck chucking all of our food in the lake."

"Ha!" I say. "Seriously?"

"Seriously," Marco says.

"He had a flair for the dramatic," Remi says, pretending to flip his hair. "It was a passionate affair."

Taylor snorts. "Right."

We step onto the trail and Marco lets go of my hand to walk single file behind me. "Didn't he send you a video of him burning the hoodie you left at his house?"

"Passion!" Remi cheers, throwing his arms in the air.

"Sure, Rem," Taylor says. "You two were a train wreck waiting to happen from the moment you left the station."

"*That*," Remi says, "is the cheesiest thing I have ever heard."

"Also," Marco says, "Lucille isn't planning to throw all our food in the lake. Are you, Lucille?"

I laugh. "Probably won't set anything on fire either."

Remi spins around, taking two steps backward on the trail to blow me a kiss, then spins back and says, "Except for Marco's loins."

"Rem!" Marco yells.

I blush.

Remi cackles.

I look back at Marco, who, smiling, meets my eye. He's blushing too.

The eight-mile hike takes us all afternoon. We stop for breaks, catching our breath as the elevation gains, snacking on trail mix, using Marco's and Taylor's water filters to refill our bottles from a stream. I love every step of it.

I love the heat in my lungs when we gain elevation, the smell of the sage, the dirt, and the feel of the sun on my arms and heavy pack on my shoulders. I love how much Remi and Taylor and Marco bottom-line *like* each other, how comfortable they are, and how easily I seem to fit. I especially love how huge the sky is and how, depending on where you look, it's all different hues of blue.

LUCY

Standing outside Dad's apartment's door that evening, I hesitate. The moment's too potent. Lucille's memories, two days before the Mimeo, are too assertive. I can feel her lingering nausea, her disgust. When she made this memory, I was in pieces. Intestines, rib cage, kidneys, ovaries and uterus (Functioning? Will I ever get a period? Be able to have kids? Live long enough to do either?), eyes, spine, all in their own blue hydrogel-filled pods.

Keys in hand, I take deep breaths (*in, one, two, three, out, one, two, three*). The Life^2 phone buzzes in my bag. But it isn't them, reading my nerves about meeting Dad in my heart rate, it's Bode.

But, his text says, *will the octopus army overcome their primary obstacle? Can you really see them conquering Idaho?*

I can't remember how it started. Someone at lunch saying something about how smart octopuses are, how they problem-solve, and how the one in Japan that got famous predicting World Cup games ended up being eaten. Then Bode turned to me and joked that they'd probably already been plotting their revenge before that for humans turning the oceans into plastic soup.

Smiling, I write back: *They won't need to. They'll use their superior intellect to lure us into the sea.*

The three grayscale dots appear immediately on the screen.

True. Plus their land dwelling allies, the spider horde, will eat those of us who manage to escape.

I mean, we probably deserve it, right?

Definitely. The election of that sentient skid mark sealed it. It's time for another species to get their shot.

I gave him this number yesterday. It feels bigger than it probably should. It's just a few texts, right? One small thing. One tiny secret. But it's mine. I write back: *All hail our eight legged overlords. Both the exoskeletoned and tentacled sorts.*

We had a good, well, no, a totally mixed review run. Art is cool.

And ice cream, I type. *Put that in the win column.*

Yes. Ice cream and art. The rest is a wash.

Heading into my dad's. You should probably stop texting me now.

Okay stopping.

I mean it.

Me too.

Sure you do.

Do you ever think about how we eat crabs but we don't eat spiders even though crabs are basically giant spiders that live in the ocean?

I laugh and type: *Yes. All the time. I think of literally nothing else.*

I bet the crabs side with the octopuses at first then swap sides when the spiders join thanks to centuries of resentment for being eaten.

Probably. Or they'll start eating us too for revenge. Also now I'm thinking about what eating a giant spider would be like. Would you boil it?

I wonder if he's smiling. If he's home or skating with Aran or at work at the print shop. If his coworkers are watching him, wondering what he's smiling at, asking *What's so funny?* But Bode doesn't answer them because, like me, he wants this weird little pocket of space to be no one's but ours.

He responds: *Crack its exoskeleton and dip its flesh in hot butter?*

Do spiders even have flesh? Or just goo.

Gross Lucy. Who wants to think about spider flesh?

Don't judge me Bode. For all you know I'll side with the spiders.

Lucille's phone chirps in my bag. I pull it out and see a message from Dad, wondering if I'm here yet.

I text Bode: *Okay I really do have to go now.*

Good. This was boring anyway.

I'm telling the spiders you said that.

Do it. I dare you. Gray dots. *Actually no don't. I take it back.*

I put my key in the lock and open the door, eyes on the screen.

Lucy?

LUCY??

I reply with a line of spider emojis.

The apartment smells like chicken and roasting onions, set to the sound track of a sizzling pan.

"Hey, Kid," Dad calls from the kitchen. He rinses his hands, dries them on a dish towel, and comes to meet me in the entryway. I hold my breath.

But he doesn't notice. Doesn't go wide-eyed or start screaming. Just opens his arms and waits for me to drop my bag before wrapping me in a warm hug. I'm glad when he lets go and turns away without studying my face, because I'm not sure how I'd explain away my expression, the tears in my eyes. With his back turned, I wipe my eyes and fix it.

"How was school?" he asks, in front of the stove again.

"Good." I take a seat at the counter. "Though I can already tell AP bio's going to be tough."

He laughs. "Well. Isn't it supposed to be?"

"Yes. Fair." Not like I'll need to remember any of it anyway. Though I am taking detailed notes like a good little life surrogate.

He flips the chicken in the pan, asks something else, I answer. And like with Mom, it's easy.

Honestly, it's cruel. I catch myself wishing they'd failed. Or that they hadn't succeeded quite so well. Would it be better if they'd spared me the capacity to love? If they'd cut it out and replaced it with obligation or some brand of benevolent apathy instead? Why make me capable of feeling, deep in my manufactured bones, that he's not only Lucille's dad, but my dad too, that it's my life too, if it isn't?

Maybe my quiet and pretending, my keeping the depth of myself a secret from Life^2, isn't power but foolishness. If they knew, they wouldn't do this, would they? Put an expiration date on me as a daughter, a friend. A person.

Later, after we've washed dishes and are watching TV for a bit before I need to head home, he asks, "How's Mom?"

"Fine, I think. A little lonely."

He nods, gazing, unfocused, at the TV. "I feel like we never talk about it. The divorce. You've handled it so well. Sometimes I worry, *too* well."

"Too well?"

"Your mom and I dismantled your normal, Lucille. And through every step, you've just been . . . fine."

I could laugh. Lucille dealt with that "dismantled normal" by letting a secret company literally duplicate her. Which, of course, *reeks* of being "fine."

"Yeah," I say, because he's waiting and I have no clue how else to fill this empty air.

"You know, it's okay to not be fine. Pretending to be when you're not can really screw things up in the long run. That's a big part of what happened with Mom and me."

"I know."

He looks at me with love and concern. But, he's not looking at *me*. He's looking at Lucille. "Do you?"

"I think so." I smile, small and solemn, and he leans over to squeeze my (3-D-printed) shoulder. But of course that's a lie. What's the "long run" in my situation? Three more weeks living half of a life as half of a person before getting turned into a product sample?

We settle back in to watch the show. I hear my phone buzz in my bag and get up to check it, hoping it's Bode. *Reminder. In-person check-in Friday, 5 p.m.*

I text back a thumbs-up and dump the phone in the bag.

LUCILLE

We brush our teeth using water from Marco's Nalgene, spitting into the grass, then pack even the toothpaste into the bear-proof canisters he, Taylor, and Remi brought.

"It's fun," Remi says, "because while the bear tears open our tents like a Snickers wrapper and munches us up like the tasty treats we are, at least our food will be safe."

Taylor rolls her eyes. "That's why we'll leave it over there," she says, pointing to a group of bushes a hundred yards off from our campsite.

"Ah yes, the relative safety afforded by a short distance of flat, easily crossable ground."

"Hey," I say, "at least with all that candy you ate, the bear will probably munch you first. Giving the rest of us a chance to escape."

"True," Marco adds. "Thank you in advance for your sacrifice."

We finish packing up the food, and Taylor and Remi carry the canisters to the designated bush while Marco and I triple-check that the fire's out. We're quiet. A little awkward. He asked if I'd rather share a tent with Taylor, but I blushed—so much blushing, it's my default now—and said no.

Walking back, Remi starts shouting at the top of his lungs. "Stay away, bears! Nothing to eat here, bears! No sweet treats or savory human meat!" His voice echoes a little, rebounding off the shallow hills surrounding the lake.

"Great job, Rem," Marco says as they near. "You've scared off all the bears while alerting every forest-dwelling psycho, alien, monster, or ghoul in a ten-mile radius to our presence."

Remi shrugs. "If I'm going to die in the woods, I'd rather it be a horror-movie-level death than a basic-ass bear mauling."

"Yes, please," Taylor says, "let's discuss the merits of death by bear-eating versus being skinned by a mutant hill person. I so want to have this conversation. Right now. Out in the open. In the dark. Miles away from anyone who might hear us scream."

"Except for the other ghouls," I say. "Ghoul and monster and mountain-serial-killer party!"

"Okay, this is fun," Taylor says, "but also stop."

Marco takes my hand. "On that note," he says, and waves to Taylor and Remi while pulling me away toward our tent.

"If you two decide to bone," Remi says, "keep it down, okay?

Or, no. On second thought, don't. We all know what happens to teens who have sex in horror movies."

Marco holds his free hand up, giving Remi the finger.

Remi calls, "Thank you in advance for your sacrifice!"

Marco drops my hand to unzip then rezip the tent door after we climb in. We're quiet, listening to Remi and Taylor talk as they head toward their tent. I sit on the end of my sleeping bag to take off my hiking shoes and set them in the corner by the door. I wonder if my feet smell, if *I* smell, then decide not to worry about it. If I do, Marco does too. Level playing field. He sits on the end of his sleeping bag beside me, taking his shoes off like I did and setting them neatly in the other corner of the tent near the door.

"So," he says.

"So."

The quiet's so loud I think my ears might pop.

"I'm going to change," I say, then turn to my pack to pull out the old T-shirt and terry-cloth shorts I brought to sleep in. Behind me, I hear him shift too, unzipping his pack to rummage around like me.

I change, pulling my shirt over my head, not telling him not to look because, well, I *want* him to look, but waiting to take my bra off until after I pull my sleep shirt on. I crawl into my sleeping bag to change my shorts.

Marco climbs into his sleeping bag beside me and takes his pants off inside, then folds them neatly on top of his bag. He's changed into a clean shirt. It's plain, white, and looks bright in the dark.

We watch each other. His deep brown eyes look black in the night. My gut heats. I can feel it in my spine. "I've never . . ."

"Me either," he says.

"Really?"

"You don't believe me?"

I snuggle down into my sleeping bag, and Marco does the same in his. We don't break eye contact.

"Of course I believe you. I'm just . . ." I shrug.

"Surprised?"

"Maybe." He waits, and I continue, "Not that you seem like, I don't know, seem like you should have. You're just . . ."

He fights a smile. "What?"

"Um, hot?"

He laughs. Breathily, still quiet. "Well, likewise."

I grin. Embarrassment tingles in my cheeks, but I don't try to hide it. I want to be me with Marco. Not Lucille Harper, Overachiever, or any other iteration. Just *me*. "Sometimes it feels like I'm the last one. Like everyone is off doing things I'm not."

Smiling, he frees an arm from his sleeping bag, reaches over, and runs his fingers through my hair. "Um, have you *met* my friends? Those two oversharing weirdos a couple yards over?"

"Yeah, they're a little intense."

He grins. "They're . . . something."

"Have you ever gotten close?"

"Once," he says. "But it didn't feel right. Not like the situation was wrong or we were drunk or something. I just . . . didn't want to."

I swallow. His fingers keep moving, methodically combing through my hair. "Do you want to with me?"

"Yes. Do you? With me?"

"Yes," I say. "But maybe . . ."

"Maybe not tonight."

I nod. Even though I'm half on fire. Even though I mean it. I want to. I so want to. Someday.

His hand pauses. "Can I kiss you?"

I nod again, leaning forward, closing the narrow space that separates us. And we kiss. Slow and sweet. Then, deeper. His hand in my hair, mine on his chest, the sleeping bags unzipped so we can get closer.

LUCY

Isobel knows the instant I meet her eyes.

Friday, eight days since I went "home," and I still haven't looked at it.

I follow her down the hall toward the conference room. "I'm trying to help you," she says, voice low. "To help you help yourself."

"How can anyone help me?" I whisper back.

She glances at me over her shoulder for the span of a footstep, then looks forward again. We're quiet the rest of the way.

Drs. Thompson and Kim wait at the table in their usual seats. The pseudo-formality of it, of Isobel escorting me, of following this protocol every single time, is ridiculous. Like they didn't grow and assemble me three doors down.

"Hello, Lucy," Thompson says, smiling. "No Lucille today?"

I take the chair across from Thompson and say, "Nope. She's been backpacking with her new boyfriend all week."

Thompson's smile shifts, brows lifting, eyes genuinely curious. "Really?"

"Yes."

"And that's going well?"

"No pitchforks yet."

Kim snorts a laugh, and I turn to him, shifting my head with the unnatural precision of a robot in the way he hates. He catches me staring and clears his throat. How he's still creeped out by me, I have no clue. Lucille could be sitting here, pretending to be me, and he'd never know.

"That's . . ." Beaming, Thompson shakes her head. "Impressive, Lucy. Well done. Why didn't you share this in your daily check-ins?"

"You didn't ask what Lucille was doing."

"Right," she says, "well, it's wonderful news. Lucille's absence proves you're doing even better than expected, that your integration is . . ."

I stop listening. As the sun dips lower in the sky, shadows cast the courtyard in a variety of grays and diluted blue.

I painted my portrait in blues today. From a watery, early-morning sky to the deepest midnight, near-black and spectral. I felt a flow, an obsession I know Lucille has never felt. Like being in a bubble at the bottom of the ocean. Dark and quiet and insulated. But not empty. Because everything that makes me *me* was in that bubble. A life that felt like mine. Every convoluted thought. Every duplicated memory. Every laminated feeling, layer after layer of emotions and reactions and questions. All those questions. About what I am. Who I am. If I'm more than Lucille, different or identical. If, even though I'm her, from my cells to my thoughts, I'm also my own. . . .

"That's incredible," Bode said when he saw my portrait.

He stood behind my bench, staring at my blue-covered canvas. I got up to stand beside him, shoulder to shoulder. He looked at me. "Go out with me. Tonight?"

"Lucy," Thompson says.

I blink and shift my focus back to her. "Yes?"

"A memory?"

She thinks I've glitched. "Nope," I say. "Just bored."

She and Dr. Kim share a look, then tell me I can go.

LUCILLE

I learn that his middle name is Yasiel after his dad's grandpa, who was apparently an "epic badass who fought with the army in World War II."

And that his favorite flavor is vanilla. "Really?" I asked, sitting with him on a rock in the sun, hair crisp from the drying lake water. "*Vanilla?*"

"Oh, and what's yours? Chocolate? People always say chocolate. Like that's somehow less boring than vanilla."

"Except my favorite flavor isn't chocolate," I said. "It's pistachio."

"No."

I laughed. "No?"

He shook his head. "Yes. I mean, right, *no*. Just no. Pistachio cannot be your favorite flavor. It's unacceptable."

"Ah, well," I said. "Then, coconut."

And he pretended to die, dramatically, like with blood spurting and convulsions, until I grabbed his face between my hands, kissed his lips, and he told me I was forgiven for my "ghastly taste."

I learn that his dad left when the twins were two and he was nine. "But it's not awful or tragic or anything. Though we don't see him enough." And his mom got remarried when he was twelve, but they divorced after a year.

I learn that he wants to study to be a nurse. "Not a doctor?" I asked in the dark as we talked late into the night Thursday.

"Nope," he said. "People need nurses. I mean, they need doctors too, of course. But there's something I like more about nursing. I don't want to be the captain. I'd rather be part of a team."

I stayed quiet for a while, thinking. "I guess I always figured everyone wants to be captain."

I learn that he snores. That's it, just that he snores. Until I shove him hard enough that he rolls onto his side.

I learn that he hums while he brushes his teeth and hates sleeping in sweatpants, even when it's cold. That he knows how to braid hair way better than I do. That he can recite on demand every coffee order for the regulars at the shop where he works and that he's allergic to cats.

And all I can do is lie.

At least, that's what it starts to feel like. In the beginning, it was easy. Then he started asking questions about school, meeting

Boris, meeting my mom and dad, what they think of me going backpacking with a guy they've never met. And every time I can't answer, it's a whisper. A little bite of doubt, saying, *If she's you, and you're here, then who's the secret?* And, *Three more weeks, but then what?* Will I go right back to where I was before? And if I do, then is this feeling even real? Or is it as manufactured and temporary as she is?

I shake my head—*forget it, forget her*—and settle into Marco's and my sleeping bags. It's Friday, our last night, and I don't want to waste it worrying. A breeze slips along the thin walls of the tent. Our nylon cocoon, self-contained and cast in gray scale from the light of the stars and moon. Marco climbs into the tent after helping Taylor stow the bear canisters and zips the door closed behind him. I watch him and think, *I could stay here forever.*

"Hi," I say.

"Hi," he says back, and takes off his shoes, tucking his socks into them, stowing them in the corner beside mine. Then he pulls his shirt over his head and reaches for his bag to grab the white one he's been sleeping in.

I touch his arm, grip his wrist, pull him toward me.

He turns, kneeling on the sleeping bag next to me. I sit up and slide my hand up his arm to his bare shoulder. He reaches with his other hand and weaves his fingers into my hair, leaning down as I stretch up. We kiss. Once. Twice.

I whisper against his lips. "Do you want to?"

"Yes," he whispers back. "Do you?"

"Yes," I breathe, and kiss him again.

He moves his hand from my hair to reach into his bag,

digging around. He pulls out a condom. I swallow, purse my lips. Shift to the side to give him room to join me in the sleeping bags. He does, leaving the condom on the tent floor by his pillow, reaching to touch my face, my hair, to pull my lips toward his again. "You'll tell me," he says, mouth against mine, "if you want to stop?"

I nod. "You too?"

He nods back.

We kiss. And kiss. He helps me pull my shirt over my head. His hands are warm on my bare skin. I taste salt, faint, on his neck, his shoulder, feel the heat of the mild sunburn on his back. Eventually he reaches for the condom. It's everything and nothing I imagined it would be at the same time. It's eagerness and hesitancy. Quiet and closeness and a little awkward.

Afterward, lying together, looking at each other, silent and still, arms entwined, bodies tucked up tight, I feel completely different.

Yet exactly the same.

LUCY

"Have I met him before?" Mom asks.

Sitting beside her at the kitchen island while I wait for Bode to pick me up, I think through Lucille's memories. "I don't think so. He's friends with Cass's boyfriend."

She nods, slowly, appraising, and takes another sip of beer. "You're bouncing."

I still.

She laughs. "Nervous?"

I shake out my shoulders and suck in a breath. "Sort of? Maybe not nervous. Bode doesn't make me nervous, exactly."

"More . . . jumpy? Twisty? Excited?"

I smile. "Twisty. Definitely twisty. But in a good way."

"Of course. Good twisty. Like your stomach might squirm its way down and out of your butt."

I laugh. "Mom!" Lying on the kitchen floor, Boris looks between us and wags the curled end of his tail.

"What?" she says, smiling. "It's an awful feeling. And one of the best."

Lucille's never had a conversation like this with Mom before. And, I realize, I'm taking this from her. First official date, first known boy. She's never going to get this moment back. But I don't think I care. She has her whole life for conversations like this, moments like this.

The feeling blooms like a tiny, rotting flower in my gut. Bitterness. Resentment. She's so terrified of not meeting expectations, of saying the wrong thing, doing the wrong thing, of her own inadequacy and being judged as not enough. Yet here I am with nothing but scraps, and I'm supposed to be okay with that? Or, I'm supposed to be nothing. A nonentity.

I run a finger along the condensation on my water glass. "Anyone making your stomach squirm out of your butt these days?"

She gives me a reticent grin, laugh-sighs out her nose, "No," then takes another drink of her beer. "Tell me more about Bode.

Does your going out with him mean you've patched things up with Cass?"

"Nice segue."

"I try."

"Yes. Sort of. We haven't really talked yet. But I think we will."

"Are you ever going to tell me what happened there?"

I hate that memory. It's so abrasive. Lucille was awful. Cass was awful. Louise was awful. It was all just awful.

I sigh. "We had a bad night. I was the odd one out. And Cass was mad because I didn't tell her about the divorce before Ava did. And . . ." This memory, this scar . . . I have it. But it wasn't me. The things Lucille felt, the things she said. I wouldn't have felt them, wouldn't have said them. Maybe it's hindsight? A mix of clarity thanks to two weeks locked up in a white room with few distractions but my thoughts and a perspective honed by my ticking clock. But even while those dulled it, made the divorce and Cass and all the fallout feel less raw, the signs were there.

Mom and Dad living like roommates. The date nights that ended years ago. The silences at dinner, not awkward or strained, just . . . empty. Long hours and mismatched schedules and those Venn diagram circles drifting farther apart while no one cared to force them back together. "We fell out of love," Mom told Lucille one day, and I can feel how that memory sat in her head. Like a shard. Incongruent and irritating. But if she'd bothered to look past her obsession with "perfect," she'd have seen how well it actually fit.

"I get it," Mom says. "Or, I get that things are complicated and friends fight." She finishes her beer, gets up, and rinses the bottle in the sink. "So, Bode."

I can't help my grin. "Bode."

"That bad, huh?"

I breathe a laugh. "He's okay."

"The kid with the weird T-shirts."

I showed her his Instagram the other day, and she'd looked at his pictures and nodded. Which she does again now. "What's that mean?" I ask.

"Just . . . I'm surprised? That you're all floppy-stomached about a kid who wears shirts with killer unicorns on them."

"Remember, he doesn't just wear them," I say. "He designs and screen-prints them too."

"Even better."

I hear a buzz in my bag and pull out my phone to check it. Bode's text reads: *Almost there.* "That's why we're going out so late," I tell her. "He was working at the print shop tonight."

She nods again.

I raise my brow and widen my eyes at her. "What?"

She purses her lips. "I'm not sure. The boy, the dress, the notebook." Bode, the pink T-shirt dress with a massive black kraken printed on one side that I bought this afternoon, the rapidly filling sketchbook in my bag. "You're different. . . . Not in a bad way," she rushes. "Just different."

Pins and needles, in my cheeks, across my scalp, and up my spine. As though my skin's gone transparent, and when she looks at me, she can see my infant bones, my neonate organs, my jigsaw parts pieced together to build my made-to-order body.

As though she can see that *I'm not her daughter.*

"Must be my newly floppy stomach."

She nods again, unconvinced, then the doorbell rings.

Boris scrambles to his feet and charges into the foyer, barking his huge, barrel-chested, I-will-eat-you bark. Mom follows a pace behind, with me (heart rate shooting to a hundred and thirty, Life^2 phone buzzing in response in my bag) bringing up the rear.

Mom waits back a step. I wave at Bode through the window, shove Boris out of the way with my hip, and open the door.

"Hey," he says, smiling.

He's dressed in his normal clothes with his hair damp like he just took a shower. Around six, not long after I got home from Life^2, he texted: *Don't get too fancy. Which is my nervous way of saying wear something you can get dirty. Ok not DIRTY dirty but paint. I mean ink. WEAR SOMETHING YOU CAN GET INK ON.* Followed by a gif of a cartoon person blushing so fiercely he bursts into flame.

I grab Boris's collar and pull him back so Bode has enough room to squeeze inside. "Hi."

He eyes Boris, who's stopped barking but is now doing his eager whining, anxious thing while trying to inhale Bode and/or force him back out the door. "Is he going to eat me?"

"Maybe," Mom says behind me.

I laugh. Bode does not, which makes me laugh harder. "He's not going to eat you," I say. "Right, Bobo?" And I squeeze Boris's fat head. He's already calming down. Bode holds his hand out for Boris to sniff, then pats his head cautiously.

I turn to Mom, Bode follows suit, and Boris, sated, stands between us like a fourth person. "Bode," I say, "meet Nancy. Nancy, meet Bode."

He sticks out his hand. "Nice to meet you, Ms. Harper."

Mom grins and takes it. "Nice to meet you too, Bode." They shake hands, then she turns to me. "Home by one."

I raise my eyebrows.

"Yes, really. Just answer if I call. Drive safely. And don't do anything that might end in you needing my services. Got it?"

I nod once. "Got it."

"Great. Have fun."

"Thanks, Ms. Harper." Bode opens the door for me.

"Bye, Mom," I say, and follow him through.

After he closes the door, he asks, "What are your mom's services?"

"She's an OB."

He opens the passenger door of his old Subaru Forester. "As in obstetrician?"

Climbing in, I nod.

He swallows. "Ah. Okay."

I smile as he rounds the front of the car and gets in the driver's side. He pulls out of the driveway onto the road, and I say, "So. Ink?"

"Yeah. I started something at work today I'm hoping you'll help me finish."

"Okay."

"But first, food."

We stop at a tapas place and order three-quarters of the menu to go, then take our drinks and boxes of food and drive the short distance to the print shop where Bode works. He unlocks the door with his key and flicks on the lights.

"I love it," I say. The walls are painted an awful neon green and decorated with dozens of framed prints. It smells like ink and is packed with equipment and merchandise. At first glance, it looks haphazard. But it's actually immaculately organized. Bottles of ink and solution are arranged by color and product on a wall-sized shelving unit. Racks of T-shirts and hoodies and scarves and other odds and ends populate the floor between the entrance and the long clerk's counter, which is tidy but covered in graffiti, its every available surface doodled on in every color of permanent marker. A bucket of them sits on top with a printed sign inviting customers to add to the counter's artwork.

Bode locks the door behind us and takes our bags of food past the sales counter to a drafting table behind it. I follow him, admiring the printed apparel that's for sale, the art on the walls (much of it Bode's), and finally the screen-printing equipment itself.

"Wow," I say, "check this thing out."

Bode comes up close to me. "Rad, right? It's a six-color, four-station silk-screen printing press. I'll show you how it works after we eat. That's why we're here."

We sit on stools beside each other, the tapas spread out on the drafting table, and eat, passing the boxes between us, trying some of everything and competing with each other for extra bites of our favorites. Bode plays music from his phone over a Bluetooth speaker mounted to the back wall.

We talk art class and the octopus army and favorite bands while we finish eating. This whole week has been so easy, and tonight's no different. Except, now we're alone and free to brush knees while we're at the table and hands while we're cleaning up. Free to stand closer than we need to while he explains the print we're going to make, arms touching, fingers lacing, while we survey the colors and pick the six we want. Free for him to stand behind me, arms reaching around my either side, hands on mine, as he shows me the right way to pull the squeegee (least sexy word of all time) up and down the screen to spread the ink evenly.

Free for me to twist in his arms after he lifts the screen and, stomach to stomach, close the narrow gap between our lips.

By the time we're done, we've printed a dozen shirts with his new design, my face hurts from smiling, I've memorized the taste and feel of Bode's lips, and I've missed four more texts and a voicemail from Life².

While Bode rinses out the screens in the slop sink, I scroll through the texts, then listen to the voicemail, lifting a finger to touch the lump of the BAN chip in my neck.

"Lucy," Dr. Thompson's message says, "responses to wellness inquiries are mandatory. Your heart rate and hormone levels fluctuated multiple times this evening with no acknowledgment or reply. As they've returned to normal and we know from your GPS that you're located at Squid's Print Shop, and not likely in duress, we must assume you are in good health. Know that if you continue to fail to communicate as dictated, we will take measures to protect our investment."

I lower the phone from my ear. Behind me, the sound of Bode washing out the screens continues.

Protect our investment.

"Hey," he says, coming up behind me and looping his arms around my waist. The skin on his hands and forearms is still warm from the water.

He rests his chin on my shoulder and asks, "What's Life Squared?"

"Nothing," I answer, and put the phone away. "Probably a scam."

CHAPTER TWELVE

LUCILLE

"Here's fine," I say, and Taylor glances back at me, skeptical, before shrugging and pulling over at the curb instead of turning into my driveway.

My knee bounces. I unbuckle my seat belt and scoot forward. Both garage doors are shut. That's the signal. If Mom's not home and it's safe for me to come in, the garage door should be open, something we never do since Boris likes to wander.

Marco reaches for my hand, but I wipe my sweaty palms on my shorts and climb out. At least the house isn't on fire, right? Or surrounded by reporters.

He meets me at the back of Taylor's Highlander and opens the hatch to grab my pack. I let him, then pull the door closed. As I reach for the strap of my backpack, he grins and refuses to let it go, instead pulling me closer and leaning down. His lips meet mine.

And I feel it, low in my stomach, in my arms and hips and hair. This new thing we share. Not necessarily a secret, but a thing, a moment, a whole series of moments that are only ours.

"We can see you, you know," Taylor calls.

"And hear you," Remi adds.

Marco's lips stretch in a smile against mine. He pulls back enough to yell, "Don't care!" Then kisses me again, quiet and slow.

My car drives past.

My car.

With Lucy in it.

Marco moves, starts to turn toward the road. But I yank at my pack's straps, and he turns back.

"Better go," I say, and struggle to loop a strap over my shoulder. My car rounds the front of Taylor's SUV, pulling into the driveway as the garage door opens.

"Was that your mom?"

I shrug and turn to go.

Marco reaches for my pack again. "Let me carry that. I'll come up." He holds his hand out. "I want to meet her."

"No." I take two steps away, pausing by the passenger door and Remi, who's sitting with the window down. "She's at work."

"So who—" he starts, while I say, "Call you later?" and Remi leans out to ask, "You coming tonight?"

I arch a brow. Behind him, Taylor clarifies, "End-of-summer party."

Remi gives me a sly smile. "Taylor and I forced Marco not to say anything. In case you were awful." He shrugs. "But you're okay. So you can come if you want."

"Thanks. I think."

"You're welcome."

Marco stands back from me, hands in his pockets.

"Call you later?" I ask again.

He nods.

I walk through the side yard up to the garage with its still-open door. My mom's SUV is gone—*thank god*—and Lucy's climbing out of my car.

"Hey."

She flinches, banging her head on the doorframe. "Fuck!"

"Sorry."

Rubbing the back of her head, she turns to me. "Hey."

"Where were you?"

"Getting dog food." She moves to the side so I can see the giant bag of dog food in the backseat.

"Where's Mom?"

"Having lunch with Ava."

I nod.

We're quiet. So quiet I can hear Boris in the kitchen, waiting for me—her? us?—to come inside.

"How was backpacking?"

"Absolutely *amazing*. We hiked to a lake tucked into this shallow valley. The water was frigid, but so clear. And we were the only ones there. We swam and laid out and ate bad dehydrated food that somehow tasted so good. Marco's friends Taylor and Remi are hilarious, and we all—"

"Sounds great," she interrupts.

Okay . . . "How was, uh, home?"

"Fine."

"Did something happen?"

"What kind of something?"

"Something to make you . . ."

"What?"

I swallow. "Never mind. Do you have my phone?"

"Yeah." She reaches into my bag she's using, pulls it out, and offers it to me.

I step closer to take it from her hand. "And the notebook?"

"Upstairs. I haven't updated it yet."

"Oh." I check my phone, but there are no notifications. "Why not?"

"I was busy."

"Doing what?"

She shrugs. "You planning to go to Dad's tonight? I'm on the schedule, but then your trip came up, and I don't know if that changed things."

"I'm not sure yet. Marco's friends invited me out."

Her eyes narrow. "Okay. Well, Mom thinks I'm heading over there now, so."

"Right. I'll go take a shower and let you know." I drop my pack on the garage floor. "Can you take this up to the apartment? I'll deal with it later. Just, it smells like campfire, so I don't want it in my room."

She pauses. Her face goes blank. Isobel blank. Then she smiles and nods before turning back to the car to grab the bag of dog food.

Inside, Boris greets me, whining and dancing and mashing his big wet nose into my legs as he smells the mountains. "Hi, Bobo," I say, hugging him. I push past, heading toward the stairs, expecting him to follow, but he lies down and waits by the garage door.

I hurry up to my room. I don't know what to do. Go to the party? Go to my dad's? I could laugh at even having this "problem" but I already feel too much. Tired, sweaty, sore. Happy, nervous, confused. What was that in the garage? Is she pissed at me? Is she . . . anything? I don't know where the line is. I mean, she's me. But is she, does she *feel* things? Separate things? Or, well, *different* things? Usually she's so flat and stoic. But down there she seemed almost annoyed. I wanted to tell her about my trip. Or, I don't know. Maybe I just want to tell *someone* about it and she's the only one I can. But I also figured she'd want to know.

My phone buzzes in my hand.

A text from Cass: *OMFG!!! You two are SO CUTE!!!* followed by at least twenty heart-eye smileys and a link to an Instagram post.

A post on *my* Instagram.

I click the link and see a picture of Bode and . . . not me.

Bode and *Lucy*.

Bode and Lucy in the print shop. Her, smiling with her arm held out to take the picture. Him, kissing her cheek. Both, wearing matching T-shirts printed with the image of some 1950s-looking white guy sitting down to a dinner of a giant spider. The post's caption reads BON APPÉTIT.

LUCY

I know when she sees it. Not from a blood-curdling scream ripping through the house (that's not Lucille's style), but because she starts liking comments. I stand in the apartment, Instagram app open on my phone, and watch it happen.

Cass: A line of dancing red-dress ladies and *FINALLY!*

Liked.

Aran: *Gross. Not you guys. But dude @BodePrints. Gross.*

Liked.

Louise: *cute.*

Liked.

Finn: *pls respect the no pda at lunch rule.*

Liked.

Matt: *Aw!!*

Liked.

I know *exactly* how this hurts her. But, after the way she looked at me in the garage. After days of being a whole person, of expanding to fill an *entire* space. After *take this up to the apartment, it smells like campfire, and I don't want it in my room.* I dumped the pack by the door and hurt her on purpose if only to get back at her for being oblivious to the fact that I'm also capable of being hurt.

When Bode comments with a line of spider emojis and a single black heart, I grab my bag and head downstairs.

I text her from the driveway: *Heading to dads. Enjoy your night.*

LUCILLE

Heading to dads. Enjoy your night, she texts. I sprint across the hall into the guest room in time to watch her back into the road and drive away.

I stare at the empty driveway until I remember to close my mouth.

Lucy went out with Bode.

Lucy went out with Bode, then posted a pic of it on Instagram.

Oh my god. What if Marco sees it?

I open my app and delete the post. Before I can think twice. Before I can wonder what that'll mean for . . . who? Bode? *Lucy and Bode?* It already has over forty likes. Eighteen comments. Bode shared it on his feed.

Is this a panic attack? The racing heartbeat, pulsing head, and the air's too tight. Too heavy.

The sound of the garage door again, Boris whining again. But it isn't Lucy.

It's Mom.

I stumble back from the window, and before I fully register what my body's doing, I'm downstairs, pushing past Boris, opening the sliding glass door, and ducking into the yard. *I'm going to puke.* Crouching low so she can't see me through the kitchen window, I cross the yard to the gate and let myself out, closing it as quietly as I can behind me. I run around the side of the garage to spy through the door.

Mom sits in her car for a minute, looking at her phone, then she hits the button on her visor to close the garage door and goes inside. I open the side door and creep up to the apartment, using the X's I taped on the stairs to pick the quietest steps.

My backpack leans against the wall on the floor to my right. The bed's still half-made, how I left it on my way out the door Wednesday morning. I tiptoe—step by marked step—over to sit on one of the bar stools and stare at my dirty cereal bowl, still on the counter beside the sink, while my heart rate slows.

LUCY

I feel electric. Like a closed circuit with a current sprinting round and round inside.

I may be the only one who sees it, but Lucille and I, we're on either side of a teeter-totter. Until this is all over, the fulcrum's our one, shared life. And I just yanked a whole load of shit (Dad, Bode, even the car) over to my side.

My phone buzzes. I check the screen (current circling), but it isn't Lucille or Life^2. I pull over to read Bode's text that he'll be at the print shop tonight making more spider shirts, do I want to join?

Of course. But I write back, *Why are you so obsessed with me?*

Boredom. Probably.

Fair enough. Too bad you'll have to suffer through it tonight. I'm hanging with the Male Paternal Unit.

What a bizarre way to say dad.

Okay fine. Father dearest. Better?

Yes, he writes back. *And not at all murdery.*

Total "I do creative taxidermy in my basement" vibe.

Hey. ALL taxidermy is creative taxidermy.

I laugh, then write, *Cool. Please start a new hobby and make me a dolphin-jaguar.*

That's horrifying. Poor dolphin. Poor jaguar.

I know. I'm a monster.

The second I hit send, my gut drops. Freudian-slip much, Lucy? I drop the phone onto the passenger seat, hear the buzz of Bode's reply, but shift the car into drive and pull away from the curb, cranking the stereo to drown out my thoughts.

Because no matter how much weight I plunder from Lucille's side and hoard to mine, we're still sharing the same scale. I'm still partial. I'm still temporary.

I'm still only half.

CHAPTER THIRTEEN

LUCILLE

It's crowded. Hot. Not so loud that a neighbor's going to call the cops, but loud enough. And I know exactly three people here. Remi, Taylor, and of course, Marco.

I hover with them, each of us nursing a cup from the keg. Then Taylor peels off after some guy they all know, and five minutes later, Remi vanishes. Like, into thin air. One second the three of us are talking, I take a sip from my cup, then I look up and he's gone.

"Wha—"

Marco grins. "Yeah, Remi does that."

"It's like a magic trick."

"It's an I-got-bored trick."

"Ah," I say, and take another gulp of my drink. Beer is gross. But I'm halfway through my first cup, and the wriggling bucket of maggots that is my state of mind right now has stopped feeling so . . . wriggly.

It's gross in here, too. Small house with smaller rooms, low ceilings, and smashed full of people, it's a sauna. "Can we go outside? Or just somewhere less . . ."

"Suffocating?" Marco offers.

"Yeah, that."

He nods, then offers me his hand, and I let him lead me through the house to the back door.

Outside, groups of people huddle in the small, overgrown backyard. They talk in low voices with the occasional laugh, cautious of the neighboring houses, tucked up close on all three of the yard's sides. Marco makes his way over to a raised flower bed built against the rear of the house. We sit on the edge. "So," he says.

"So." I tip my beer gently from side to side, watching the foam. He doesn't want to be here, didn't want to come. When I called this afternoon and asked if he wanted to go, he suggested a movie at his house, saying it'd be loud and crowded and wouldn't it be better to be alone? But I'm a writhing quagmire, and I knew that if I were stuck somewhere quiet with him, something would slither out.

"Want to know a secret?" I ask.

He looks over at me. It's full dark, the yard lit by two porch lights and the orange-black city sky. "Always."

"Okay." I take a sip. "This is my first beer."

"Ever?"

"Yep."

"You've never even, like, stolen a couple from the fridge when you were twelve and chugged them with your cousin upstairs in your room only to end up hurling in your trash can and getting caught by your mom?"

"How specific."

He shrugs. "Oh, you know, happened to a friend of a friend."

I breathe a laugh. "Your mom still pissed about it?"

"Till the end of time."

I lean into him, resting my head on his shoulder. I feel like an unfinished circuit. What am I doing here? What am I doing, *period*? I didn't sign up for this mess. I signed up for time. And validation. To top off the stale hollow of Lucille Harper, Fill in the Blank. But maybe that's bullshit, too, since what'd I really do besides swap Lucille Harper, Overachiever, for Lucille Harper, Life^2's Ideal Candidate. Different shades of the same blue.

Part of me thinks, *I can fix this.* Three more weeks, and I can fix this. Break up with Bode, reclaim my life, move on and numb the sting that my clone—my *self*—hates me. That she's . . . *the better Lucille.*

I can barely make myself think it. But that's what she's doing. Taking my classes, dating Bode, friends again with Cass, at Dad's right now being the dutiful daughter while I'm here, at a party with a boy, neither of which my parents or best friend knows about. Like I've slipped through a crack and suddenly all the time I spent thinking I was getting to be *more* like myself feels like fiction, and instead I'm less. Still left out and separate, just telling myself a different lie.

I take a sip of beer to stifle a bitter laugh, because at least we're acing Life^2's test, right? At least we're excelling. Proving they were right to want me. But if that was ever going to feel like an accomplishment, it's soured now. *Three more weeks, and I can fix this.* Sure, great. Except "fixing this" starts with sending her back. And while that always felt like a simple given, in ways I can't explain it feels far less simple now.

"You were right," I say. "We should've stayed at your place and watched a movie."

"Definitely. Or—" He cuts himself off.

I look up. "Or?"

"Your house." Marco fidgets with his cup, making the plastic dent and undent, clicking it in and popping it out again and again.

I can't do this. I stand up and chug the rest of my beer. My throat stings from the carbonation. Liquid sloshes in my gut. "Time for a refill," I say, and head back into the house before he can stop me. In the kitchen, one of the guys hanging out around the little keg fills my cup back up. I take a long drink as Marco joins me. My stomach is too full. My head's already started to spin. I set the cup on the counter and grab Marco's hand.

"Come on," I say, and tug him out of the kitchen toward the living room and stairs.

"Lucille," he says, but I don't stop.

The hall at the top of the stairs is narrow, with half the doors closed. It's quiet, no music, no conversation. I try the first door: locked. The second: closet. The third is a bedroom. Probably Marco's friend's. The bed's messy and there are dirty clothes on the floor. A poster of the Wasp hangs on the wall over his dresser, another of Black Widow is taped to the ceiling above the bed.

I pull Marco in, close the door behind me, and kiss him. I need this. I need out of my head.

He pulls back. "Lucille. What's—"

I move in to kiss him again, but he lifts a hand, puts it between us.

"Stop," he says.

I back up a—wobbly—step. "Why?" I ask. "You're supposed to want me. That's basically the whole point of this."

"Of what?"

"All of it. Her, them, the whole *thing*. I'm supposed to finally get to be the *right* Lucille. The version people want."

"What are you talking about? I *do* want you, Luce, but I—"

"Don't call me that."

"What? Luce?"

"Yeah. Don't fucking call me that."

"Jesus," he breathes. "Fine." He pushes away from the door and moves farther into the room, away from me. He still has his half-empty cup in one hand. "What is going on with you? Last night, we— Then at your house today, it's like . . ."

My cheeks are hot. Not just my cheeks, my eyes too. And I swear to god if I start crying, I'll— "What?"

He doesn't answer, just stares at me.

"It's like *what*?"

"Like I'm your dirty secret!" he shouts. Really, shouts it. "You went *backpacking* with me. For *days*. And yet you won't let me walk you to your door! Let alone let me meet your mom. Are you going to tell me there's nothing weird about that? Nothing *wrong*?"

He waits, but I don't answer.

"What's wrong with me that—" He stops himself, shifting his eyes away from me. To the carpet, the wall, the ceiling. Looking anywhere but at me. And my heart—*a heart, my heart, suspended in blue goo*—breaks.

"This isn't how it's supposed to go," I say. "None of this is working."

"*What* isn't working?"

"Everything." And I yank open the door and leave the room.

Back in the kitchen, I grab my cup, dump it in the sink, and shove it at one of the guys—watching me, wide-eyed—by the tap to refill. He does, hands it back, and I swallow as much of it as I can, coughing as I force the beer down. My stomach feels too tight, my face is hot, but I don't care.

A group of people share a bottle in the living room. I ask to join and they hand it over. It's worse than the beer. Like drinking cough-syrup-flavored fire. I hand it back and turn away. I think I hear Marco in the kitchen saying my name? I don't know. A Rihanna song comes on, someone turns the stereo up, a few others start singing, and I move on. Back through the living room, thinking, Go outside. Go home. Go.

I hit the entryway just as someone's coming through the front door, and I stumble out of the way. "Whoa," the guy laughs, reaching out, grabbing my arm. To steady me, I guess. But I shake him off, then round the corner, using the wall for support, and follow him downstairs.

My feet feel, they feel, they don't.

I'm loose. Taffy muscles. Taffy joints. Wax-paper skin.

The basement ceiling's low. Popcorn ceiling. Paneled walls. Old carpet. A thousand percent sure it's gritty. I can feel it through my shoes.

"Lucille!"

Remi. Smashed with three other people on a dumpy old couch. They're passing a bong between them. "Join us!" he says.

Perfect Lucille. Uptight Lucille. Stretched-thin, straight-A, stick-up-her-ass Lucille. Lucille Harper, Overachiever. Lucille Harper, Turned Down by Her Own Boyfriend. Lucille Harper, Second Place to Her Own Fucking Clone, flops down on Remi's lap, listens to the instructions, and puts her mouth to the glass.

Then I'm coughing, my lungs squished flat. My thoughts go oblong.

"Remi! What the fuck?"

Marco grabs my arm, pulls me up off Remi's lap. The girl next to Remi on the couch reaches for the bong before I drop it.

"Dude, what?" Remi says.

I sway next to Marco. Who still has my arm. Who says . . . something. Don't know. Don't care. The room's a comforter. A duvet. Warm and small. And constricting.

". . . seemed fine to me," Remi is saying. "Sorry. Okay? I'm sorry."

And I'm moving. Feet following my upper body. Upper body following my arm. Arm held by Marco. He pauses at the bottom of the stairs, loops his arm under mine, around my chest.

"I think—"

"What?" Marco asks. Breathy. Next to my ear.

The stairway spins.

"I'm going to throw up."

He groans. "Awesome."

Then we're hurrying. Up, up. Through the entryway. Out the door. Fresh air, dark sky. Cement stairs, sidewalk, grass. I lean over and lose it.

Marco grabs my hair. Rubs my back. When I'm done, he sits me on the bottom step of the porch and crouches in front of me. Eye to eye. "Stay here. Got it?"

"You're mad."

He huffs a sigh. "Just. Don't move."

Then he runs back into the house.

She's there right now. Dad's apartment. In my bed. I picked those sheets. Purple sheets. Purple floral comforter. Texting Bode, probably. Being the right me.

I lean my head against . . . something. Railing? Cold, hard. Uncomfortable.

"Come on."

I open my eyes. Marco offers his hand. "We're going. Come on."

I reach for his hand. Noodle arm. Taffy fingers. He leans down and helps me up.

He buckles me into Taylor's SUV. "Taylor says if you throw up in her car, she'll gut you."

"Ouch."

"Yeah."

He closes the door, goes around, gets in, starts the engine, drives. Drives. Stops. Cuts the engine. Gets out. Opens my door. Unbuckles my seat belt. Helps me out.

"No."

It's my driveway.

My house.

"No," I say, pulling back. "I can't—I'm not—Lucy—"

"Please, Lucille. You're wasted," Marco says. His voice hurts me. Not an angry voice. A sad one.

Up the stairs, on the porch, he rings the bell.

Boris. Losing his shit, charging through the house, barking, barking, barking with his big fat lungs. Then the porch light. The click of the dead bolt. Mom.

"Lucille?"

"Ms. Harper," Marco says. "I'm so sorry. I'm so—"

"What's going on?"

"She drank too much. And smoked some weed." Marco, ashamed. Marco, devastated. Marco, meeting my mo—

I throw up again. All over my mom's peonies.

"For fuck's sake, Lucille," she groans, and grabs me. Roughly. Yanks me inside. "Thanks," she says to Marco. At him. "Whoever you are."

"Sorry, ma'am. I'm—"

"Not the time," she says, and slams the door in his face.

Marco. My mom. *Lucy.* I'm supposed to be—

She drags me through the entryway. "What were you *thinking?*"

"I—"

"Rhetorical, Lucille. Clearly, you weren't. *Jesus.* Does your dad know where you are?"

I gag. "No."

She half carries, half pushes me up the stairs, down the hall, into my room. I check my pocket for my phone. "Clean yourself up," she says, and leaves.

I pull my phone out. Call Lucy.

"Lucil—"

"Out," I say. "You have to get out."

"What?"

"Dad's apartment. I'm home. With Mom. She's calling Dad. Get out."

"WHAT?"

"Now. Leave the car."

LUCY

Leave the car. And do what? *Walk?*

Then I hear it. Dad's phone rings, shrill and grating through the apartment's walls. Three rings, four. A pause as he misses the call. Then it starts up again.

I go. In my jersey shorts and an old T-shirt, keys and phone in hand, sneaking down the hallway, through the dim kitchen-slash-living-room, flip-flops snapping at my heels. I pause and take them off to go barefoot.

The ringing stops again. I hear Dad's voice, muffled, then louder.

I reach the door, unlock it, heart pounding. (Cue Life^2 text in three . . . two . . . one . . .) I slip out into the hall and ease the door closed behind me with a hushed *click*.

Then I run.

Down the hall, the elevator, through the lobby. Outside, I stop.

Does she expect me to hide out in the courtyard? Curl up and sleep between the bushes? I slip my flip-flops back on and call her. It goes straight to voicemail. I'm so mad it takes every argument I can conjure to stop myself from charging straight back upstairs and telling Dad the truth.

Fuck Lucille for this. She gets everything. Freedom, control, this life, the "official" life, *a* life. While *I* get . . . "I." Fundamental issue there. That pesky "not an individual" thing. My phone buzzes again in my hand. The text reads: *Drastically elevated heart rate. Report.*

I write back: *Nightmare.*

This is just fabulous. I have no money. No car. And it's 1:02 a.m.

I could call Bode. And say . . . what? *Hey, I need a ride across the city in the middle of the night for reasons I can't explain and, oh, what? Yeah, that is my car, but I'm not allowed to use it because my Original—you know, Lucille? The girl you still think I actually am? Yeah, her. She's a self-centered piece of shit who royally fucked me over, and my alternative is sleeping outside. Oh, yeah, and by Original I mean she's the "real" Lucille and I'm a fucking clone.*

I sit on the sidewalk next to my car, cross-legged, staring at my phone in my lap. I have five numbers: Lucille's, Bode's, Life^2's main number, Dr. Thompson's cell, and . . . Cass's.

I put it in there after school on Friday. After a week of loaded but friendly smiles and stilted but hopeful conversations. I hadn't been avoiding her, exactly. But I wasn't going out of my way to talk to her either. Because every time I imagined talking to Cass, even our fake conversations revolved around that night in the park. And every time I thought about that night in the park, it was in third person: *She* felt like this. *She* shouldn't have said that. *She* wishes it'd been different. I couldn't own that fallout because it wasn't mine.

I hesitate, my thumb over the button. Then call.

It rings three times before she answers, groggy, confused. "Hello?"

"Cass?"

"Yeah. Who's this?"

"It's Lucy."

"Lucy," she repeats. "Whose phone are you calling from? What's going on?"

"I, uh . . . need a ride."

"Wait. What? Start from the beginning."

"I . . ." I let go a slow breath. "God. This is so shitty. But, I can't. I need a ride. From my dad's to my mom's. But I can't tell you why."

Silence.

For so long that I pull the phone away from my ear to see if she's hung up.

Then she asks, "Are you okay?"

"Yes. I'm okay. Nothing happened. Nothing's wrong, exactly. It's just . . ." I roll my eyes. "A logistics issue."

"You're serious."

"As a platypus."

Quiet again. It's our (*their*) word, like a promise. She and Lucille came up with it when they were little, a way to say "trust me and have my back, no questions asked." Like anyone actually drops "platypus" casually into a conversation, but they both liked the word, so it stuck.

"Text me your dad's address," she says. "I'll be there as soon as I can."

She pulls up in her mom's car at 1:47, rolling to a stop behind mine. I stand, open the passenger door, and climb in. "So," she says, leaving the car in park. "You're really not going to tell me?"

I sigh. "I really can't."

Her eyes narrow behind her thick-lensed glasses (the ones she hates, the ones she only wears in dire circumstances once she's taken her contacts out). There's a dark smudge under each eye, makeup she didn't wash all the way off. "Can't. Not won't?"

"Can't. In this case, semantics matter."

She stares out the windshield. Everything is tinged orange from the streetlights. "Fine," she says, and finally shifts into reverse, backing away from my car before pulling out into the street. "Late-night drama." She glances at my lap. "Second phone. Aren't you just an International Woman of Mystery all of a sudden."

"International? I wish."

She laughs, but it's not funny. It was just a thing to say. "Where are your glasses?"

I reach for my face. A reflex from memories of years of wearing glasses. "Put my contacts in."

"Before I picked you up in the middle of some covert 'logistics issue' at two a.m.?"

I shrug. And there's a beat. A skinny blip in which her acceptance goes brittle.

"For real, though," she says. "You've been MIA for months. And now?"

"And now I call you for a ride in the middle of the night?"

"Yeah. That. Why didn't you call Bode?"

I look at my phone. Nothing new from Lucille. "Because I can't tell him why either."

"And you worried he might not be as amazingly understanding about it as yours truly?"

"Yup."

She smiles over at me. I lean my head against the window.

"So," she says, "can we talk about our stuff? Or is that a secret too?"

"It's not a secret. I just don't know how to talk about it."

"Easy. You form thoughts in your head and use your breath, vocal cords, and mouth muscles to project them into the world."

"Yeah."

"That was a joke, Lucille."

Lucille.

How jarring. Such simple proof that she's talking to "me" instead of *me.*

"I know," I say. "But I meant it, I don't know how to talk about it."

Cass sighs. An annoyed sigh. Because I'm avoiding this the way she and Lucille avoided it all summer. "She—" I start, then shake my head. "*I* should've told you about my parents. Right away. But things between us . . ." I search for the right way to say this. "They were weird. I stopped knowing how to talk to you about stuff."

She sighs again, sad this time. "I really want to say that's not fair. I tried. You know? Again and again, I tried. To include you. To invite you. And you checked out! Like you were so jealous of my being with Aran you'd rather ditch our friendship altogether than deal with it."

It's a jab. And even though it's *Lucille's* hurt, I still feel it. "I know," I say. "But it felt . . ."

"Like pity?"

"Yes. And then you told Louise about my crush on Bode and—"

"Wait. What?" She pulls over, shifts into park, and turns toward me. "What are you talking about?"

It's late. I'm tired. And I have to concentrate too hard on using the right pronouns. "I heard you. After we fought. I came to find you, and I heard you and Louise talking about my 'pathetic' crush on him."

"That's not—I don't think that's what we said."

"Maybe. But it's what I heard."

"Well," she hedges, "I mean, it kinda worked out . . . didn't it?"

I laugh, off-kilter and jagged. Here I am, having this heart-to-heart with Lucille's (not my) best friend about an event I wasn't present or even *alive* for, about a shitty thing Louise said about Lucille (me but not me) that's basically nullified since I'm with Bode now, supposedly satisfying that crush, except I'm not "me," not Lucille at least, which means she's still the one on the outside. And, honestly, I'm pretty focused on hating her right now, and that stab of empathy isn't helping.

"That's really not the point," I say.

"Then . . ." She slumps down in her seat dramatically and groans. "What *is*?"

"That you told Louise. That she . . ." I swallow it. I could break something. I'm stuck in this rancid swamp of Lucille's making, and I'm tasked with *defending* her? Except, that's pretty perfect, isn't it. I don't just exist because of her. I exist *for* her. "Can we not do this right now?"

"Do what?"

My throat constricts. Not doing it now pretty much means not doing this ever. Not for me. I'll never get to know her. Sixteen years, a thousand memories, but I'll never actually know her.

And she'll never know me.

"Have this pseudo heart-to-heart."

"*Pseudo?*"

I stare out the windshield at the tiny universe lit up by the car's headlights. I can feel her attention on me.

"What the hell happened to you this summer?"

"You wouldn't believe me if I told you."

"Try me. I've known you your whole life."

"Yeah, well. Maybe I'm not the Lucille you think you know."

LUCILLE

I wake with a start, like I'm rising from the dead, which is fitting since that's how I feel.

I'm in my bed. At home.

Oh, shit.

I'm home. In my bed.

Where's Lucy?

I search for my phone. Not on the bedside table. Not on the floor. *There.* Wadded up in my comforter. God, is that smell *me*? Beer on my shirt. Smoke in my hair.

Clean yourself up.

Mom said that. At least, I think she did. *Clean yourself up.*

Then she left to call Dad. I check my call log. It shows me calling Lucy at 12:58 a.m. The record says it was thirty-six seconds long. *Did she get out?*

I make myself still. The house is quiet. There're no sirens or shouting or . . . I don't even know. What the hell happens when you get caught having a clone? What's the precedent for that?

It's early. Six-thirty. The sun's still rising. I get up, creep to the door, crack it open, and listen hard. Boris snores downstairs on the cool tile floor of the entryway. The refrigerator kicks on in the kitchen. And . . . nothing.

I tiptoe down the hall, the stairs, through the kitchen, and out into the garage. My car isn't here, at least. I make my way up the stairs to the apartment, following the X's, and ease open the door.

I cover my mouth to mute my relief. She's there. Asleep in the bed, our shared long brown hair fanned out over her pillow.

I pull the door shut with a quiet *click* and sit on the landing, my throbbing head in my hands.

Lucille Harper, Off the Deep End.

Lucille Harper, In Over Her Head.

Lucille Harper, A Metaphor for Drowning.

I take long, slow breaths—*in, one, two, three, out, one, two, three*—but it doesn't help. With the panic, or the nausea. *What am I doing?* I hold my hands out, like I'll be able to see them. All of my problems cradled in my palms. But all I can see are the lines. All those lines. Thousands of them. While hers, except for the ones from SemblanceSync, are perfectly smooth.

When my stomach finally settles, I get up to go deal with the only one of my problems I might actually be able to solve.

LUCY

My buzzing phone wakes me up. I grab it off the nightstand. *Gone to see Marco. Drank too much last night and screwed everything up. Mom's pissed.* There's a pause followed by a second buzz: *I'm sorry.*

I stare at the ceiling, counting breaths until I'm calm enough to keep from smashing the phone against the wall. It takes me fifty-two.

"Lucille!" Mom shouts from the kitchen. She must've already checked Lucille's room. I consider not answering. What do I really owe her? What (else) goes wrong for me if Mom finds me up here? If she finds out I'm not Lucille?

They'll send me back.

The thought's like swallowing sour milk. She won't want me. I'm not her daughter. They'll send me back, and that'll be it for me. No more anything, not even this partial, stand-in, semblance of a life.

I hurry down the stairs, pausing on the landing before stepping into the garage, listening for Mom, who calls for Lucille again, but it's so muffled she must be downstairs.

I hurry inside, aiming for the stairway, walk halfway up, then turn around back toward the kitchen and call, "Mom?"

We meet in the empty space between the kitchen and the stairs.

"Where were you?" she asks. Arms crossed, jaw tight, one brow arched. Still supremely pissed. I wonder if she slept at all.

"Bathroom," I say.

"I checked your bathroom."

"Guest bath—"

She shakes her head. "Never mind. I don't care." She points to the kitchen. "Sit your ass down. I'm ready to yell."

I sit through it, staring at the color variations in the island's marble countertop, veins of gray twisting through the white. The yelling isn't what gets to me. She doesn't even shout that much. A few variations of *How could you?* and *What were you thinking?* Then her voice lowers. She switches to bewildered disappointment.

And *that's* what sours my guts.

I didn't earn this. Her "loss of trust" or the look in her eye while she says it. As though I'm a stranger. Which I am. I'm not her daughter. (*I'm not. I am. I'm not. I am. I'm . . .*)

She pauses, waiting for the apology she deserves. But I don't give it. Because *I'm* not sorry.

"Nothing?" she says. "You don't have anything to say?"

I glare at the countertop and shake my head.

She scoffs. "Fine. You're grounded for the next two weeks."

"Great," I say.

"Yeah. Great."

I get up, push past Boris (who's hovering, anxious, since he hates it when any of us fight), and am halfway up the stairs when she calls, "Who is he? The boy who brought you home."

I pause on the fourth step. "Probably Marco."

"*Probably?* What the hell does that—"

But I'm done having this conversation. I run up the rest of the stairs and close myself in Lucille's room. Half an hour later, Mom knocks and says through the door that she's been called in to work. Ten minutes after she leaves, I start walking toward the bus stop.

LUCILLE

I call, text, call again while I ride the bus into the city, but he doesn't answer. When I knock on his door, Ariana answers with her eyes narrowed. "Marco missed curfew last night because of you. Mom's still mad this morning."

"I'm sorry. Is he here?"

"No."

"Work?"

"Why should I tell you?"

"So I can go grovel for his forgiveness in person?"

Arching one brow like a pro, she considers me. If only missing curfew was all I needed to ask forgiveness for. Finally, she sighs and cocks her hip like she's bored with me and says, "Yeah, he's at work."

"Great. Thanks, Ari." And she shuts the door.

I walk to the coffee shop—a dozen-plus blocks from his house—take ten deep breaths outside the door, then go in.

Behind the register, he looks up when the door's bells jingle, sees me, and frowns. I wait a handful of paces back, unsure if I should order or wait or what, but he finishes with the customer at the counter and turns to his coworker. I hear him ask her to cover while he takes a break, then he comes out from behind the counter, pulling his apron off over his head and holding it, wadded up in his fist.

He walks past me, out the door.

I follow.

Don't cry. Don't cry. Do. Not. Cry.

Outside, around the corner from the entrance, he stops and leans back against the brick, arms crossed.

"Hi," I say.

He won't look at me. When he swallows, I watch his Adam's apple bob. "She didn't even know who I was."

"What?"

"Your mom had no clue who I was. Did she even know we went backpacking?"

"I—"

"Don't lie," he says. "Please."

My throat aches. I have to push the word past it. "No."

He nods, still staring at the sidewalk. "Also, turns out my friend Grant's cousin goes to a school in the same district as Lakewood, and last night when I got back to drop off Taylor's car, when people were asking about my girlfriend and what the hell was going on with you, he mentioned that his cousin started classes last week, so."

"So."

"So you just skipped your first week of school?"

"Not exactly."

"Jesus, 'not exactly'? What the hell does that even mean?"

"I don't know what—"

"Save it. I thought—" He stops himself, clears his throat. "I thought we were . . ." He shakes his head. His eyes are wet. "I thought we were real."

"We *are*, Marco. We are!"

"How am I supposed to believe you, Lucille? What the fuck was that last night? What is *any* of this? It's like—"

"Like what?" I whisper.

"Like you're *ashamed* of me. Like you don't even want me in your life. Like I'm just one more of your lies!"

"*What?*"

"Oh, come on." He glares at me, then lifts a hand and wipes his eyes. "I've never been inside your house. Every time I picked you up you told me to *park down the fucking street*. You won't let me meet your parents, your friends. I've never even met your *dog*."

"That's not— It's not y—"

"It's not you, it's me? Are you kidding?"

"No, that's not what— I mean, it *is* me. But it's . . . complicated."

He pushes off the wall and moves to leave.

I grab his arm. "*Please.* Wait. That's not what I . . ."

We're only six inches apart. Touching. But the distance is brutal. "Did it, did Friday, *us*, even matter to you?"

"*Of course.*" I keep my hand on his arm, and I have to believe it means something that he lets me.

"I don't know how to believe anything you say."

"I'm not lying about that. I would *never* lie about that!"

"Except, that's what you do, right? Lie. All the time."

"Not about us. Not about how I feel about you," I say. I'm losing it. My tears brim, then fall. "I *swear*. You have to believe me."

"Then tell me," he says. "The truth. Promise."

"Tell you what?"

"If your mom doesn't know you went backpacking with me, where did she think you were?"

I purse my lips. "She didn't know I was gone."

He stares at me. And slowly removes his arm from my grip.

"I'm not lying," I say. "That's not a lie."

He coughs a laugh. "Now you're lying about lying."

"Please, Marco. I want to tell you the truth! I *am* telling you the truth. My mom didn't know. I just can't tell you the rest of it. Okay? *I can't.* I'm not *allowed* to tell you."

"What the hell does that mean?"

"I—" I'm desperate, flailing. The current's raging, my head's submerged, and I don't even know what the expectations are anymore, what I'm trying to do, who I'm trying to be. No matter what I say now, if I give in, tell him, violate the NDA and risk that "shitstorm," even the truth sounds like a lie.

"I'm going to go," he whispers, moving around me. "I need to go."

And he does.

I watch his back, but I don't follow.

I slide down the wall, brick snagging on my shirt, and sit on the sidewalk. I was supposed to be done failing, done coming up short. With two of me, there wasn't supposed to be any question.

Do more. Be more. Both, everything, all of it. Perfect girlfriend, perfect daughter, perfect student, perfect friend. This was my way to be perfect. And yet. How can there be two of me, and I'm still not enough?

My trek home feels mechanical. Walk, bus, transfer, bus, walk.

I call Lucy when I'm at the end of our block. She answers on the first ring. "Yeah?"

"Is Mom home?"

"No."

Boris greets me when I come through the front door. I push past him and find Lucy waiting for me in the kitchen, leaning against the counter.

With shoulder-length pink hair.

CHAPTER FOURTEEN

LUCY

Her jaw drops.

I strike a pose. "You like it?"

She makes an incoherent sound in her throat. Boris noses at her hand, but she ignores him. He plods over to me, sitting by my feet and leaning his heavy body into my leg. I rub his head absent-mindedly. Lucille's attention flicks from him to my hair again, and I say, "You don't have to do it too, you know."

"How would that work? You stay in the studio for the next eighteen days?"

"Or you send me back early." It's a bluff. Or self-destruction. I honestly don't know. When I went to the salon, I knew this would be something. A way to shove us off the teeter-totter. It was reckless and terrifying, and I'd do it again and again. Because while I want those eighteen days, I need her to see me. Not her reflection, *me*.

For the first time, I can't tell what she's thinking, feeling. There's an emptiness to her expression. Shock, maybe. Then her eyes go glassy. She pulls out her phone, closes the gap between us, snaps a few photos of my hair, and turns back toward the door.

"Don't forget to go by Dad's and get the car," I call after her.

"And I left your history homework in your room. You have a quiz tomorrow." She doesn't look back, but I hear a quiet "Thanks" before she slips out the door.

I wait for a count of five (For what? In case she comes back in and asks me to keep her company? For her to change her mind and say, "Forget it! Let's come clean!"), then head to the studio. The garage is hot and smells like dog food and dust. My hair feels light around my shoulders. But when the loose curls bounce in rhythm with my steps as I climb the stairs, when I close the apartment door behind me and they float, so obvious and pink, into my vision, I can't even feel satisfied.

I just feel alone.

LUCILLE

"Cute," the stylist says, looking at my phone. She runs her fingers through my hair. "Your hair's so healthy and long. When was that?"

I huff a laugh. "That's not me."

"Oh. So a twin?"

"Something like that."

Send her back. That's the easy answer, right? It's not even like we failed. But the thought makes me sick to my stomach, not in small part because I'm realizing it should've made me sick all along.

Mom finds me in my room when she gets home from work. "What the fuck, Lucille?"

I have no explanations, so I just say, "Sorry," and close the history book I had open—reading and rereading the same three paragraphs—on my lap.

She shakes her head and lifts her hands in a helpless gesture. "What is this about? Some delayed reaction to the divorce?"

"No."

"That boy who dropped you off last night?"

I bite the inside of my cheek—hard—to keep my expression empty. "No."

She stares at me like she's trying to read the real answers on my face. I shift my gaze to the cover of my history book, letting my eyes go unfocused and refusing to blink until they start to sting. "You used to tell me things," she says.

"You mean I used to be easy."

"No, Lucille. I mean that you used to let me be there for you. You've always been so practical and efficient. I never thought you'd use those traits to shut me out."

I say nothing.

"Damn it, Lucille! *Talk* to me."

I open my mouth. But I can't. I won't. She didn't do this, I did. I can't ask her to fix it. *How* would we even fix it? I signed an NDA, the contract. Sure, it's void since I lied about my age with the fake ID, but all that does—I looked it up on the way to the salon—is make it fraud. And since I'm a minor, that means Life^2 wouldn't come after me, they'd come after my parents. I had a company make a *person*. And if I come clean, that same company could turn on my family. How am I supposed to drop that on her?

So I reopen my book.

"Really?" she says.

I don't look up.

"Fine. You're grounded for an extra week. Like you'll respect it, but here we are."

The next morning, we sit at the counter eating cereal in silence. She glances at me sidelong, narrowing her eyes at me like I'm a stranger. No, worse. Like I'm altered. Like however she meant to make me, shape me, I came out in a way she didn't expect and isn't sure she wants.

LUCY

I sit at the counter and eat my cereal in silence, listening for the sound of them leaving. When I hear the garage door open, I walk over to the window (following the X's like a good little secret) and watch through the crack as first Lucille, then Mom, backs out and drives away. Ten deep breaths later (*in, one, two, three, out, one, two, three, helps with the panic*), I head inside.

LUCILLE

School is a stress dream come to life.

I park my car and rush straight to my first period—eyes following my pink hair like I'm glowing—which, since it's a green-block day, is history. History with the reading I couldn't make myself finish and the quiz I couldn't force myself to study for. And

I seriously doubt Ms. Martin will take "I was distracted by my clone" as a valid excuse.

I find a seat I can't be sure is "mine," set my book on my desk, hunch down, and chant *please, please, please, please* in my head while I wait for the bell to ring, begging Providence to shine on me by giving both Cass and Bode a different class this period. When the warning bell rings, I watch the second hand circle the clock, relaxing with each tick.

Then Louise walks through the door.

I look away, tuck my head, pretend to study. But she turns down my row and slows by my desk, nudging my shoulder as she goes. I glance up.

"Love it," she says, gesturing to my hair.

I manage a smile—I think—and as the final bell rings, she slides into a desk one row over and two seats back.

Louise too?

Out of fifteen questions on the quiz, I know the answers to three.

LUCY

Boris stretches out on the carpet of Lucille's room and huffs a contented sigh. I open her laptop, type in her password. Stare at the flash drive on the palm of my too-smooth hand. Then plug it in. Click the icon. Open the first folder, a video.

And press play.

Isobel sits eye-level with the camera. She's wearing a white doctor's coat, with her hair down in tight curls and dangling orange earrings in her ears. Her expression is stoic. "Stardate nine five seven three seven point—" Then she's laughing, smile spreading bright and quick. "Sorry, okay." She clears her throat. "Today is February nineteenth, two thousand eighteen, it's"—she glances at her watch—"a little after ten-thirty in the morning, and I am Dr. Olivia Mitchell, lead geneticist at Life Squared."

LUCILLE

I sit at my regular table in the library, chewing a bite of granola bar, looking up the answers to the history quiz questions that I didn't know. But I can't focus. *What have I done, what am I going to do, what have I done, what am I going to—*

My phone buzzes. I flip it face-up on the table. It's Cass: *Bode's wondering where the hell you are, says you won't answer any of his texts. So . . . You coming to lunch or?*

I stare at it, chewing the second half of my granola bar, then tap a two-letter response.

"Yeah, I didn't think you were."

I look up, nearly choking on my mouthful. "Jesus. Creepy much?"

"The pink hair's interesting."

"Thanks?"

Cass smiles. "Let's ditch."

I arch an eyebrow. "Really?"

"Yes. Really. What do you have next?"

A tightening spiral into my massive existential and legal crisis. "Independent study."

"Seriously?"

"Convinced admin I needed it for History Day and Science Fair and such."

"Well, then, what are we waiting for? Get up! You can take me to get frozen yogurt in your fancy new car."

"What do you have?"

"Choir. I'll tell Mr. Campbell I have cramps. Which I do, so it's not even lying."

I roll my eyes.

"Come on. You know you want to."

And I do. I *so* do.

LUCY

There are hundreds of them, each one time-stamped, spanning more than two years.

On February 22, 2018, at 11:37 p.m., she started without preamble: "Major breakthrough. And I mean major." Her expression is ecstatic. She can barely sit still. "It's a match! I almost can't believe it. A fully functional human kidney. Grown from scratch. And matched specifically to the recipient." She (Olivia not Isobel, Olivia not Isobel, Oliv-*liv-liv-liv*) huffs an astonished sigh and leans back in her chair. The room around her is dim, gray, her face illuminated by what I'm guessing is the computer she's using to record and maybe a desk lamp. Apart from her, the frame is empty.

"The implications of this are . . ." Her eyes go unfocused, aimed somewhere up and beyond the camera. She shakes her head, purses her lips. Blinks away tears. "It's life-changing. *Humanity*-changing." She looks into the camera again. "No more transplant waiting lists. No more donor databases." She laughs, overcome by amazement. "We can cure . . . *cancer*. Replace amputated limbs. Cure heart disease, lung disease, cirrhosis. Jesus. We could do transfusions with the *patient's own blood*. Limitless. The possibilities are truly limitless. We've just made the human body a machine with entirely replaceable par—"

There's the sound of a knock and a door opening. Olivia sits ups, looking beyond the camera to her right. "We're going to celebrate. Coming?" someone asks, and I recognize Dr. Adebayo's voice.

Dr. Mitchell nods, and the video cuts off.

I open another, dated about six weeks later.

"Sunday, April eighth, two thousand eighteen. Two twenty-two"—she snorts a laugh, shakes her head—"a.m. No, wait. That makes it Monday. The ninth." Dark circles under her eyes, she blinks rapidly a few times, then yawns. "It's official. The kidney failed.

"Well, the *kidney* didn't fail. The suspension process failed. Had we had a recipient ready six weeks ago, a *month* ago even, I feel confident it would've worked. But if the aim is to create a delicate organ like a kidney or a lung or . . ." She trails off, a slight crease appearing then disappearing between her dark eyebrows. "Or a brain. We'll need—" Her eyes go wide and she leaps out of her seat, running out of the frame. Ten seconds later, her arm cuts in front of the camera, maybe reaching for the keyboard, and the screen goes black.

The next one's dated three days later. "I knew it! It's the

hydrogel. The organs need to stay alive. Without a host. For an extended period of time. So." She shrugs like it's nothing, then her expression brightens with pride and she starts dancing in her chair. "Tailor the hydrogel! Genetically! To mimic the future host! Circulate oxygenated donor blood and there we go. We still need to test it, but it's perfect. I know it is."

I skip ahead two months, to one dated June 5, 2018, 1:33 p.m. "It's digesting. Di-gest-ing. Fucking unreal. Sorry, language." She laughs. "Kim's planning to attach the small and large intestines tomorrow. Thompson says it's time to shit or get off the pot. Ha. What she really said was something like *What are you waiting for? Shanghai and Stockholm already have functioning livers.* Which was a completely wasted opportunity when discussing the digestive system, if you ask me."

Grinning, she drops her eyes to her lap.

"I wish I could tell someone about it." She lifts her eyes to the camera again. "I know why we can't. It's all proprietary. And we're in competition with the other branches. Not to mention the chaos leaking any of this to the public would cause. I'm not even supposed to be keeping this video journal.

"I just mean . . . the work we're doing is light-years beyond what I thought possible six months ago. It's not groundbreaking, it's *earth-shattering*. The minds at work here?" She shakes her head. "Baffling. I'm part of the team, and I'm baffled. Awestruck."

July 1, 2018, 1:12 a.m., and she glares at the camera for a full minute before beginning to speak. "Fucking money. A river of it coming from the investors, whoever the hell they are, yet we can't spare a single kidney? A heart? Some kid with shit lungs dies on a waiting list while we could grow him a new pair in a matter of months. Burn victims languish in agony while we could print them a *whole new suit of skin*. And *I'm* the ridiculous one? For suggesting that all of this amazing shit we're doing be used for more than some megalomaniac's immortality wet dream?

"Thompson says to be patient. They get what they want, make their money, then, eventually, let the benefits trickle down." Jaw tight, she shakes her head. "Some of us know that's not how this shit works."

She leans back, resting an elbow on the arm of her chair. I watch her shoulders rise and fall with deep, calming breaths. Still looking away, she says, "I should delete this one. Even with Damian's encryption." Then she reaches for the keyboard and the screen goes black.

Boris snores on the carpet behind me. Great blubbering snores. Paws twitching as he chases something in his dreams. I check the time (almost noon) and skip ahead six months, to January 7, 2019, 8:15 a.m., and Dr. Mitchell starting the video off with a truly epic yawn. She sips from a hot mug, eyes bleary behind the rising steam. "It's done. Assembly on BF1901 completed at"— she looks at her watch, blinks, looks again, gives up—"twenty-ish minutes ago. Now we just wait for, well. Everything. We wait for everything."

BF1901.

01.

The first clone.

Face-up on the desk, my phone lights up. I glance at it. Three unopened texts from Bode and a new one from Life[2].

I open the next file.

"Like dominoes," she says, miming it with a sweep of her hand. "One after another. Kidneys, liver, pancreas, intestines, stomach, lungs, heart. Brain. It'd have been impressive if it didn't mean watching months of relentless work literally die. Necrosis and catastrophic organ failure. Even his—*its*. Sorry. Semantics matter. Even *its* skin. Which was . . ." She shakes her head, takes a deep breath, then cuts the video off.

I start skipping. Looking for clones two through nine.

March 12, 2019, 9:55 a.m.

"Progress. That's what we focus on. Progress. Stanch IE1902's necrotic spread, only to watch her fall apart at the seams." She barks a dark laugh. "You forget. You know, of course. But. Five liters feels like so much more when it's oozing out all over the floor."

June 2, 2019, 4:32 p.m.

Dr. Mitchell sits with her forehead in her hand. Her hair's pulled back into a (Isobel's) tight bun. "We learn so much. Each time, we learn *so much*. Twice as much since we did AA1903 and GT1904, concurrently this time. But it still feels . . ."

Inhaling deeply, she sits back, a slight smile on her lips. "They tease me for being squeamish. Because I usually spend my time at a microscope instead of elbow-deep in guts. I like to remind them that despite my being sans MD—all PhDs all the time over here—I've become quite the adept surgical nurse in recent months. Besides, it wasn't me who lost it on the lab floor today." She arches a brow and quirks her lip. "That was Thompson."

August 17, 2019, 1:12 p.m.

"It's the brain. Which we all know, even without what happened to JO1905. All of it. Lymph nodes and endocrine glands and perfectly formed heart valves. It can't work in concert without the brain." She huffs a breath out her nose. "Everything we've already done. Enough to save millions. Yet, *without the brain, they'll always be parts*," she mimics someone. "As though those parts aren't already a miracle."

October 9, 2019, 7:58 p.m.

"You start to wonder what the point is. You start to wonder . . ." She swallows thickly. "You disassociate. You have to. Because if they're people, then— Are we murderers? Seven of them. With RK1906's removal from life support yesterday and NK1907 . . ." She takes a deep breath. "And NK1907 gone today, that makes seven. Karlsson immediately went into research mode, wanting to open it up and find out what happened.

"I found Kim in the hallway afterward. Crying. And when I set a hand on his arm, he said, 'I don't know what's wrong with me.' I said something about it being normal and we laughed. Because none of this is normal. Five minutes earlier, Kim had watched himself die. Watched his Facsimile suffer consecutive grand mal seizures and go into cardiac arrest. There's no way that doesn't fuck you up. Even if they aren't—"

She shakes her head. "That's the crux, right? Are they people? Are they individuals? Do they have souls? Does it make a difference either way? They're just bodies, Karlsson says. But we can't know that. Not until one of them succeeds long enough to be able to converse. Until we can prove consciousness, cognizance. Would that simplify it? The individuality question? They're still exact replicas of preexisting individuals. NK1907 was Nathanial Kim in every physical aspect. A duplicate. But so are identical twins. Genetic duplicates. Yet we'd never say that neither was an 'individual.' So what are they?"

Dr. Mitchell frowns at her lap. "The truth is, I don't know. None of us do."

December 23, 2019, 11:55 p.m.

Her face is blank. No, not blank, frozen. I check the time bar, but the video's still playing. Then she blinks. "He woke up. Patel's. But . . ." She swallows. "All he did was scream."

December 26, 2019, 2:32 a.m.

"Onward. It's what we all say. Even *cheers*ed to it tonight after our mandatory day off. Thompson was right, of course. We needed it. I've never seen her this affected. Not even by GT1904. But I can't tell if it's because we got so close only to fail again, or if RP1908's conscious state disturbed her the way it did the rest of us.

"Anyway. Tomorrow's my full-body mold, and I'm trying not to get preemptively claustrophobic. Adebayo's been teaching me breathing techniques, and I practiced wearing the face mask yesterday."

She pulls one foot up onto her chair and hugs her knee to her chest. Her eyes go wistful. "I asked tonight why we don't have funerals for them. Karlsson shot whiskey out her nose, then cursed me in Swedish while tears streamed down her face. It turned the mood. Adebayo said that when it finally works, we'll have things to consider. Kim said it's the Board's job. Patel said it's also the client's.

"Then I asked, 'Not the creators'?' And the table went quiet."

February 1, 2020, 6:01 a.m.

She's dressed in Life^2 scrubs. White and soft. I remember the feel of them against my skin. Her hair is down, her eyes bright. "Today is the day. Kim and Adebayo have made substantial adjustments to the Mimeo since RP1908, and honestly, despite all of it, I'm feeling . . . excited? Hopeful. Truly. OM2009 is almost done. And she's . . ." She shakes her head, grinning, almost proud. "Magnificent."

Then there's a two-month gap.

I click the next video file, dated March 29, 2020, 5:58 a.m.

She's in the scrubs again. Hair pulled back in a tight bun. Expression blank. I wait for her to say something, anything, as seconds, then minutes, tick by in utter silence. Then I recognize it.

That stillness.

That quiet.

It isn't Dr. Mitchell. It's Isobel.

LUCILLE

"So," Cass says as we walk to the parking lot, leaving through the empty gym to avoid passing the main office. "Pink, huh?"

I reach for my hair, self-conscious. "Yeah."

She nods.

"What?"

"Remember in first grade when we both wanted those ridiculous winged unicorn things?"

"I remember."

"Good. So, then you remember that when we got them, you threw this epic fit—"

"I did not. I was just—"

"—about how you wanted the purple one because you hated

pink and I got the purple one and that wasn't fair. And I was, like, *Forget that I hate pink too,* so finally we both ended up with purple ones and we colored the hooves on yours silver with a Sharpie so we could tell them apart?"

"What's your point?"

She stops between two cars and turns to face me. "You hate pink! You have *always* hated pink. So . . ." She waves a hand, urging me on. *"What's up with the hair?"*

I squeeze past Cass and start walking again. "I wanted to do something different."

"Bullshit."

I scoff.

"Don't get me wrong," she says, "it looks awesome. But . . ."

We reach my car. I look at her over the roof. "But what? I'm not allowed to do something different because that's 'not like you'?"

"Well, *yeah.* You've been a lot 'not like you' lately."

"What does that mean?"

"Come on. Really? Bode. Art. Saturday. The hair."

Wait, what? "Saturday?"

The look she gives me—like I've lost half my head or sprouted a second one—sends a spark up my spine. *Cass is how Lucy got home.* I duck down and climb in the driver's side. My hand shakes as I put my key in the ignition to start the car and roll the windows down. After a beat, Cass opens the passenger door and gets in.

I sit, trying to order my thoughts, and finally say, "How do you know what is or isn't *like me* when I don't even know myself?"

She's quiet for so long that I purse my lips to keep from filling the silence with something I shouldn't say. Sitting like this, quiet and alone and close, I realize just how much I *miss* her. All summer. Last year. Right now, even though she's right next to me.

I miss her.

Cass, the person I shared not just inside jokes but whole stories, whole imaginary universes with. Cass, who cried with me when my first dog, Nellie, died; who called the only boy I ever asked to dance—and said no—a "human suit filled with rancid turkey fat" to his face; who told me about her first kiss in the seventh grade before she told anyone else, then cried on my couch when he broke up with her a week later.

Cass, the person I used to tell everything to, shared everything with. Cass, who now knows nothing—about my parents, Marco, my *freaking clone*—beyond a series of flimsy lies.

Then she says, "I know that even *thinking* about *Dumbo* makes you feel like you're going to cry. I know that you think Twizzlers are good in theory but make you sick to your stomach. I know that while your mom loves *Gilmore Girls* and has made you watch the whole series with her, you think Rory's a self-absorbed snob. I know that when you flipped over your handlebars and got that cut on your temple, you didn't even cry.

"I know because I was *there*. For all of it. I've watched you cry watching *Dumbo*. And *Inside Out* and *WALL-E* and, which I will never believe or let you live down, *Cars 3*. I've listened to you argue with your mom about *Gilmore Girls*. I've eaten Twizzlers with you, then regretted it twenty minutes later. And when you went over your handlebars, I took off my sock to sop up the blood."

I snort a laugh. "So sanitary."

"Yeah, well, you ruined my sock."

"Sorry."

"You know what else I know?"

I shake my head.

"There is something going on with you. Something big. Maybe your parents' divorce, but I don't think so. You're . . ." She stares out the windshield. "*Different* isn't the right word for it. Because you aren't totally. Yet you are. I don't know. But it's like since the first day of school some switch flipped. Then, for some reason, today it flipped back."

I mean to laugh, but it comes out broken. "I messed up, Cass. I did something, and . . ."

"And?"

I wipe my eyes, but the tears keep coming.

"Can you fix it?" she asks.

"I don't know if I want to. I mean, I have to. I can't do nothing. But I don't think the easy fix is the right one anymore."

"It usually isn't."

"I've really missed you," I say.

"I've missed you, too."

We're quiet for a minute, a breeze blowing through the open windows of my car. "What did you say about art?"

LUCY

It's unbearable.

Watching her.

Her halting speech (six videos until she can complete a coherent sentence), her erratic movements, and finally, her grief.

May 1, 2020, 10:17 p.m.

She sits, shoulders straight and chin parallel to the floor (this, I learn, the fastidiousness, the attention, is how she controls the tremors and tics), with her hands in her lap. "I don't know . . ." She pauses, collects herself. "Metaphors are still difficult for me. But I feel hollow, as though the bulk of me either never was or has been . . . scooped out. Dr. Thompson says this is because my my my . . ." Isobel stops again. Aiming her eyes as far down as she can without shifting the set of her head. I can almost hear her thinking, searching for the right word, forcing her synapses to connect. She looks up again. "My connectome is incomplete. But I know it's because you're gone."

The muscles in her chin shiver. Then she's crying. Silent rivulets slipping down her cheeks. "To never get to know your self, to lose that self without ever . . ."

She closes her eyes. I watch her throat bob as she swallows. Then she looks directly into the camera and says, "The misery is acute."

The Mimeo killed Dr. Mitchell.

Halfway through, thanks to a catastrophic amount of brain swelling brought on by excessive radiation. I find the write-up in the files. Not a traditional medical report, rather a series of events included with a diagnostic report on the machine: elevated heart rate, reduced oxygen rates, seizures—followed by the cessation of the procedure, administration of medications, CPR, removal of a portion of her skull to reduce pressure, and finally, death.

I think about what it would be like to lose Lucille. There's a flash of satisfaction (a glimpse of how easy it'd be if, suddenly, I was the only one) followed by a chasm.

Not the same as losing a sister. A best friend. A confidante. Because she's none of those things. I honestly can't even be sure that I like her. I *know* I resent her, envy her, maybe even hate her.

But she's also me.

Losing her would feel like having my life string cut. And without that tether, I might simply float away.

There's more. Beyond the video diary. Massive PDFs filled with pages and pages of indecipherable (to me) data, rosters with the names and personal information of the Life^2 investors, much of it dated after Mitchell's death. And a separate video titled "Presentation OM2009, 5/18/20."

It opens on a conference room, bright and sterile like the one at Life^2 but bigger. The table stretches at least ten seats to both the left and right of the camera, with every seat filled. Across from it, back a few paces from the middle of the table, between it and a glass wall, stand Dr. Thompson and Isobel.

Isobel's dressed in her familiar skirt suit and modest heels. She stands stiffly, with her hands clasped before her hips. To the audience, I'm sure her expression appears stoic, composed. But as the camera zooms in slowly, before it rewidens the frame, I see how her right eyebrow twitches. There's a sheen of sweat on her upper lip.

"Begin," says a deep male voice, out of frame, at the right end of the table.

Dr. Thompson nods. "Thank you, to the Board and other

gathered investors, for allowing me to present the American branch's successful Facsimile"—she makes a sweeping gesture—"Isobel."

The awe is audible, gasps and disbelief. People talk over one another. Isobel's left knee begins to shake. "How do we know it's real?" shouts a man over the rest. "She could be anyone."

Thompson lifts her chin. "You'll find all relevant verification materials in the introduction packet on your tablet."

"How long did it take?"

"Can it talk?"

"Does it have preferences?"

Until they're all talking over one another, rabid. A cacophony. And Isobel begins to panic. I watch her hands shake, her eyes dart from point to point, face to face, never pausing long enough to focus. I can feel it. How she must've felt. The pressure of all that attention, all those questions, dozens of Thompsons wanting something from her, something she couldn't give, couldn't be, all at once.

"This says there were complications. What were those complications?"

"How long until the service is available to clients?"

She's about to lose it, lifts her hands as though to cover her mouth or grip her head.

Then a deep male voice from the right-hand head of the table asks, "Where is her Original?"

Isobel opens her mouth and begins to scream.

The screen goes black.

From a follow-up report, I learn that Thompson nearly lost her job. What had she been thinking, presenting a Facsimile for a dead Original? What use was RapidReplicate if it killed the client? There's no praise, no acknowledgment of Isobel, only censure. Deserved, maybe, but the tone is vicious.

Then there are Isobel's videos about Lucille. About me.

They start in June, the day of Lucille's first appointment. "They've found a new candidate" is all she says. In the following entries, she calls Lucille "young" and "naïve" and "self-involved," which is "exactly what Thompson wants. She doesn't even care that the girl's a minor, though who knows if the Board will. Not like legality is a big consideration here. And even if Lucille were of age, it isn't like Thompson would honor the contract if it tipped suddenly out of her favor. In the end, all that matters is Thompson's ability to deny knowing, and leverage Lucille's lie against her. She only cares about winning, about being first. And for that she needs a willing participant. A candidate who won't think too hard about the implications. Who's only flattered that she's been chosen, who doesn't know that Thompson's search turned up dozens of candidates and she's the only one who took the bait. One who's a stranger. Ignorant of the risks, easy to manipulate. Whose Facsimile won't be . . ." She pauses, takes a quick deep breath. "A shadow."

The last one is dated Wednesday, August 12, 5:45 p.m. The day before I went home.

"I'm not sure why I keep making these. As a testament to my existence? Habit? Both Olivia's and mine. And as a contingency, I suppose." She sighs, and her shoulders relax. She lets her head tilt to the side, eyes appraising, like she's studying her own image on the screen. Her movements are fluid. No more careful, incremental shifts. No more preternatural stillness. Her hair's in its usual bun, but she's shed her suit jacket and undone the top button on her blouse. She looks . . . not like Olivia, exactly. But more like herself. "I went back and watched a few of my first videos. I won't call it humbling, to see how far I've come. It's infuriating. Though, helpful in some ways. Only yesterday Thompson left me alone in her office yet again. Because she still sees me as she did that first day, when I woke up and she figured out I'd have to relearn how to speak.

"And thanks to that, I now have this." Smiling, she holds up a flash drive similar to, if not the same as, the one she gave me. "The failsafe codes for Cindy. And with Lucy heading home tomorrow, I imagine I'll get my opportunity to use them soon."

LUCILLE

I walk with Cass back through the front doors, then turn toward the wing with the art room instead of following her toward the junior lobby to wait for our next classes.

"Where are you going?" she asks.

"I need to take care of something."

She smirks. "Lucille Harper, ditching two class periods in one day?"

"Guess so. I'm a real wild woman."

"International Woman of Mystery, right?"

I smile but don't say anything. It's a Cass-and-Lucy joke. I'm not sure how I know, but I do. Cass waves and I head for the art room.

When I walk in, it's empty, lights dim, Mx. Frank's planning period or something, and I'm glad for it. I hesitate inside the door.

No clue where I'm going. I've never been in this room before. It smells like mud and dust and paint. Sunlight comes in through the windows facing the courtyard. In a weird way, it reminds me of the conference room at Life². The size, maybe. The courtyard, the light. Like, if that's the fake version, this is the real one.

The easels are all pushed together against a wall, but they're empty. To their right are drying racks with canvases in each slot. I stride over and start searching.

I know which one is hers right away. And not just because it's . . . me.

I don't know what I was expecting. Cass told me about it, confused why I was asking her to explain my own painting but humoring me anyway. She told me how Bode's apparently obsessed, how he kept talking about it at lunch and asking Cass why I hadn't signed up for art before. She told him the truth, that I couldn't draw anything better than a janky stick figure to save my life. But, of course, she was talking about me. This is Lucy's. And it's gorgeous. And ugly. And strange. And interesting. But mostly it's real.

That's what I settle on.

It's *real*. And Lucy made it.

Her self-portrait's done entirely in shades of blue, from a near-black to the bleached blue of a sun-drenched sky. Her—not my—head is tipped to the side, her—not my—brow is tight with eyes slightly narrowed, considering. Skeptical. And her—*not my*—edges are liquid, blurred into the all-blue background.

What the hell color is the sky, anyway?

She looks like me. But the longer I look at it, the less I recognize her.

"Lucy?"

Bode stands in the doorway to the storage and kiln rooms, backlit by the overhead light. "What are you doing? Aren't you supposed to be in physics or something?"

"Yeah."

I stare back at the painting. It's just pigment. Strategically placed, in varying shades. And looking at it makes me want to pull my heart out of my chest with my bare hand.

She made this. All this while, I've treated her like a thing. A placeholder. My stand-in. And she's capable of *this*. I shake my head. It shouldn't matter. It doesn't matter. This thing she did, it's not what matters. It's incredible, but it's a symptom. A side effect.

I wipe my cheeks with my free hand and—taking the painting—turn to go.

"Lucy," Bode says, "wait."

Almost to the door, I glance back. "I'm not Lucy."

LUCY

My phone buzzes on Lucille's desk, snapping me out of the stupor I've been sitting in for the last twenty minutes. It's Bode: *Where are you?*

I unplug the flash drive from the laptop and make my way back out to the studio, wanting, what? A moment alone? Seems superfluous. But I guess I just want to be somewhere that feels even a little bit like mine.

Walking up the stairs, minding the X's out of habit, I text back: *In class.*

What are you talking about? No you aren't. I just saw you.

Where?

Are you joking? In the art room. You took your painting. Kickass hair btw.

My throat goes thick. Can't swallow. Can't breathe. I run the rest of the way up the stairs, dialing Lucille's number as I go. The phone buzzes with a text while I hold it against my ear. She doesn't answer. I check the message, from Life²: *Severely elevated heart rate. Please report.*

But I can't think clearly enough to come up with a lie. I can feel my pulse inside my head. *If she, if she, if sh-sh-sh-sh—*

The garage door opens. I hold my breath, hear a car pull in, the engine cut, door open and close. Then, footsteps on the stairs.

LUCILLE

I close the door to the studio behind me. Lucy's eyes flick between mine and the painting. She's terrified. And it breaks my heart that she thinks I'd hurt it, hurt her. But I suppose I've set the precedent, if not for hurt, then for total disregard.

"The strangest part is that you know," I say. My throat aches. I can't stop my tears. "You've known all along how I thought of you. How I *didn't* think of you. I don't know how to say I'm sorry for that."

She stands still, both feet on a blue X between the counter

and the back of the love seat. "So that's it? You see a picture I made and suddenly decide I'm human?"

"It's not about you not being 'human.' It's understanding that you aren't . . ."

"That I'm not what?" She swallows, jaw tight.

"Me. You aren't me."

She loses the battle, tears welling in her eyes. "Aren't I?"

"No. Maybe. Maybe you're both. Maybe I'm both too. Me, not me. Lucille, Lucy"—I cough a laugh—"Lucille Harper, Overachiever. Lucille Harper, Perfect Daughter. Lucille Harper, Trying Too Hard. Maybe I'm all of it, or none of it. Maybe I have no fucking clue."

She purses her lips, and I can still feel the gesture, taste the salt of tears on her lips, because I'm doing it too. "Sounds about right," she says.

I hold up the painting. "This is amazing. *You're* amazing."

"Same apple," she whispers. "Same tree."

I swallow, letting my eyes blur as I stare at the blues. "What the hell do we do now?"

CHAPTER FIFTEEN

LUCY

Lucille sets my painting on the counter carefully, wipes the tears from her cheeks with a hand, and crosses the room to sit on the love seat. I watch her. Feeling my heart rate slow, my tension ease, then join her. My phone buzzes in my back pocket. I check the screen.

"It's Life Squared," I say.

"About what?"

"Elevated heart rate." I type out a quick text, telling them someone slammed a door and scared the shit out of half my class. Seconds later, I receive a reply: *Please advise, new in-person progress appointment scheduled for 6 p.m. today.* "They want me to come in later."

"Why?"

I shrug and breathe a deep sigh. The quiet between us goes slack.

"I figured you'd be an extension of me," Lucille says. "All the parts I needed and none of the ones I don't. Or, I hoped you wouldn't get those. I don't know. They kept saying 'copy,' 'duplicate' . . ."

"Facsimile."

"Right. And I thought that meant . . . exact. An exact reproduction of me. Who I thought I was, at least." She pulls her feet up onto the couch and hugs her knees to her chest.

"Is that why you were okay with giving me back?"

Her eyes brim again. "How's that for a healthy sense of self-worth, huh?"

"Something preaching something something choir."

Lucille breathes a sad laugh, then shakes her head. "I'm so sorry. But, if I'm honest, I'm not sure what for. I don't regret doing what I did. You're here because of it."

"You don't?"

She turns her head to look at me, and I know our expressions are a perfect mirror for each other, just without the images being reversed. The same, but different. "No," she says.

We close the gap between us at the same time, looping identical arms around identical backs, breathing with identical lungs, identical blood pumping through identical hearts. Loving each other and trying harder to love ourselves.

When we let go, we sit shoulder to shoulder, sunk low together on the worn-out cushions. I ask her about Marco, and she tells me about the party, breaking up. "I slept with him," she says. "The last night of our trip."

"Really?"

"Yeah." She picks Boris hairs off her pants. "I think . . . I thought he was the answer. Which seems pretty ridiculous now. I mean, I really like him. He's funny and kind and decent. I don't necessarily wish I hadn't done it. I guess I wish I'd done it all differently. I dove headfirst into it, into him, because being liked by him, wanted by him, by *anyone*, felt like the solution. Like if he wanted me, then I was finally doing everything right. Like I finally deserved to be wanted by someone.

"I know that's why I answered Thompson. As pathetic as it sounds, it's because she, Life Squared, wanted me. Because she said she *needed* me. That I was their *ideal candidate*. The best."

I grab her hand, stop her picking at her pants. It's both weird and not weird, touching her. Weird because my brain says *mine*, but not weird because it's like touching anyone. Just warmth, just skin. I turn her hand over to look at her palm, holding it flat beside mine. "I don't know," I say. "I think we're kicking this trial's ass."

She laughs, then stares at our hands like I am. "You know enough about me—"

"Understatement."

"Tell me about you."

Twenty-six days of consciousness. Fourteen at Life^2. Twelve here. But there's a lot. I tell her about Facsimilate and how her memories shift and recolor until they feel like mine. I tell her about how it feels to spend time with Mom and Dad. "I can feel their love, but it's for you. Not me," I say, and her brow curves before she rests her head on my shoulder. I tell her about school, about art: "I think I love it so much because I *know* you've never felt it. Which sounds kind of shitty, I guess. But everything about me is either copied or repurposed, while this is entirely and purely mine." Then, about Bode: "I don't know why he likes me. I like being liked. He's fun and interesting and creative. But there's that extra thing where he thinks I'm you."

She listens to all of it. Letting me talk, meandering along the tangents of my thoughts, without interrupting. Just being here with me. Proving that neither of us is alone.

Finally, I talk about me: "You talk about feeling partial. Or, I *know* how you worry about being inadequate. I can feel it in a way that's more than empathy. Like I can pull the feeling on and wear it around for a while. But I also know that I *don't* feel that way. After all of it, how and why I exist, Life^2's incessant attention to semantics. 'It.' 'Life surrogate.'

"I know I'm not a thing, Lucille. I know I'm a person. A *whole* person. Not you, just me, but—"

I take a deep, centering breath, and stand up. "I need to show you something."

LUCILLE

Closed in my bedroom, I sit in my desk chair, laptop open. Lucy leans over to plug in a flash drive. "From Isobel," she says, then stands back to watch me watch them. Video after video. Dr. Mitchell, BF1901, AA1903, GT1904, and the rest.

I feel sick.

I mean, I knew. Not details, but I—*we*—knew, right? That they'd have had to do tests. That Isobel wasn't their first attempt. But that's not what turns my stomach. It is, but it isn't. What makes me cover my mouth in shock is the heartbreaking callousness of it. With my own Facsimile at my back, I want to scream at every single one of them, *Don't you care? About Olivia? About Isobel? About Lucy? About* yourselves?

I feel painfully, impossibly naïve. I can't even blame just

Thompson or Life², because while they were using me, I was using them, too. For validation. To loosen the knot in my chest. To feel complete. I share that guilt. I didn't think of my Facsimile, of Lucy, as a person. Not one with thoughts and feelings. She was temporary. An extension of me. A *thing*. And irreparably wrapped up with my own sense of deficiency. She was partial, but supposedly the perfectly shaped piece to fill in my own gaps.

I look up at her. "How do we— What do we do with this?"

"I don't know."

"Why'd Isobel give it to you?"

Lucy lifts a shoulder. "So I'd know? She said she was trying to help me. Help me help myself."

I look back at the computer, the video of Isobel's presentation paused near the end. "It's proof. Gigabytes of it."

"The NDA."

"Void. Since I used the fake ID. But that means Life Squared can sue Mom and Dad. I looked it up yesterday." I meet her eye. "You think they'd do that?"

"I think Thompson used it as a way to make you feel important. In on it. And to scare you into keeping your mouth shut."

"So, then what? The contract's void too, but it's not like they're going to give a shit about that. Say *Whoops! Guess we'll let Lucy go!*" I push the heels of my hands into my eyes, and try to picture it. The fallout of what we're both refusing to say outright. I drop my hands into my lap and look at her, eyes slowly refocusing. The pink suits her. "We both know the issue isn't the paperwork."

Lucy purses her lips. "So we publish it. Go public."

"You'd do that?"

She gives me a helpless look. "Do we have a choice?"

That's when we hear it. We'd been so focused we must've missed the garage, the door to the kitchen, Boris's whines. Now there are footsteps on the stairs, and, "Lucille? Are you home? I got a text from the school . . ."

The bedroom door opens.

Together, we turn. "Mom?"

She sees us. Both of us. For one wide-eyed second. Then faints dead away on the floor.

CHAPTER SIXTEEN

LUCY

Dad comes back into the dining room from the kitchen and sets a bottle of whiskey on the table with a *thunk*. "You won't blame us, will you?" he asks.

Mom unscrews the cap, takes a shot straight from the bottle, then hands it to Dad, who does the same.

They sit beside each other, across from Lucille and me. Mid-afternoon sun falls in through the windows at their backs, illuminating the occasional dust mote and Boris hair floating through the air.

"I'm going to need the original Lucille to put her hair up," Mom says. "Please." Beside me, Lucille pulls her hair back into a short ponytail.

"So," Dad says, then stops.

It's been like this since Mom came to. We both rushed to her. A beat later, she blinked the focus back into her eyes, looked between us, and screamed, crab-walking into the hall as fast as she could. I backed away. Finally, she stopped screaming long enough to shout, "*What the fuck?*"

Then Lucille called Dad, and we waited in silence, with Mom in this weird orbit, not too close, not too far, until he showed.

"Clone," Lucille supplies. "Lucy's my clone."

Dad nods. "Ah."

Mom swallows. "I think I'm going to throw up." She runs from the table to the main-floor half bath. We hear the fan turn on. A few minutes later, the toilet flushes and the faucet runs. Then she's back and reaching for the bottle again. She sips it more slowly this time. "Sorry," she says, leaving the cap on the table, then gestures to Lucille. "Continue."

Lucille explains about Life^2, punctuated by frequent interruptions.

Mom: "It's not fucking possible. It's just not possible. This is decades beyond today's science. An ear, some skin. An artery. Even a miniature human heart. They're doing it. I know this. The foundation is there. But . . ." She gestures (purposefully not looking) at me. "She's— A complete *brain*? An *entire human body*? In *weeks*?"

And Dad: "You're a minor. Nothing you signed is valid."

Lucille shifts in her chair. "I used a fake ID."

He throws his hands up. "Oh, good! Fraud!" He pushes away from the table and starts to pace.

I wish Lucille would take down her hair. Because the way they look at me, the way they *won't* loo-oo-oo-oo— Her hand finds mine beneath the table, our fingers lacing. She squeezes once. When I turn my head to meet her eye, she smiles.

"Dad," Lucille says.

He keeps pacing.

"*Dad*," she says again, louder. He stops. I glance up at him, then at Mom, who's looking between us like she's trying to solve a riddle that's actively breaking her heart. Lucille checks the clock. Somehow, it's almost four. "You should probably know that Lucy has an appointment tonight at six, and . . ."

She looks at me.

"And?" Dad asks.

"I kind of forgot to mention that in two and a half weeks, they'll want her back."

In unison, Mom and Dad yell, *"What?"*

LUCILLE

They excuse us to my room. Like I'm seven again. Lucy and I plod up the stairs, Boris following, and I close the door behind us.

Immediately their voices rise.

There are whiffs of accusation, of "How didn't you notice?" and "How didn't *you* notice?" Until we hear Mom call a truce and their volume lowers to a murmur.

Lucy leans her back against the wall and slides down to sit on the floor. Boris curls up next to her, and I join her on his other side. "What do you think they're talking about?" she asks. "Us?"

We laugh, then quiet, both of us petting Boris.

"You really think we should go public?" I ask.

"If that's how I get out of being Life Squared's floor model? Yes."

"That's who we'd be forever. Lucille Harper, The Girl Who Got Cloned, and Lucy Harper, The Clone."

"That's who we already are."

"But not just."

"No. Not just." She stares off into the middle distance, eyes unfocused, then grins. "Think of the hook, though, Lucille. Think of the college essays. Guarantee, every single Ivy would be banging down our door."

I laugh, shaking my head. "Ah, well, if anything's going to make a worldwide media cluster worth it, right?"

"I don't even have a birth certificate. Or Social Security number. Or, you know, legally exist in any way. Plus . . ."

"What?"

She shakes her head.

"Yeah, well," I say, "you don't have loads of stuff. Your own clothes. Room. Bed. Classes. Not to mention all the stuff you've only done and tried in memory. Like, pistachio ice cream. What if you only think you like it because I do? What if you try it and end up hating it?"

"Only the most important considerations, I see." But she smiles, which was my goal.

I pet Boris's so-soft ear, and he groans happily, mashing his head into my leg. "I'm scared."

"Me too."

Forty-five minutes later, there's a knock at the door.

"Come in," I say.

Dad opens the door. Sees us on the floor and cringes.

Lucy's shoulders droop as she averts her eyes.

"Time to figure this shit out," he says, and turns back into the hall.

I get up first and offer Lucy my hand. Together, we follow Dad back down to the dining room.

As we settle into our spots, I watch them watch her. I still have my hair pulled back, but I can see from the way they look between us that it's barely anything. A tiny signifier. That if I took it down, if they left the room and we switched places, they wouldn't have the faintest clue which of us is which.

"So," Mom says.

Lucy tenses, and I get it. That "plus" in my room. She's worried they don't want her, that they'll decide to send her back.

"How do we fix this?" Mom asks. "How do we get you out?"

Lucy looks up. "Me?"

"Both of you."

"But I'm not—"

"Not our daughter? In what way?" Rhetorical, but Mom waits anyway. Lucy's eyes start to tear, and I feel it too. My own eyes going sour and tight. "That's what I thought," she says. "So. How do we fix it?"

Lucy and I share a glance, and I start.

LUCY

I'm surprised my phone isn't buzzing as we pull up to Life² because my heart is a jackhammer in my chest, but we (me, Lucille, my mom and dad—*mine*, it's still surreal) decided it was better to come. Skipping out would tip them off, right? And this way we can maintain appearances while we sort the rest of it out.

Stuff like what to leak and to whom, whether Lucille and I should come out bursting like a *Ta-da! Human clones are real!*

firework, or if we should just use Isobel's info to out Life^2, doing our best to protect her and Olivia's identities as well. Dad mentioned a college friend, Mitch, who apparently works for CNN; Mom countered with a plan to leak info through a masked IP for anonymity; and we argued fun stuff like what to do if the shadowy übercompany capable of printing people on demand decided that a media shitstorm wasn't enough to let me go. Or, better, if it would warrant my disappearance followed by a tragic "accident" for the remaining Harpers.

Then five-thirty rolled around and we all chose *Put a pin in it till we're back home.* So here we are.

We look out at the Life^2 building, Lucille in the driver's seat, me riding shotgun. "Well . . . ," I say.

"Time to make sure all your guts are still in the right place," she finishes, and we share a look, heavy with everything we both know now, everything we've decided, then climb out.

The gate and doors open for us as they always do, and we find Dr. Thompson waiting in the lobby beside Drs. Kim and Karlsson. Isobel stands off to the side. Our eyes meet, and I can tell the moment she realizes that I finally watched the videos. Her eyes widen a fraction and she nods, tipping her chin a few faint millimeters. The feeling, the recognition, I don't want to say it feels like power because it doesn't. It isn't as potent as that. It's more like sloughing off my passivity. There's tension in sharing this secret with her, with Lucille, like pulling a spring taut, knowing that, if we wanted to, we could release it and let it snap.

"Hello, Lucy," Thompson says. "You look well. The hair is . . ." She tilts her head, amused. "Was that your decision or Lucille's?"

Lucille and I look at each other. "Mine," I say, while she says, "Lucy's."

Thompson smiles. "Fascinating. With that and your recent deceptions, I've begun to wonder just how much of your docility and acquiescence was for show."

"Deceptions?"

"Of course. Just today you replied to a status inquiry with a lie. Or were you really in class yet somehow left your GPS chip at home? Not that it matters. It's honestly more intriguing than anything else." Lucille looks at me. Heat buds in my cheeks. Thompson waves me forward. "Time to go, Lucy. Thank you, Lucille, that'll be all."

"What?" we say.

"Lucille's role with us is finished. We're terminating the field test and moving on to the next phase."

"*Excuse me?*" Lucille shouts while my hearing goes hollow. Kim crosses the lobby to us in wide strides, aiming for Lucille. She tries and fails to dodge his grip. I lunge for him, feeling too slow, as though we're all underwater, in a dream. But Karlsson grabs me, hauling me back.

There's screaming.

Mine.

Lucille's.

Then the doors close between us, and it's only me.

CHAPTER SEVENTEEN

LUCILLE

Kim pushes me outside and shuts the exterior door in my face. My breath burns in my throat. My heartbeat is too big for my chest. I want to lose it. Scream and kick and pound my fists on the door.

Instead, I close my eyes, clench my jaw, and take ten deep breaths.

In, one, two, three, out, one, two, three.

Then I back up until I'm in clear view of the camera mounted over the door and glare into it, imagining Thompson staring back.

I call Mom on the way to our car. "Change of plans."

LUCY

Karlsson lets me go when the door closes. I want to run at it, yank the handle, scream until my throat bleeds. But I make myself still, from the soles of my feet to the ends of my hair, feeling my heartbeat in my fingertips.

"Ready?" Thompson asks.

I turn. It takes everything in me not to spit in her face. "For?"

"Your final BodyProg and SyncroMem appointments before I present you to the Board tomorrow morning in New York." She smiles, close-lipped and mirthless. "You should be proud, Lucy. You're more than I dared hope for, and I make a practice of aiming high."

"You're kidding, right?"

"About our success? Never."

In, one, two, three, out, one, two, three. "You're a remarkably shitty person. I feel like you should know that."

"Perception is subjective. Apparently, even for you," she says, then gestures to the sci-fi door. "After you."

I refuse to cry, through the body scan verifying that all of my parts are present and accounted for, while Adebayo sets the sensor halo on my head and asks me questions I choose not to answer. "I like the pink," he whispers as he takes the halo off.

"Did it bother you when they died? When *yours* died?"

I wait for him to ask how I know, but he only says, "Yes. The last one especially."

Kim walks me to my room. "Here," he says after pressing his hand to the hidden panel and opening the door. He holds out a phone. "I turned off the signal jammer. You have two minutes."

"Why?" I ask.

"Because you deserve the time to say goodbye."

"Since when do I deserve anything? Aren't I just an 'it' to you?"

He swallows thickly. I watch his throat move. "I spent a lot of time convincing myself exactly that."

"But?"

"But, you remember. You were conscious. When you woke up in the hydrogel during the final stages of your assembly, you remembered it. And I started to wonder, did mine remember too?"

I consider telling him that's bullshit, too late, not enough. That a phone call is a shitty consolation prize, one that won't fix his guilt. Instead, I take a chance and move to close myself in the bathroom. He doesn't stop me.

LUCILLE

We're spread out at the dining room table, each staring at a laptop, each with our own task. Mom researches the laws about cloning and minors entering into legal contracts in Colorado while Dad digs deep into the conspiracy sites, following every thread with even a kernel of truth. I compile a compendium of information for release.

My phone rings. The number's blocked. "Hello?"

"Lucille." Her voice breaks.

"Lucy, thank god." I push back from the table, standing before I realize I'm doing it. "Are you okay?"

"Yes," she whispers. "No. Kim gave me his phone so I could say goodbye."

"Fuck that. We're moving for—"

"She's flying me out sometime tonight. To New York. To present me to the Board in the morning."

"Okay." I swallow. "Okay. We can work with that."

"I don't think—"

"No. I'll fix this. We'll get you out. I promise."

Her breath hitches.

"Lucy, I mean it. I'll fix this."

She hangs up. I set my phone down.

"Well?" asks Dad.

"They're flying her to New York tonight."

Mom: "When?"

"She didn't know."

She looks to Dad. "She doesn't have ID. Could they fake it? Say she's Lucille?"

He shakes his head. "I don't know."

"So we report it. Call the police and say Lucille's been kidnapped."

He picks up his phone. "I'll call Emma." Mom and I listen, unmoving, barely breathing, as he talks to my aunt who's a pilot. He hangs up and reports, "She says they'll probably fly private. Get her out under the radar. Not DIA, there's too much security." To my mom he says, "Research regional airports." Then, to me, "Start searching the flash drive's files for anything that mentions a plane. We need to know what kind they're taking so we can narrow it down. You get enough info put together to release?"

I nod.

"Great." He stands up, taking his phone with him. "I'm calling Mitch. We can't let them leave."

LUCY

The air in my room smells stale. I wonder if it always has, or if it's just that my perception's changed. The walls seem to encroach, their glow emanating out, closer and closer, as though it's trying to touch me. Swallow me up.

The memory of Isobel's scream in her presentation video plays in my head on a loop.

You are the sum of your purpose.

Tell yourself a lie enough times and it becomes your truth.

But which is my truth? That I'm nothing but my purpose? Or that I'm more? Everything I thought I knew, thought I'd learned to believe since I was last in this room, feels so insubstantial now. Like those days, the ones in which I had friends, a family, where I could settle into myself, feel whole and solid instead of a patchwork of mismatched pieces and haphazard seams, were a mistake. Like they were the lie, while this is what's real.

What if Lucille can't get me out?

The door slides open.

"Come on," Isobel says, "we need to move quickly."

I follow her down the hall, running every few steps to keep up. She's dressed in jeans, a T-shirt, and bright orange sneakers, and carries a laptop under one arm. "What's—"

She looks back, finger to her lips to quiet me. We pause at the corner while she checks to make sure the next hall is clear, then we're hurrying again. At the end of this hall, she stops, places her palm to a hidden panel. A door slides open, revealing a dim stairwell. Motion sensors catch our movement as we step through, and the lights flicker on to reveal walls painted industrial beige, metal railings, and concrete stairs leading down.

"I need your help, if you're willing to give it," Isobel says.

"Obviously."

She grins. "Downstairs is the Life Squared mainframe computer. I'm going to upload malware designed to leak all of the company's information onto various online channels, then destroy the supercomputer housing Olivia's and Lucille's connectomes by triggering the doomsday failsafe."

"Sounds like an oxymoron."

She starts down the stairs, moving gracefully. Her stiffness is gone. Gone or left behind, like a costume she doesn't need to wear. "It's a program written for the sole purpose of covering Life Squared's tracks should some aspect of the operation be compromised."

"Fantastic. I'm in."

I can hear it when we reach the bottom of the stairs, even through the walls, a deep, resonant hum. "How long have you been planning for this?" I ask.

She glances back at me as we jog down the long hallway. "Since the moment I was capable. With only half of Olivia's connectome uploaded before the Mimeo killed her, I ended up with half a blank slate. Which took . . . time. To fill back up."

"That's why Thompson needed Lucille and me?"

"Thompson . . ." We round a corner into a second, identical concrete hallway. The humming gets louder. "Thompson needed a successful Facsimile *and* a surviving Original. She didn't care how she got it. But after Olivia, she ran out of volunteers."

We pause before a set of double doors with a scanner pad mounted on the concrete wall, and Isobel says, "All entries into this room are monitored, and ours is unsanctioned. Our clock starts now."

"Our clock to do what, exactly?"

"I'm going to go straight to the mainframe and upload the malware. I need you to find everything you can to keep these doors propped open. The failsafe can only be triggered remotely by a pair of senior Life Squared members. I have Thompson's codes, but no second party and no Life Squared tablet to enter them. I have a way to do it alone and with this"—she holds up the laptop—"but it means doing it from in there. Any tampering from inside the room, and the doors are mechanized to seal shut."

My brow rises. "Why?"

"To lock whoever did it inside."

"Dark."

"Yes." She pulls something out of her back pocket and unfolds it. It looks like two thin sheets of plastic with a semi-translucent handprint between. She peels the sheets apart and, very carefully, matches her hand to the outline of the print. "Thompson's handprint," she says. "They conveniently keep all of the prior Facsimiles' genetic and physiological data filed away, and no one ever bothered to remove Olivia's security clearance upstairs or ask if her knowledge of the ITOPs transferred to me." With Thompson's print layered atop her own, she lifts her palm to the pad. "Ready?"

I nod.

The door's lock clicks. When she opens it, the hum becomes a roar. We step into a room the size of a super Walmart. Or three.

"What is that?" I shout.

"Cindy," she shouts back, gesturing to the supercomputer filling the entirety of the space. "This way!" She heads left, jogging toward a glass-walled room at the far end, and I follow. I look for things to shove in front of the doors as we go, but there's nothing.

At the room, she pulls open one of the glass doors. Inside, the roar is muffled. "Its real name is *syneídisi*, or 'consciousness' in Greek," she says. "But they call it Cindy for short. It's where the connectomes are stored."

She takes a cable from her back pocket, plugs one end into the mainframe computer and the other into her laptop. It's not an average computer. Two full walls of the room, larger than our basement at home, house its processors. A desk built into the third holds a series of monitors and video screens displaying images from all over the building upstairs. The fourth wall, comprised entirely of what must be soundproof glass, looks out at Cindy. "The malware won't leak the connectomes?" I ask.

"No. For one, the files are too big to go anywhere else. And Cindy is air-gapped. Meaning she's entirely self-contained, not connected to any server. Unlike this one."

"Where did you get that?" I ask, eyeing her laptop. "And your clothes? Where'd you get all of it?"

"My brother."

"Olivia's bro—"

"He's mine, too." Holding the laptop with one hand and typing with the other, she glances back at me. "Get going. Grab whatever you can."

The room's sparse on furnishings, but I start with the chairs, running them out to prop open the doors, then coming back for more. Next, I take the drawers from the desk. Then, once Isobel okays it, I take the monitors, ripping their cords from the wall. Finally, Isobel sets her laptop down and helps me pry the table itself from the wall. We carry it out together, cramming it into the doorway until it's wedged in tight enough that we can't move it.

We take one more trip back, and I catch movement on the video screens. Thompson, walking from one camera's range to the next, from the lobby toward my room.

Isobel pauses at my side. "You need to go."

"But—"

"The malware's running. We're almost out of time. I need to trigger the failsafe. And I need her"—she waves at Thompson, now rounding a corner into a hall near mine—"not to stop me. Can you do that?"

I take a breath. "Yes."

"Goodbye, Lucy. Good luck."

"You too."

I go, sprinting across Cindy's warehouse, crawling over the table wedged into the doorway, and charge up the stairs to head Thompson off.

LUCILLE

Dad strides back into the dining room, sets his phone on the table, and slides my laptop over in front of his chair. "Mitch is intrigued. To say the least. I'm sending him the doc you compiled." He looks to me. "What'd you find about a plane?"

"Not much. Something about a King Air?"

He nods. "Good. Nancy, airports?"

"The closest to the Life Squared building is one just southeast of DIA, about twenty—"

Her email notification dings. Again. Again, again, again. "Google alerts," she says, focusing on the screen. "All for Life Squared."

We crowd around her as she pulls them up. "That's from the flash drive," I say, pointing at the screen my mom just opened. It's screenshots of receipts: bulk orders of chemicals spread out across multiple wholesalers, all placed by a company called MegaSyne but under a link with LifeSquared in the site address. To most people, it wouldn't look like much of anything, but Kim liked to talk. "Those are polymers," I say. "Ingredients for the—"

"Hydrogels," my mom finishes, and clicks the next link.

My throat goes dry.

"That's the contract I signed." Next, schematics for what looks like the BodyProg scanner. Since we opened the first one, my mom's gotten at least twelve more emails. "Someone's leaking . . . everything."

Dad moves around the table to grab his phone. "That's it, we're going. Nance, start calling the airports. We'll drive toward the most likely one."

My dad wanders off, talking into his phone. "Mitch, we have to move. Are your contacts ready?" Meanwhile, Mom talks to someone at the airport.

What if we don't make it? What if I lose her?

"Lucille," Dad says. "Get your shoes."

I head to the garage to grab my shoes. My hands shake when I grip the doorknob. Behind me, Mom says, "Ryan." And I turn. She looks at him, panicked. "They have a King Air flying out, for New York. In less than an hour."

He checks his watch and hurries toward me.

Mom, voice thin, says, "I'm calling the police."

LUCY

I reach my hallway at the same time Thompson does from the opposite end. Glaring at her phone, she doesn't see me at first. But even when she does, looking up to find me before her instead of buttoned up tight in my room, she doesn't seem to care.

"Time to go," she says, and turns on her heel, expecting me to follow.

And because Isobel needs me to be the distraction, to let Thompson think she's still winning for as long as Isobel needs to finish the job and get out, because I trust Lucille and our parents, I do.

We stride down one hall, then the next, deeper into the building and down routes I've never used before. As we turn another corner, making sure I'm utterly lost, an alarm sounds. Pulsing wails reverberate off the walls. Red replaces the soft white glow.

"What is *that*?" I ask. But I already know. Isobel's tripped the failsafe.

Thompson halts midstep. She looks up at the lights, jaw

clenching, then reaches back and grabs my arm, yanking me down the hallway with her and out a back exit to a waiting car. The driver's already holding open the rear door. As we climb in, her phone rings.

"Thompson," she answers. The driver closes the door behind me, then speeds around the building toward the road. "No, it wasn't me!" she says. "Why would I—"

There's yelling on the other end, loud and panicked.

"*Isobel?* How?" More yelling, then she says, "I don't care! *Figure it out!*" She hangs up and answers another call. "Thompson," she says again. "Yes, sir, we're aware." A pause, then, "Sir, with all due respect, security breaches do not fall under my current job description. I'm not sure what you expect me to—"

Shouting, loud enough that I can hear the timbre of the man's voice. "Sir," Thompson yells above it, "of course it wasn't me! I'm in the car with LH—"

She holds the phone away from her ear, expression impassive while the man on the other end screams. "Sir," she says, then louder, "*Sir. Sir!*" She shouts over him, "LH2010.2 and I are in the car on the way to the airport now, we'll be there in the morning." And she hangs up.

Her phone rings again immediately, but she silences it and drops it into the pocket on her door. "Back roads, Darren. As fast as you can." The car speeds up.

"Problems?" I ask.

She meets my eye. "You cannot comprehend how hard I've worked to get here. To this moment. The failures I've overcome. The expectations I've surpassed. As a woman in a male-dominated field, I enter every room at a deficit. Having to claw my way up to equal before I can even think of excelling. Yet, I have. Succeeded, excelled. And still, the moment anything goes wrong, who's the first to be blamed?"

"Seems like a lot's going wrong."

In the dim, throbbing light from the streetlights we pass, I see the muscles in her jaw flex. Her breathing's too quick and she holds her hand in a fist at her side. It's crumbling. Behind us. In front of us. But the car's a bubble, suspended in between.

I shift in my seat, angling to face her. "So, that's your excuse?"

"What could I possibly need an excuse for?"

"For using people, killing people, to get where you are."

Shaking her head, she breathes a laugh. "Killing people? You mean the failed prototypes that came before you?"

"I mean Dr. Mitchell."

She raises her brow at me, then looks away. "Olivia knew what she was signing up for."

"That's convenient."

"Do you also know that I was the first by *six months*? More, if the rumors out of Shanghai are the bloated fictions I expect they are. OM2009 was complete, *is* complete. But the Board couldn't see it, *refused* to see it. Because when you're expecting failure, that's all you see. Anything less than perfect was unacceptable even when I was the only one remotely close to completion."

"Her Original *died*."

"You can't understand. Your connectome is too young."

I laugh. "Right. And you know exactly how young, don't you?"

"Of course. Do you think I wouldn't do my research? Lucille

was so easy. So *desperate* to be chosen, to do it all right. The contract never mattered, and the NDA was a scare tactic. All I needed was for her to feel beholden. To show up and keep her mouth shut. And, here we are. Here *you* are. Alive and *perfect*. Thanks to me."

"I can't tell if you're a sociopath or you just have no shame."

"When you're playing by other people's rules, ambition necessitates sacrifice. That's the nature of it. What you call shame is little more than a set of subjective, personally imposed constrictions most people of power and influence eagerly disregard. If that's the cost of greatness, I'd do it over again a hundred times."

"Is that what I am? Greatness?"

"Aren't you?"

"I think I'm an example of all the things you could choose to do right if you felt like it."

She breathes an acerbic laugh. "Enlighten me."

"The tech that made me could change the world, save untold millions of lives, yet you're hoarding it away for money."

"You sound like Mitchell."

"Well, she was right."

"What do you know about what's right? What do you know about anything? You're a sixteen-year-old consciousness in a body that's less than a month old. A body *I made*." We turn right onto an empty road. In the dark, she continues, "Money is power. And the people with power decide how the world works."

I settle back in my seat, wipe my sweaty palms on my jeans, and stare out the window. We're far enough away from the city out here that I can actually see the stars.

"You're judging me," she says.

"Absolutely."

"Incredible. Truly. From the first sentence you spoke, you've astonished me. There were times even I didn't think it was possible, that we'd never—"

"Do you think you'll still get your power with all of Life Squared's secrets laid bare?"

"The world is a remarkably predictable place, Lucy. Some will hate us, call what we do an abomination, the work of the devil. Some will call it a miracle. There will be protests, debates, resolutions, maybe a handful of actual laws. And all the while a line will be forming at our door."

I watch the stars until I see the lights of a tiny airport in the distance. Then I begin to panic. If she manages to force me onto that plane, that's it. I'll be gone.

The car drives straight out onto the tarmac where a jet awaits, door open, stairs down. I consider running. Heart beating like a sledgehammer, skin on fire, I feel like I could sprint to the moon.

The moment we stop, I yank at the handle. But the door's locked. The driver climbs out, goes to open Thompson's door, and I scramble over his seat, out his door. Feet on the pavement, I go. He reaches for me, gets the hem of my shirt, and I spin, screaming, fighting with everything in me as his arms circle my waist, as he lifts me off the ground and around toward the plane. Which is when I see them.

A line of flashing red and blue lights.

The sirens swell as they near. I begin to sob.

LUCILLE

It happens in flashes of red and blue. Running footsteps and incoherent shouts. Police cars circle the plane. Staff sprint out from the terminal. Officers yell at Thompson and the man who is holding Lucy to show their hands.

She sees me through the crowd and we race for each other, slamming together. Matching tears on identical faces.

Then, the news vans. The one tipped off by Mitch and the others that caught whiffs, chasing Isobel's leaks or news of a kidnapping on the police scanner, and followed along. Cameras and questions are aimed our way. But not because the stolen girl—Lucille Harper—has been miraculously saved.

But because there are two of us.

Lucy and Lucille Harper, different yet exactly the same.

CHAPTER EIGHTEEN

LUCY

"How many today?" Lucille asks.

"Six news crews, twelve abomination picketers, eight miracles, and that guy who sells sandwiches."

She joins me at the window of the former guest room, now my new bedroom. We look through the half-closed blinds, her re-dyed brown head beside my pink one. "We should put out chairs and sell tickets."

"Put on a show?"

"Recite *Hamlet* or something."

"Like you didn't forget every syllable of that monologue the second after you performed it in lit last year."

"True." She nudges my arm. "Come on. Everybody's downstairs."

I hesitate. Three and a half weeks, and the daily crowd's finally starting to wane. Week one, we had to enlist the Lakewood Police Department for help managing it all. They were clogging up the whole street. Lucille and I couldn't leave the house for days. Mom and Dad talked about moving. The second week we spent at Dad's, because at least there we had the cushion of the lobby, like a moat. But then reporters and a few fanatics slipped through, made it all the way upstairs, and scared the absolute shit out of us by banging on the door one day while Dad was still at work. So, we're back here. And now Mom and Dad take turns staying with us while a police cruiser camps out at the curb.

I won't say it's easy. We've all had to change our numbers at least four times each. There are extra locks on all the doors now, and a state-of-the-art security system on top of that. Lucille and I finally gave in and did a morning show last week, hoping it'd calm some of the fervor. The camera crew set up in the living room and we did the whole *Look, she's a living, breathing, feeling person* thing. But I'm not sure if it made it better or worse. They asked some fluffy stuff, some funny stuff, then some stuff that made my skin crawl, and finally made Mom shout that they could "shut the fuck up and get out." The clip of her went super viral within the day.

It's like because I was made as a commodity, I should expect to be one still. Everyone thinks they're owed a peek under the hood. Nothing's off-limits. And, well . . . I guess I still struggle sometimes to remember I'm more than parts.

It's not all bad. Like, before my Life^2 phone quit working, about a week after all the shit hit all the fans, I got a text from a blocked number, and when I opened it found a picture of Isobel with her brother. In it they both look so damn happy I immediately started to cry.

I also think it's pretty great that Thompson ended up being wrong. Not about all of it (she nailed the devil, miracle, protests, and debates stuff), but there's no line at Life^2 because there's no door. Isobel and her brother's bug ended up doxxing the whole lot of them, and with nowhere to hide, the Board and the president, an old white guy (of course), are having to answer a shitload of questions about a whole mess of dubious ethics and legit crimes. They immediately threw Thompson under the bus, which was unnecessary, since she was arrested for kidnapping at the scene, but it looks like she'll end up with plenty of company. Plus, most of the doctors have flipped and are assisting the investigation— first Adebayo and Kim, then the rest. But it's hard to say what will stick, since the laws are unclear or nonexistent.

News crews have been all over the Life^2 facility, so Lucille and I got to see the aftermath of the doomsday failsafe, which was, honestly, pretty rad. Whatever switch Isobel managed to flip caused Cindy to self-destruct, most likely with fire, as evidenced by the burn patterns on the walls, then a sprinkler system coated the whole thing in a kind of expanding foam that dried as hard as concrete. Isobel made it to the Mimeo machine, too. That was harder to watch, because Lucille and I could both imagine how she must've felt while she smashed as much of it as she could to pieces.

There's something comforting about knowing it's all gone. And something unsettling knowing there are other branches out there, undiscovered, maybe under different names, with their own Thompsons and teams still pushing forward. Then a feeling of flat confusion in the middle, which is where I sit most of the time. I can't regret my life, but do I think they should make more of us?

The short answer is no.

The longer answer is that I hope they'll use all they've learned for actual good. But none of us think that'll be the end.

"Luce!" Lucille calls up the stairs.

"Coming!" I turn away from the window and head downstairs, pausing in the kitchen. I can hear them down in the basement. Cass, Bode, Marco, Lucille. They're laughing.

"Hey, sweetheart," Mom says from the counter, where she sits with a book and cup of tea. I cross over to her. She opens her arms to pull me in for a hug.

"Love you," I say into her hair.

"Love you, too."

And I think, *It's worth it.* All of it. Every mess. And the good stuff, too. This feeling, laughter downstairs and the press of my mom's love.

I'm worth it. We both are.

ACKNOWLEDGMENTS

Book two! How did this happen?? Well, with a lot of help.

First, to my agent: Melissa Edwards, over five years and now two books in, I still feel so lucky to have you in my corner. You're fabulous. Thank you.

To my editor: Kelly Delaney. What do I say here that won't feel insufficient? *Half Life* became the book that it is today because of you. I'm pretty sure you understood this book's heart before I did, and your thoughtful feedback and encouragement pushed me to find that heart, too. This was a true collaboration, and I am incredibly proud of how it turned out. Thank you, thank you, thank you.

To everyone at Knopf BFYR and Penguin Random House: Jessie Sayward Bright and Angela Carlino for the *gorgeous* cover art and design, thank you! It's more perfect than I dared hope for. Iris Broudy, Artie Bennett, and Alison Kolani, thank you for your careful attention and polish. Thank you to Emily Bamford for all you did for me and *Immoral Code*. Sarah, thank you so much for your insights. And a huge thank-you to everyone else who has had a hand in bringing my debut and now *Half Life* into the world.

To new friends: Debut year is a wild thing. Highs and lows, messy expectations, and a lifelong dream achieved. And through it all, I was lucky enough to meet some incredible people. Erin and Jenn, thank you for chats with 100-plus notifications and for being your endlessly brilliant and lovely selves. Gita, getting to know you has been a joy, and I appreciate your kindness and support more than you know. Sara, our rambling emails and chats never fail to brighten my day. I swear we will have that cup of tea soon. Gabriel and Heather, it was so wonderful to meet you, and I cannot wait till we get to see each other again. Rebecca, I'm so glad we met and am thankful for your friendship! Hooray for clones! To everyone in the Novel19s and especially Class 2k19 (Nikki, Gail, Quinn, Sarah, Leah, Victoria, Keena, Kara, Claire, RuthAnne, Tiana, Alex, Katy, Naomi, Jessica, Jennifer, Erin), thank you! These groups were like, to use an eye-roll-inducing cliché, oases in the desert. Corny, but true! You're amazing, and I feel so lucky to have found you all.

Kelly: You are a gift. Words can't convey how grateful I am for your friendship. Meeting you has been one of the absolute best things to come out of this experience. Your insight, support, enthusiasm, commiseration, encouragement—it's all priceless. You're a wonderful person and friend. LOVE YOU, LADY!

Mandy: My fabulous friend! You are such a kind and generous and deeply genuine person, and I am lucky to know you. You are a bright spot in my life. Thank you for everything. I am a better person for knowing you. (Please read this and imagine it as basically a heart-filled glitter bomb. Not the, erm, other kind. HA.)

Stacey and the ladies of Oula: Your class felt like salvation this past year. It was a year filled with new stresses and digging up old insecurities while I worked on this book, and dancing it out with you, surrounded by such strong and supportive women, was an outlet and a balm. Thank you.

To my family: Thank you for your unfailing belief in me. Even when I falter, you don't. Words are my livelihood, but I can't properly express how much that means to me. Erik, thank you for being there for me through every high and every low. You and Owen mean everything to me. I love you both as big as the universe.

Thank you to every single person who gave *Immoral Code* a chance and showed my debut some love. To Shaun David Hutchinson, Caleb Roehrig, Brenda Rufener, Lianne Oelke, Rachel Lynn Solomon, Jared Reck, and Sarah Porter, thank you so much for reading my book and liking it enough to lend your words and support.

And finally, a note to my readers: In so many ways, *Half Life* is a book about self-acceptance, especially for young women, but really, for anyone who's ever worried that you were failing to meet expectations. It's a book that forced me to dredge up and work through so many of the doubts I have about myself, ones I've clung to since I was a teen. Lucille's worries mirror many of my own, most potently her fear that no matter what she does, she will always come up short. Life gives us so many opportunities to feel inadequate, it questions our value and challenges our worth. Too often, we end up chasing expectations, jumping hurdles that grow higher with every pass, aiming for a finish line that inches ever farther out of reach. But as Lucille and Lucy learn, external acceptance pales in comparison to the feeling of finally accepting and loving yourself.